EX LIBRIS

ALSO BY WALLY LAMB

We Are Water

Wishin' and Hopin'

The Hour I First Believed

I Know This Much Is True

She's Come Undone

BY WALLY LAMB AND THE WOMEN
OF THE YORK CORRECTIONAL INSTITUTION

Couldn't Keep It to Myself:
Testimonies from Our Imprisoned Sisters

I'll Fly Away:
Further Testimonies from the Women
of York Prison

I'll Take You There

WALLY LAMB

HUTCHINSON
LONDON

1 3 5 7 9 10 8 6 4 2

Hutchinson
20 Vauxhall Bridge Road
London SW1V 2SA

Hutchinson is part of the Penguin Random House group of companies whose addresses can be found at global.penguinrandomhouse.com.

First published in the UK by Hutchinson in 2016

www.penguin.co.uk

Published by arrangement with Metabook Inc.

A CIP catalogue record for this book is available from the British Library.

ISBN 9781786330642 (hardback)
ISBN 9781786330666 (export trade paperback)

Designed by Fritz Metsch
Printed and bound by Clays Ltd

Penguin Random House is committed to a sustainable future for our business, our readers and our planet. This book is made from Forest Stewardship Council® certified paper.

For feminists everywhere, of every era

I'LL TAKE YOU THERE

I turned sixty [illegible]
of course [illegible]
her [illegible] people's [illegible]
are [illegible]
the [illegible]. Another [illegible]
Pound—once you [illegible]
eligible, or more [illegible]
you're eligible [illegible]
so. Let's [illegible]
be. Take, for instance, [illegible]
Odysseus [illegible]
years. We are [illegible]
age. Then, at about [illegible]
showing up [illegible]

PROLOGUE

I turned sixty earlier this year, an age that brings deficits, of course: creaky knees, a temporary inability to remember familiar people's names, a *second* colonoscopy. But there are benefits to reaching this age, too. One is wisdom, or so they tell me. Another is the senior citizen discount at Dunkin' Donuts—once you survive the shock of being asked if you're eligible, or *more* shockingly, the cashier's assumption that you're eligible *without* asking. Geezerdom's got a third perk, too. Let's call it a bemused appreciation for how ironic life can be. Take, for instance, adult diapers: from Pampers we came, to Depends we shall return. Ironic, no? It's the same with tears. We cry easily when we're kids, not so much as grown-ups. Then, at about the time those AARP magazines start showing up uninvited in the mailbox, the lachrymal glands come alive again. Mine do, anyway. I can tear up at sappy commercials, sentimental newspaper articles, Facebook posts about some family's decision to have their dog put down. And when the TV news shows one of those surprise reunions between a soldier returning from the war and his kids—or her kids—man, I lose it.

Hmm? Oh right—excuse my manners. I'm Felix Funicello. If you're wondering why my surname sounds familiar, it's probably because my family had a famous cousin. *Annette* Funicello? *The Mickey Mouse Club*? *Beach Blanket Bingo*? No? Well, never mind. But mark my words: someday when you're my age, you'll mention Miley or Bieber and some future youth will look at you blankly and say, "Who?" Take it from me. The accelerating passage of time will astound you.

So where was I? Oh yeah, tears. I was on a plane a while back, flying out to California for a film conference, and one of the in-flight movies was that Disney-Pixar film, *Up*. So I start watching it. *Studying* it, you know, because I'm a film professor—and the author of three scholarly books on film history—and these Disney-Pixar flicks are considered by some to be both entertainment and art. So what did I care what that teenage boy sitting next to me with the earplugs and the fauxhawk and the skateboarding magazine in his lap thought about some old dude watching a cartoon? What's it to him, right? But then, when the film does that "married life" sequence between the old guy, Carl, and his wife, Ellie—shows them from the time they meet as kids to when they wed, lose their baby, grow into middle age, and then, in old age, she dies—I began blubbering. Over a cartoon movie, for crying out loud. And in my peripheral vision, I could see the fauxhawk kid staring at me. I felt like saying to him, "Wait until you're my age, you little doofus, and we'll see how dry-eyed you stay when *you* watch a sequence like this. Or De Sica's *The Bicycle Thief*, or Schlesinger's *Midnight Cowboy*, or Jim Sheridan's *In the Name of the Father* instead of *Iron Man 12* or *X-Men 27* or whatever the hell last summer's pubescent blockbuster was. Maybe by then you'll have picked up a little cinematic discernment. And by the way, your mouth-breathing's annoying and your haircut looks kind of stupid." But when I look over at him, I see that he's not watching me watching the film. He's watching the film. And then he taps me on the arm and says, "This movie rocks. That part they just showed? First time I saw it, I was like *crying*."

By the time you're sixty, you have, of course, encountered the reality that life can be unfair or even tragic. Bad things *can* happen to good people. Bad people sometimes *do* thrive and get away with terrible transgressions for which they should be punished, cosmically or legally. But life can also be amusing—hilarious even. Beautiful and sublime. All you have to do to realize that is take out those tattered family photo albums or pop in that VHS tape from 1983 or thread the old film projector, that vintage opto-mechanical Bell & Howell from the early sixties, say, and watch those home movies your dead dad took back when you and your siblings were kids and he was still in his thirties, and he aimed, shot, and captured for posterity who you all were back then.

That's what movies are, right? Thousands of still pictures taken months or years or decades before—streams of images burned onto celluloid that are reeled in front of a lamp and projected onto a screen, allowing us the illusion that they're alive. Flickers of light and dark. Brightness and shadow that won't stand still—like life itself.

ONE

Hooray for Hollywood! That screwy ballyhooey Hollywood . . .

Oops. That's my phone. Excuse me for a minute, will you?

"Hello?"

"Hi."

Weird pause. "And, uh, who is this?"

"Kenneth."

"Kenneth . . . ?" That REM song starts playing in my head. *What's the frequency, Kenneth? Is your Benzedrine uh-huh . . .*

"From the Monday night movie club."

"Oh. Hey, Kenny." (Speaking of what's the frequency?) "What's up?"

"I lost that schedule you gave us, so I wanted to know what movie we're seeing this coming Monday night. Because I can't find the schedule and I think my mother might have thrown it out, but she says she didn't. She told me to decide whether to go to our group or to a graduation she wants me to go to."

Kenny's a community college kid going on middle-aged, which more or less puts him in the same demographic as the rest of the gang in the Monday night film group I run. Interesting young man, though—movie-obsessed, although he's a specialist, not a generalist. He's the only twenty-one-year-old I know who can speak in detail about the *oeuvre* of Russ Meyer, the breast-obsessed director of such films as *Faster, Pussycat! Kill! Kill!*, *Wild Gals of the Naked West*, *Mondo Topless*, and *Beneath the Valley of the Ultra-Vixens.* If you want to talk Russ Meyer, Kenny's your man.

"We're going to be watching *Ben-Hur*," I tell him. "Not the Charlton Heston one. The silent film from the twenties with Ramon Novarro and Francis X. Bushman. It's pretty amazing visually, given the limitations of moviemaking back then. It's got the sea battle, the chariot race, a cast of thousands. A lot of the big stars from that era are in the crowd scenes. The Barrymores, the Gish sisters, Mary Pickford and Douglas Fairbanks." None of whom he's ever heard of, I'm sure. Kenny's somewhat dismissive of anything that came before Russ Meyer's first film, *The Immoral Mr. Teas*, a nudist comedy.

"Wasn't Charlton Heston in *Bowling for Columbine*?" he asks.

"Was he, Kenny? Let me think."

"He was. Michael Moore went to his house and tried to interview him because he was the one who said they were going to have to grab his guns out of his 'cold, dead hands.'" Kenny worships at the altar of Michael Moore, too, which is not something I necessarily would have assumed.

"You're right. Now I remember. But Heston was a big action star before he became an NRA pitchman. Westerns, war movies, Bible epics. He won the Oscar for *Ben-Hur* and he had the lead role in the original *Planet of the Apes*."

"He was in *Touch of Evil*, too. He had a mustache."

"I forgot about that one. Classic film noir, right?"

"Silent movies don't really interest me. I guess I'll go to the graduation."

"Okay, sure. We'll see you next time then. Who's graduating?"

"Me."

"Oh. Well, sure then. You should definitely go to your own graduation."

"That's what my mother says, too."

"And congratulations. I hadn't realized—"

Click. End of conversation.

The Monday night movie club? Kenny came on board about a year ago, but I've been getting together with my little band of regulars for the past several years. First I introduce some great old classic—*Stagecoach*, say, or *Sunset Boulevard*—and talk about the technical innovations or camera angles they used, the historical or cultural significance of the story, the dialogue, the director's other films. Then I screen it for them, after which we talk about what we've just seen. I don't so much steer the conversation as let it go wherever it wants to. We meet in New London at the old Garde Theatre. They got some significant grant money a while back that allowed them to renovate and refurbish it and install state-of-the-art sound and digital projection, but they hung on to all the old equipment, too, and that's what I prefer to use. For authenticity's sake, you know? It's called *film*, right? As in celluloid, not pixels. It's getting harder to find distributors of the old film reels, and the shipping costs for those clunky metal canisters are ridiculous. But to me it's worth it. If you're going to show an audience the vintage stuff, they might as well see it the way it was meant to be seen, not with some technology that came along sixty or seventy years into the future.

I really enjoy my Monday night regulars—more so than, say, the college kids I teach at Hunter. Of course, those students have their charms, too, if not a whole lot of life experience yet. But by and large, the Monday nighters have some considerable mileage on their odometers so they've seen more, know more. Marilyn has her SAG card and was on a couple of *Law & Orders*, once as a socialite and another time as a corpse. JoAnne and Murray's daughter is a big-time casting director. Reggie fell in love with old movies via TCM while he was doing a six-year bid in prison for check kiting. He carpools with Tony, a cop who retired with a work-related disability, paid for culinary school with his settlement, and opened a gluten-free bakery. Ed, a weightlifter who was once Mr. Rhode Island, mans the projection booth for me, hitting the foot pedal so that as reel one runs out, the second projector starts running reel two. They'll start out talking about the film we just watched and end up talking about themselves. It's the same with me. Hey, movies are touchstones, right? Triggers that have the power to transport us back in time. Songs can do that, too, of course. And music videos. The other day, I was looking for something on YouTube and I stumbled onto that old Tina Turner video for "What's Love Got to Do with It." Remember that one? Tina's strutting through some urban landscape wearing her jean jacket and shaking that wild hairstyle she had back then, doing that sexy little two-step of hers. *What's love got to do got to do with it? / What's love but a sweet old-fashioned notion?* I watched that video and bam! It was 1984 all over again. Ronald Reagan in the White House and *Cheers* on TV and my then-wife Kat "power-dressing" for work like Joan Crawford in those suits with the shoulder pads. We couldn't really afford it back then, but I bought one of those big-ass camcorders. Lugged it around on my shoulder so that I could get a videotaped record of our daughter, Aliza, taking her first steps, blowing out her birthday candles. Of course, VHS has gone the way of the dodo bird and the 35-millimeter film projector now. One of these days, I'm going to get those old tapes converted before—

Hooray for Hollywood! That screwy ballyhooey Hollywood . . .

Excuse me. Ah, it's Aliza, speaking of whom. "Hey there, kiddo."

"Hi, Daddy. Are you busy?"

"Too busy to talk to you? Never! How's it going? Everything copacetic down there in Queens?"

"At the apartment, yes, although I didn't realize what a slob Jason is until he moved in. Dirty dishes in the sink, toothpaste dots all over the medicine cabinet mirror. He's almost as bad as Jilly."

Jason is her new boyfriend, a New York University Special Collections librarian and part-time slam poet with whom she's sharing her bed. According to my daughter, "Jason's almost as big a film nerd as you, Daddy." Jilly is one third of the trio of young career women with whom Aliza shares a four-bedroom apartment in the Astoria section of Queens. By New York standards, the place is huge. Jilly's real name is Jillian and there's

Jordana and Jen, too, although I can never keep it straight which one is which. They all have college degrees and entry-level professional jobs in Manhattan, but to me the three Js seem like twentysomething middle schoolers. They travel in a pack, check their cell phones obsessively, and giggle in unison about the guys who respond to their online dating profiles and Snapchat posts. The last time I visited Aliza, I overheard one of them tell the others that she didn't care how many pics of his "meat and potatoes" this one guy sent her, she was *not* texting him any shots of her pussy. Compared to these three, my free-spirited daughter seems so grounded, she could be the house mother.

Aliza told me that one of the Js—Jordana, maybe? Jen?—categorizes herself as "polyamorous." Because this term was new to me, I had my daughter define it. "So in other words, she sleeps around a lot?" I asked. Aliza shook her head; it was about nonexclusive *loving* relationships, not hookups, she said. When I mentioned Mormons and sister wives, she rolled her eyes and said no, that polyamory didn't make women subservient; it *empowered* them. I still didn't get it. If this is the "new woman," then thank god I'm a couple of generations removed. As far as I can see, Aliza doesn't have much in common with the three Js, but she seems to get along with them fine. Get along with her boss? Not so much.

"I'm calling because I need to vent about my stupid, sawed-off little shit of a managing editor," she says.

I squint at the clock. "Better keep your voice down. Aren't you at work?"

"Yeah, but I'm so pissed off right now that I'm walking up and down Varick Street, trying to shake it off so I don't go back in there and tell him what a dick he is."

"Wow. What's he done?"

"So we have this huge special issue coming up, okay? Stories about retro Manhattan? It's called the 'Yesteryear' issue. I'm finally going to get my first big print feature. A couple of days ago, they posted the articles they're planning: the Warhol Factory, Al Sharpton and Tawana Brawley, the Copacabana, the Subway Vigilante. And the one I wanted—and was like ninety percent *promised*—was the history of the Ansonia Hotel."

Is it possible to break down a promise into percentage points? Whoa, look at that. My toenails are starting to turn yellow just like my father's did—yet another indignity of the aging process. Yecch.

"—because I was the one who fucking *pitched* it. Right?"

"Right. What drew you to that—"

"A ton of things! When it opened in 1904? It had a farm up on the roof. I mean, the concept of sustainable farming all the way back then? Shut the fuck *up*! They even had a special elevator for cattle."

Which hotel is she talking about? Not the Algonquin. That's the one that had the literary round table. Starts with an A, though. And there's another thing. Your short-term memory goes to hell in a—wait. It's got the same name as a town here in Connecticut. The Ansonia? Yeah, that's it.

"Babe Ruth, Theodore Dreiser, and that opera dude Toscanini. Oh, and you know who else lived there? The one who played Glinda the Good Witch in *The Wizard of Oz*."

"Billie Burke? She was married to Flo Ziegfeld, the theater producer."

"Yeah, she lived there, too. With Glinda, it said."

"Ziegfeld was a he."

"Oh, okay. I assumed they were lesbians. But then much

later? After they turned it into a condo building in the nineties, you know who had apartments there? Natalie Portman, and that guy who played Will on *Will and Grace*, and guess who else. Someone *really* famous."

"Kim Kardashian?"

"Uh-uh. Legit famous. She won an Oscar."

"Katharine Hepburn."

"Younger."

"*Audrey* Hepburn."

"Come on, Daddy. Someone who's big *now*."

"I give up. Who?"

"Angelina fucking *Jolie*!"

"Really? No kidding. So what's with all the F-bombs lately, Aliza? You're starting to talk like some character on HBO."

"Oh, sorry. It's New York, Daddy. Everyone here swears like this."

I can't argue with that. The last time I was on the subway in Manhattan, I overheard a teenage girl complaining to her friend that the "tramp stamp" she'd just gotten was "hurting like a motherfucker." And these two were wearing parochial school uniforms. "Well, just don't curse like that in front of your Aunt Simone. She'll start following you around with her rosary beads."

"Seriously. How is she, by the way?"

"Good, I guess. Last time I spoke with her, she said she'd had a date. Got fixed up with someone at work's brother."

"Aunt Simone went on an actual date? That's huge! Did you get the deets?"

"The what?"

"The details. Like, what he looked like, what he wore, and if he said he was going to call her?"

"No, she was pretty stingy with the deets. She just said it had gone 'okay.' And that he was nice."

"That doesn't sound too promising. I forget. How long has it been since Uncle Jeff died?"

"Oh god, eight or nine years maybe? And then, right after that was when your cousin got sick and she was taking care of him. But anyway, let's get back to you. So you wanted to write about this hotel because there was a farm on the roof and Angelina fucking Jolie lived there."

She tells me about all the stuff that went on in the Ansonia's basement during the seventies and the eighties: a gay men's bathhouse and then a swingers' club for straight couples.

"Wow, quite a lot of 'polyamorousness' going on at the old Ansonia, eh?"

She ignores the wisecrack. "And how's *this* for hypocrisy? When they made it a swingers' club, they banned gay guys but welcomed lesbians. Lipstick lesbians, I'm sure. What is it with straight guys and their hot woman-on-woman fantasies, Daddy?"

Daddy thinks he'll treat that one as a rhetorical question. There's no way in hell I'm going there with the kid I used to bring to Brownie meetings.

"Sounds like you'd already done a fair amount of research."

"He had practically promised it to me!"

"Ninety percent, right?"

"Right! But then today? At the staff meeting where they were handing out assignments? This new guy, Taz, who's been on staff for like three months? *He* gets the Ansonia. And I just sat there like, *Seriously?* But he's the fair-haired boy around here. The *Brown University* graduate who's only twenty-three but already has a book contract from Knopf. Taz: that's his poseur name. You know what his real name is? Eugene. He wears a porkpie hat and a string tie and crop pants that he cuffs up. And Keesha the receptionist and I are like, *Really, dude? Could you* be *more of a hipster cliché?* Oh, and he has this wispy little mustache that makes you wonder if he's still going through puberty. I would have *killed* to write about the Ansonia."

"So what assignment did you get?"

"Some stupid, sexist New York beauty contest."

"Let me guess. Miss Subways?"

"What? No. Something that a beer company sponsored every year."

"Ah. Miss Rheingold."

"Yeah. How did you know?"

"Oh, it was a big deal back then. We voted for Miss Rheingold here in Connecticut, too. There were always six Rheingold girls in the running and the public picked the winner. They had ballot boxes in all the stores. Even kids could vote."

"For a beer queen?"

"Uh-huh. For some reason, the beer was incidental. One year, a girl from Three Rivers was in the running. She had been our babysitter when she was in high school. I thought my sisters were going to blow a gasket when she got picked to be a Rheingold girl."

"Even Aunt Frances?"

"*Especially* your Aunt Frances. She worked on all cylinders that summer to get Shirley Shishmanian elected." Aliza asks me what kind of a name Shishmanian is. "Armenian. But she changed it to something less ethnic when she became a model."

"Why?"

"Well, I guess it was because you could *be* Armenian or

Italian or Jewish back then, as long as you covered it over with an Anglo-Saxon Protestant veneer. So Sadie became Sandy, Elisabetta became Betsy, et cetera, et cetera."

"God, I had to cover the Victoria's Secret fashion show last month, and the 'Angels' were from places like Namibia, Angola, Egypt, the Czech Republic. And trust me, Daddy, none of them had changed their names. Those accented vowels drove me nuts when I was doing the write-up. So I'm curious. What did Shirley Shishmanian change her name to?"

"Can't recall off the top of my head. You know who might remember, though? Your Aunt Simone."

"I thought you said Aunt Frances was the one who was into the Miss Rheingold thing."

"She was, but Simone was best friends with Shirley's sister, JoBeth."

"Are they still friends? Maybe the sister could tell me how to get in contact with Shirley. It would be awesome if I could get a quote from her for my piece."

"I don't know if they're still in touch or not. Why don't you email your aunt and ask her?"

"Okay, cool. Hey, as long as I have to do this story anyway, you may have just given me an angle. I mean, not even straight-up supermodels like Alessandra Ambrosio and Tyra Banks could have competed for Miss Rheingold. Right?"

"Well, Alessandra could have if she changed her name and lost her accent. But Tyra? Uh-uh. No way she would have passed as a WASP from the wilds of Westchester or Westport, Connecticut. That's just what it was like back then: blacks at the back of the bus, Lucy and Ricky sleeping in twin beds, Mrs. Cleaver vacuuming in pearls and high heels while her husband was at the office earning a paycheck."

"It sounds so fucking restrictive."

"In retrospect, yes. But it wasn't until the sixties that people started questioning the status quo."

"Mostly blacks and women, according to Mom. But then again, why would white dudes want to change things when they held all the cards?"

"Well, some of us white dudes wanted to change things, too—on the political front, mostly. You know—anti-war, anti-Nixon, pro–civil rights. When I was in college, I went on strike in protest. A lot of us did. Of course, we were also putting down our placards to 'party hearty,' too."

"Wow, you hippie you," she says, chuckling. "Wait, who's Mrs. Cleaver?"

"Hmm? Oh, the Beaver's mom."

"What?"

"Never mind. But look, sweetie. I think you're onto something with this angle you're considering. You might even have some fun with it, from a sociological viewpoint. Maybe season it with a little of that smart-ass tongue-in-cheek you're so good at."

"Yeah, I wonder where I get *that* from."

"Look, all I'm saying is, keep an open mind and give it a shot. Okay?"

"It's not like I have a choice as long as I'm working for Napoleon."

"Well, if I were you, I'd keep my head down, drop my defensiveness, and let my writing make the noise. And one of these days, you'll be *giving* assignments instead of getting them."

"Not soon enough."

"Kiddo, you're writing for a great magazine, you're getting

your name out there on that blog of yours, and you haven't even hit thirty yet. You know who I saw at Starbucks the other day? That girl Kelly who was on the swim team with you in high school. She's working as a barista, teaching a couple of classes at a yoga studio, and on the weekends she moonlights as the overnight supervisor at a group home for emotionally disturbed kids. She said she's living back home with her parents so she can start digging out from under all the student loans that are burying her alive. Where did she go to school?"

"Sarah Lawrence for undergrad and NYU for her master's, I think. But I get your point. I guess I should stop complaining because I'm pretty lucky."

"What you are, Aliza, is talented. And determined. Own it."

"Okay. Thanks, Daddy. Shit, I better get back and—oh, wait. I almost forgot. Jason and I were thinking about coming up this weekend. Depends on whether or not I can get my piece done and put Miss Beer Queen back in her crypt. I have Katie's bridal shower on Sunday and Jason wants us to check out a slam show in Providence Saturday night because one of his poet buddies is performing. He said he really wants to meet you, too, so that you two can talk movies, maybe watch a few together. But if you're too busy on Sunday, he could always go down to the casino when I have the shower. Play poker or something."

"Likes to gamble, does he?"

"Jason does *not* have a gambling addiction, Daddy, if that's what you're asking. Or a drug addiction. Or a wife and a couple of kids. He hardly even drinks. Hits the chocolate milk a little hard sometimes, but that's about it."

"Well, that doesn't sound *too* worrisome. Seriously, though, if he's a film buff, maybe I could take him to the Garde. Show him around, put something up on the big screen for him. He's not afraid of ghosts, is he? Did I tell you that after *The Day* and *The Bulletin* both did stories about some of the paranormal stuff that's happened, Steve and Jeannie have been getting inquiries from that show *Ghost Hunters* about doing an episode there?"

"Oh, Daddy, that's such a crock. In all the years that you've been running your movie program there, have you ever seen any ghosties or ghoulies?"

"No, but I heard footfalls on the grand staircase once when no one was there."

"It was probably that ancient furnace making some weird noise in the basement. Didn't you say that thing makes a racket sometimes during the movie you're showing?"

"Yeah, but Steve saw a guy in a Civil War uniform up in the balcony once. Said he looked almost translucent. Like a hologram or something. And Maura, who works the box office? She saw a girl dressed like a flapper. And when Maura said something to her, she just faded away. Maura thinks it might have been this old-time silent movie actress named Billie Dove."

"Maybe Maura should lay off the hallucinogens."

"Ha! Maura's idea of tripping is taking a bus tour to Vermont during foliage season. There is a connection, though. Billie Dove was one of the stars of the first film they ever showed at the Garde—opening night, 1926. She was considered the world's most beautiful woman back in her day. Mary Pickford was so jealous of her that she began eating rose petals to enhance her own beauty."

"Yeah, and I'm sure *that* worked. Oh, look! Here comes Charlie Chaplin's ghost up from the subway. And wow, he's riding on a pink unicorn."

"Okay, ye of little faith. So how old is this Justin of yours?"

"His name is Jason, Dad. Not Justin. And he's twenty-five. Don't start with the 'cradle-snatching' jokes, please." (Fair enough. Aliza grew up on those; her mom is four years older than I am and never once thought my wisecracking about that was funny.) "Why do you want to know his age?"

"Just trying to gauge what his cinematic tastes might be. Tarantino and the Coen brothers, I'll bet. Fell in love with the movies the first time he saw *Donnie Darko* or *Napoleon Dynamite*. Right? Oh god, he's not one of those *Star Wars*–Comic Con kind of movie fans, is he?"

"He's more into Wes Anderson, actually. But I think he wants to pick your brain about films *you* like. Maybe have you make him a list of must-sees."

"Yeah? I'm starting to like this guy. Do you think I could call him Grasshopper and get him to refer to me as Master Po?"

"Don't be weird, Daddy. If you take him down to the Garde, I'm sure he'd love that. By the way, is it okay if we stay with you when we're in town? Mom says she's already got company coming."

"No room at the inn, eh? Sure, you guys are welcome to bunk in with me. Separate bedrooms, though. None of this sleeping-together-before-marriage stuff." There's a long pause on the other end. "I'm *kidding*, Aliza."

"Oh, okay. For a minute there . . ."

"Hey, I'm your cool parent. Remember?"

"Dad, you wear argyle socks."

"So?"

"With Crocs."

"Well, yes, there's that. Maybe I'm so *un*cool that that *makes* me cool. Ever thought of that? Anyway, I assume you're taking the train up. Just call me when you know what time you're getting in and I'll pick you guys up, take you two to dinner."

"That would be great, Daddy. Thanks."

"Okay, kid. Tell Justin I'm looking forward to meeting him, too."

"His name is *Jason*. Justin was the *last* guy."

"Oh right. The stockbroker with the little ponytail."

"It's a topknot, Daddy. And they know each other. Jason fucking *hates* Justin from when he and his Wall Street buddies used to go to the pub where Jason worked part-time. They treated him and the other waiters like crap and left shitty tips. So it would be really uncool if you got mixed up and called him Justin."

"Yeah, that would be fuckin' fucked up of me if I fucked up like that, huh?"

"Ha-ha. Very funny. Look, I better get back up there and start researching Miss Brewski."

"Attagirl. And do me a favor, will you? When you get back up there, get ahold of that little twerp Eugene's porkpie hat, sit on it, and when you give it back to him good and squashed, tell him it's a hello from your old man."

She laughs. "Gladly. Love you, Daddy."

"Love you more, kiddo. See you soon."

Aliza: good god, I'm crazy about that kid. Kat and I had wanted more, but we sure lucked out with the one we got. Smart as a whip, sensitive, hardworking. And I like to think I had a little something to do with that sense of humor of hers. My ex is great, but she can be . . . intense. Doesn't laugh a whole lot. She was a damned good mom, though, and, for all the things we used to fight about, we pretty much balanced each other out as far as child-rearing. We both gave our daughter quite a bit of free rein, let her figure things out for herself, and she never abused that freedom. Even during all that testing most kids do in high school, Aliza pretty much behaved herself. Avoided the mean-girl cliques and the wild parties. Did her own thing and let everyone else do theirs. She's just always been a good kid. Not that Aliza's a kid anymore. Her next birthday, she'll be twenty-nine.

Looks-wise, she's a blend of Kat and me. She has her mother's pale complexion and China blue eyes and my dark hair and long lashes. I'm not sure where that turned-up nose came from; not from either of her parents. When she was a baby and the three of us were out someplace, strangers would sometimes tell us Aliza should be on TV—in commercials or whatever. After they left, Kat would grumble about her daughter being objectified, but it kind of tickled me when someone said something like that. Sometimes when I'm feeling sentimental or blue, I'll pop one of those old tapes into the VCR I still keep hooked up to the TV and watch who she was back then, when she was my little girl. . . .

She's grown into a lovely young woman, too: tall and athletic—she ran the New York City marathon last year and recently joined a wall-climbing club. She dresses unpretentiously—more Patagonia than Prada. Hates shopping, she says, and hardly ever wears makeup. When we're doing something in the city together, going to a restaurant or an art gallery, she seems unaware that guys are checking her out. That's what's lovely about her, in my opinion.

When Kat and I split up, Aliza was in her freshman year at Connecticut College. She'd seen the divorce coming, I'm sure, but still, when the ax finally fell . . . To her credit, though, she didn't take sides. Didn't seem to resent either of us. And as divorces go, Kat's and mine was pretty amicable. Neither of us had cheated on the other; that wasn't it. We'd just grown so far apart that the only thing we had in common was our daughter. Still, we held it together until she went off to school.

At Conn, Aliza minored in creative writing, which pleased me, and majored in feminist studies, which her mother was over the moon about. After she graduated, she got a job as a tech writer all the way across the country in Silicon Valley. She lived out there for about four years. Then Yahoo laid her off and she and her California boyfriend called it quits. That was the lowest I'd ever seen her, but she came back home, got her bearings, and moved to the big city. One of her friends pulled some strings and got her a fact-checker's job at *Condé Nast Traveler.* After a while, she began writing pieces for them. And then, about a year ago, she jumped ship and landed a job as a staff writer for *New York* magazine. Much to Aliza's frustration, she's usually assigned to cover the fashion and shopping beats for their website. Still, she's maintained her feminist cred by blogging. Her Tumblr page, *Invincible Grrrl*, gets over a thousand hits a week and she has twice that many people following her Twitter feed.

Or should I say her *post*-feminist cred? I'm not even sure what post-feminism is, but Aliza's mother doesn't seem to be particularly fond of it. She's annoyed that twentysomethings like our daughter and those roomies of hers, the three Js, take for granted the rights that Kat and her "sisters" marched for in the streets back in the seventies. "The battle's far from over," Kat told Aliza a while back when the three of us met for brunch. "Not with women only earning seventy-eight cents for every dollar that men make. There's even a gender gap in nursing, for Christ's sake. Why should male nurses make more than women in a traditionally *female* occupation?" Kat got herself so lathered up that she kept forgetting to eat her eggs Florentine, which I kept looking at, wishing I had ordered that instead of my buckwheat waffles. She went on to blame pop culture for all the backsliding. "Eighteen-year-olds getting boob jobs and fanny implants, middle school girls posing on social media in their underwear. All the women in TV news squeezed into those tight sleeveless dresses. Spanx! A girdle by any other name is still a goddamned girdle. And that show *Girls* that you're so addicted to, Aliza? I watched two episodes and I was done when Lena Dunham submitted to anal sex, not because *she* wanted it but because that monkey-faced boyfriend of hers did." That was when I noticed our waitress standing there, waiting to ask us about coffee refills. I smiled apologetically at her, in case she'd just heard my ex-wife opine about Lena's up-the-butt sex.

Sounds like Aliza's new man will be an improvement over the stockbroker. That guy was a little too full of himself for my taste, not to mention way too right-wing. Listening politely to his long-winded explanation about why Obamacare was going to bring us to financial ruin felt like torture, but I held my tongue. When Aliza called to say that she'd ended it with him, I was conciliatory. Then I got off the phone and did a little happy dance. I just better not slip up and call this new one Justin. Because he's *Jason*. Jason Robards, Jason Bateman, Jason and the Argonauts. Jason, Jason, Jason.

But yeah, it would be fun to take him down to New London and show him what movie palaces *used* to be like. Maybe give him the grand tour of the "Whaling City" while I'm at it.

Show him where the bus depot and my father's lunch counter used to sit before they built that parking garage. On second thought, that probably wouldn't excite him too much. Well, speaking of Ye Olde Garde Theatre, I'd better put some shoes on, drive down there, and set up the projectors for my Monday evening movie mavens.

HEY, NOW, LOOK at *this*: a parking space right in front of the theater. Must be my lucky day. I fish out the key, unlock the side door, and walk into the lobby. Take a moment to scan the renovated splendor of this exquisite old dame: the palatial lobby with its mosaic floor tiles and grand staircase, the neon-lit refreshment counter, the framed lobby cards. They did some extensive research to find out what it looked like when it opened back in '26 as a "photoplay" house and vaudeville stage. The murals and wall etchings are done in what's called the Moroccan Revival style. Always makes me feel like I'm walking onto the set of *Casablanca*. And they've left the doors into the auditorium open, so I can see the giant screen and red velvet curtains. Sixteen hundred seats at this place, and back in the day, for the biggest shows, they'd fill every single one of them.

If Aliza wants to write about a place with a fascinating history, she should do a story about this theater. Everyone from W. C. Fields and Sophie Tucker to Itzhak Perlman and the Plasmatics have appeared on that stage up there. I was at the latter show, watching punk princess Wendy O. Williams break every taboo she could think of, including flashing the audience and taking a chainsaw to the bass player's guitar.

Over the years, moviegoers have watched flicks from Busby Berkeley to *Boyhood* and *Birdman* on that big screen. My parents used to take Simone, Frances, and me here when we were kids. We could walk to the movie theater in Three Rivers where we lived, but if it was a special-occasion film—say, *The Shaggy Dog* (with our cousin Annette!) or *King of Kings* (with Jesus!)—we saw it at the Garde. . . . The day I got my driver's license, I took my high school girlfriend here and we necked up in the balcony instead of watching that boring big-budget mess *Airport*. . . . And one summer during the seventies, when I was home from college and my buddy Lonny was on leave from Fort Dix, we saw a porn film here, *Carmen Baby*, in which the title character did her infamous "bottle dance," courtesy of a long-necked jug of wine and, I would guess, a fair number of those Kegel exercises women do. The place was in pitiful shape by then: ripped seats with the stuffing coming out, water stains creeping down the walls. Not long after that, when the Garde had reached its nadir, they showed a snuff film here. I passed on that one, but I think it was called *Faces of Death*. Something like that. There was a big brouhaha, I remember, and the cops shut it down after the first night. The theater closed for several years after that inglorious episode. Became a downtown eyesore and a target for vandals. There was talk of demolishing the place, but then a committee of locals and summer people with political pull got that whopper of a grant from some historic preservation foundation and they were able to renovate it back to its former glory. Well, I'd better get up to the projection room. Set things up for the movie club.

I love the way these old lobby cards accompany you on

your way up the grand staircase. They got some of them on eBay, but they also found a stash of them stored in the cellar when they were doing the renovation. Miraculously, the cards were still in pristine condition. Look at these babies. Gloria Castillo and Edd "Kookie" Byrnes in *Reform School Girl* ... *The Singing Nun* starring Debbie Reynolds ... Spencer Tracy and Elizabeth Taylor in *Father of the Bride* ... Mamie Van Doren in *Born Reckless.* I can all but hear Kat indicting Hollywood for only offering women two role models: virgins or whores. And, of course, that would be *my* fault.

This one at the top of the stairs is my favorite. It's the film they screened at the Garde's grand opening: *The Marriage Clause*, a Lois Weber film starring Billie Dove and Francis X. Bushman. It was 1926, so Bushman must have filmed it straight from his role as Messala, the villainous chariot driver in *Ben-Hur.* I'll have to point out this poster to my group on Monday. Maybe I could do a little retrospective on Bushman's and Dove's careers. And Lois Weber's career as a director, too. Now there's a woman who never got her due. She was a trailblazer—a female film director in an industry dominated by domineering men. She made more than a hundred movies—shorts, mostly, with social justice themes: wage inequality, capital punishment, birth control, racial prejudice. Made the censors apoplectic from time to time, too, I've read, even before the Hays Commission lowered the boom. I forget the name of it, but one of her films was the first to show full-frontal female nudity. I'd take her on as a subject for a biography if I thought I could interest a publisher, but it would be a tough sell. Maybe some university press. Speer Morgan runs essays about film history in *The Missouri Review.* I could start there. Query him to see if he'd have any interest in an article on Weber and, if he did, maybe use it as a springboard to a full-blown book.

Well, back to business. *Ben-Hur: A Tale of the Christ.* Reel number one. Let me just . . . let . . . me . . . just . . .

What the . . .

Holy Mother of God.

TWO

There are two of them. Two translucent females, vividly detailed but as insubstantial as cigarette smoke. "Greetings, Mr. Funicello."

"Are you . . . Is this a dream?"

"No, Felix," the talking one says. "May I call you that? I see no reason why we should stand on formality. In fact, I suspect we may become fast friends."

"But what . . . ? Did I die? Is that it?"

"No, no. I doubt you'll be joining our ranks for some time yet. You've conjured us from the shadow world via your cogitations about us. Had you had such thoughts elsewhere—in the grocery market, for instance, or at the college where you teach—we would not have appeared. But the Garde is so lovely and welcoming to its guests, living or shaded. I've heard the manager acknowledge that even when a show has empty seats, the theater is filled to capacity because those from our ranks are in attendance alongside you livings. And the staff never forgets to turn on the ghost light before they lock up for the night. We so appreciate such courtesies."

I stare at them, dumbfounded. The talker is dressed in a cloche hat and one of those drop-waist dresses from the twenties. Looks to be in her early forties maybe? The younger one wears a glittery evening gown and long white gloves. With her painted-on eyebrows, bow lips, and spit-curl bangs, she looks camera-ready for a close-up. Maybe I'm dead despite what she said. Ghosts are known to be tricksters, aren't they? But if I died, when did it happen? And how? And why is it I can feel my heart jackhammering in my chest? Do hearts still beat in the Great Beyond? Do the dead still get sweaty palms when they're scared?

"Oh goodness, poor boy, you're trembling," the talker says. The glamorous one pouts sympathetically. "Well, I suppose moving pictures are to blame for that. We members of the shaded world have been depicted rather malevolently in the movies: *Nosferatu*, *The Haunting*, *The Amityville Horror.* Gothic nonsense! There's no reason to be afraid, I assure you. We come in peace, dear Felix. Delighted to make your acquaintance."

How does it—she?—know my name? "Excuse me, but who are . . . ?"

"Oh, forgive my manners. In the living world, I was Lois Weber. And this was my star, 'the American Beauty' herself, Miss Billie Dove."

I point stupidly to the lobby card for *The Marriage Clause.*

"Yes, that was one of ours. It was the only time I directed

Mr. Bushman, but Billie and I made several pictures together. We trusted each other's work implicitly, which is *so* important when one of you is in front of the camera and the other is behind it." "The American Beauty" nods in silent agreement.

"I'm sorry. I didn't recognize . . ."

"That's understandable, regrettably. My contemporaries, Davy Griffith and Cecil B., are lionized. And when you livings talk about the early film actresses, the names Mary Pickford and Clara Bow are still bandied about. Unfortunately, posterity has been far less kind to poor Billie and me."

The glamorous ghost pokes out her bottom lip and stamps her high-heeled slipper. Why doesn't she say anything? Maybe it's because, in costume, she's more of a confection than a real woman—or maybe she just can't get a word in edgewise. Anyway, despite my confusion about whatever's going on, the film scholar in me can't help seizing the moment. "So you knew DeMille and Griffith?"

"Oh yes. Knew them, know them still."

"Wha . . . what were they like?"

She and her star exchange a look I can't quite read. "Well, Felix, let's just say that both men were talented moviemakers who assumed that moviemaking was a talent that only men could master. But that's the underlying assumption in Hollywood to this day as well. Is it not?"

"Well, Kathryn Bigelow won the Oscar for directing *The Hurt Locker*."

"So if one were keeping score, that would make nearly eight dozen male directors and one female. I believe that proves my point, does it not?"

"What about Pickford then? She was a producer as well as a

star." This is beyond weird. I'm playing devil's advocate with a freaking *ghost*.

"So she was," ghost-Lois says. "Little Gladys Smith from the wilds of Canada became an actress *and* an executive. She was a big chunk of cheese in the industry by all accounts, especially her own. But alas, Miss Pickford was all washed up once the talkies came along. And she was a tippler, too—the poor dear had more than a passing fondness for giggle water."

Billie's ghost tips an imaginary flask to her lips and smirks. Apparently, the dead can be as catty as the living.

"Not to toot my own horn, Felix, but my achievements far exceeded Miss Pickford's," ghost-Lois says. "At one time I was the highest-paid director and screenwriter of Hollywood picture-plays, male or female."

Am I being Punk'd? Is Allen Funt's ghost going to pop out and say "Smile! You're on Paranormal Candid Camera!"

"I also established my own production company, pioneered the early talkies with sound-on-cylinder films, and originated the split-screen technique." "The American Beauty" whispers something into her director's ear. "Oh yes. I forgot to mention that, Billie," Lois says. She informs me that she also served as the first mayor of Universal City, campaigning on a platform that advocated "cleanliness in municipal rule and cleanliness in picture making, by which I meant that filmmakers should take up the cause of making the middle class more compassionate toward society's downtrodden."

Impressive? Hell yes, but it's not like I've requested her résumé. She's a *ghost*, for Christ's sake. Or a figment of my . . . Am I cracking up? Having some kind of psychotic episode?

"Yet *Motion Picture World* and *Variety* created the myth that my chief contribution to the industry was my 'female intuition.' I was touted as a kind of clairvoyant fairy godmother who could pluck pretty *ingénues* from obscurity, tap them with my magic wand, and turn them into cinematic Cinderellas."

"I think I've read that about you. It wasn't true?"

"Complete and utter applesauce!"

"Excuse me?"

"Applesauce. Publicists' poppycock."

"In other words, bullshit."

"There's no need for vulgarity, dear boy, but yes. That's precisely what I mean. I was a hardworking professional, as were the actresses who starred in my films. To claim otherwise was condescending to me and to the ambitious players of Billie's caliber who had honed their craft on the New York stage. But Hollywood was happy to reinforce the public's cherished myths about the genders. I was the mother hen with witch-like powers and Griffith and DeMille were the geniuses."

If I closed my eyes, I might think this was my ex-wife talking. Different era, same tone.

"With the exception of myself and my stable of scribes, the screenwriters of the silents served up characters who were clichés. There were the Sheiks and the Shebas, of course, and the comedians and comediennes—Chaplin and Keaton, Marie Dressler and ZaSu Pitts. Beyond that, male characters were stalwart heroes, cads, or Caspar Milquetoasts. The females had to be Pollyanna types, as played by the likes of Miss Pickford and Miss Gish, or Dumb Doras, or conniving *femmes fatales*. Those latter roles went to actresses like Pola Negri, Dolores del Rio, and Joan Crawford. Of course in La Crawford's case, it wasn't much of a stretch. She was happy to recline on the casting couch in exchange for plum roles and worldly gain.

How else to explain the fact that her career straddled the silent era *and* the talkies?"

"Well, I hate to say so, but those stereotypes are alive and well in today's films, too," I tell her.

"Oh, yes. We keep abreast of the current fare, drifting undetected in and out of your cookie-cutter Cineplexes and the few movie palaces that still exist. When Roger Ebert crossed over not so long ago, he did so with his Netflix account intact, so we have access to contemporary films in that way, too. Ida Lupino and I watched a few episodes of your *Orange Is the New Black* recently and shared a chuckle. Among you livings, it's touted as 'groundbreaking,' but in truth, dear boy, it travels the same terrain as women's prison films from the forties and fifties and features the same hackneyed characters as audiences saw Ida, Jan Sterling, and Barbara Nichols play in *House of Women*, *Blonde Bait*, and all the others: the naïf who's been cast into an all-female hell, the motherly jailhouse protector, the tough-as-nails bully. Of course, there are many more Negresses and Spanish girls in this version, and the lesbianism is explicit rather than implied, yours being such an indecorous age."

Indecorous, eh? Well, she's got me there. A few weeks ago on Madison Avenue, I was walking behind a young guy whose T-shirt read, *I've got a PhD (Pretty Huge Dick).*

"You know, Felix, I challenged stereotypes such as these in my 1915 film, *Hypocrites*. That was the picture whose name you could not recall before when you were conjuring Billie and me. It featured a nude female character whom I dubbed 'The Naked Truth.' State censorship boards banned the film for showing a woman in her natural state. As if museums the world over weren't filled with the works of painters who had been free to do so since the earliest days of canvas and pigment."

"Sheesh," I say. "Ridiculous."

"Hypocrites indeed! My film eventually came under scrutiny before the Supreme Court, where those pompous old men ruled that picture-plays were not protected by the First Amendment. And how about *this* for hypocrisy? The mayor of Boston, a known frequenter of Bay State houses of prostitution, was so offended by my film that he ordered clothing to be painted onto The Naked Truth, frame by frame, or else it was not fit to be shown to Bostonians!"

I smile. Commend her for being progressive.

"Indeed I was, kind sir. But alas, it's always the prigs who prevail, is it not? The studio bosses saw to it that uplifting pictures like mine, which argued for the betterment of women, or an end to bigotry, or fairer treatment for the downtrodden, were replaced by simplistic stories that dared not upset the apple cart. They assumed audiences wanted to laugh or weep without having to *think*—wanted merely to cheer for the hero, boo the villain, have romantic love reaffirmed, and dismiss the picture as soon as the credits rolled."

I nod, thinking about the modern box office champs: the *Batman* franchises and *Twilight* saga. The far superior indies that make a splash at Sundance or Toronto usually fade away after a few weeks in limited release.

"I try not to be bitter, Felix, but once stereotypes and softer plotlines won the war, the industry no longer sought my services as a directress. And so, I became the silenced woman of silent films. I was so impoverished by the time I passed on that my funeral services had to be covered by my onetime *protégée* Frances Marion, whom I had hired as a screenwriter decades earlier."

"How old were you when you died?" Now *there's* a question I've never asked anyone before.

"I was sixty. Succumbed to a bleeding ulcer in 1939." She turns toward her ghostly companion. "Dear Billie here lived to the ripe old age of ninety-four." Billie's ghost shrugs and giggles in silence. "She crossed over in 1997, the year that that dreadful monstrosity *Titanic* was breaking all the records at the box office."

I remind her that '39 was a banner year in Hollywood.

"Yes indeed. *Gone with the Wind*, *The Wizard of Oz*, Olivier in *Wuthering Heights*, Garbo in *Ninotchka*." She releases a deep sigh. "Amidst all of *that* fanfare, my obituary in *Variety* merited nary a mention; I had become an afterthought in a business with a notoriously short-term memory. Alas, in today's world, my entire *oeuvre* has fallen into the black hole of oblivion. I'm barely a footnote, and who reads *them*? That's why I think it would be a *marvelous* idea if you were to write a book about me which, at long last, might set the record straight. This would be an *authorized* biography, of course. I should be happy to cooperate in any way."

I tell her I'll consider it. Then it hits me: I've just promised a freakin' phantom that we might collaborate on her biography. Oh man, if these two wraiths aren't real, then I'm in serious need of a psych eval and some heavy-duty meds. Maybe I should call 911. But what would I tell them? That I've been chatting with a couple of ghosts? That I take a size large in straitjackets?

"And goodness knows, Felix, if you wanted to travel the low road after our project is finished—pen one of those lucrative tell-alls—I certainly could provide you with some scurrilous stories about the industry. Spill some juicy secrets, if you will. Tell some tales out of school, as we used to say. The Fatty Arbuckle scandal, for instance. There's more to *that* one than the public ever got wind of. And I was at the studio when Coco Chanel and Gloria Swanson exchanged fisticuffs over a wardrobe issue. Joseph Kennedy, the future president's father, was the one who broke it up. He and Gloria were 'special friends,' you know. They had a grand old time out on the West Coast while Joe's wife, Rose, looked after the children and said her rosaries up there on Cape Cod. Oh, those randy Kennedy boys! They loved their Hollywood conquests. Poor Marilyn gave us quite an earful when she crossed over after her 'probable suicide.'"

Hey, wait a minute. I bought a drive-thru coffee on the way down here. "One cream, no sugar," I'd said, but it tasted sweet. And because I'd already gotten back on the road, I drank it anyway. Wasn't "sugar cube" a nickname for LSD back in the day? The guy at the window who handed it to me looked a little sketchy.

"So many stars, Felix, so many transgressions. Crawford's start in stag films, Clark Gable's hushed-up hit-and-run, Judy Garland's abortion of Tyrone Power's love child. And then there was Ty's affair with Cesar Romero, who, in turn, was doing the cha-cha with his fellow Cuban, a certain married executive at Desilu whose libido didn't discriminate. You could fill an entire book with the sham dates and 'lavender marriages' the studio arranged for their homosexual and bisexual male stars with starlets and studio secretaries. Oh, the list goes on and on: Errol Flynn, Monty Clift, Randy Scott and Cary Grant sharing a 'bachelor pad,' young Mr. Dean before he had that dreadful automobile accident with Mr. Turnupseed. And among Hollywood's female stars, there were part-time and full-time members of the 'sewing circle.'"

"The sewing circle?"

"Yes, dear. That was the euphemism for the lesbian stars in our industry. Dietrich, Garbo, Bankhead, Stanwyck—to name a few."

Okay, but what if I'm *not* flipping out? What if these spooks are real? It could be a win-win for me, couldn't it? A scholarly examination of Weber's contributions to filmmaking could burnish my reputation, but a *Hollywood Babylon*–type tell-all could do wonders for my bank account. Ah, the lure of the low road.

"Of course, the scandals to which I refer would be off-topic in a book about *moi*. It can all be sorted out at a later date, of course. But look, Felix. I've brought you something that I imagine will be of great interest to you."

I follow her translucent pointing finger to the film canisters stacked up against the wall of the mezzanine lobby—a couple dozen of them, it looks like. Had they been here before? I walk toward them. Each one is labeled "Funicello, F." and they're dated: 1954, 1959, 1965, and so on. I shrug. Tell her I don't understand.

"Welcome to your life, Felix Funicello! Films such as these are usually only available to those of us who have crossed over, but I've pulled some strings, called in some favors from the higher-ups, and an exception has been made."

"An exception? What kind of—"

"Your past has been preserved on film and is ready for viewing. Open a canister, take out a reel, thread the projector, and *voilà*. And these films come with a special feature that, for all the technological tricks available to today's moviemakers, supersedes anything they can make happen in the living world." Miss Dove puts a hand on her narrow hip and nods in affirmation.

"Special feature?"

"Yes, dear. Whenever you like, you will have the ability to *reenter* your past, not just view it on the screen. To access this feature, just walk up onto the stage while the film is playing, then face the screen and touch it gently with your fingertips."

"What would happen if I did that? Which I'm not saying I *would* do."

"You would be pulled back into whatever episode of your life is playing. Depending on what's being projected, you could be seven again, or seventeen, or thirty. And, of course, you can come back to the present whenever you wish. Just turn your back to what's on the screen, extend your arms with your palms out, and you will be delivered back to the present, safe and sound. It's all very fluid and flexible, dear. Very 'user-friendly,' as you moderns like to call things. And now, my dear, if you'll excuse us, we must make our exit. Billie is taking tea with her old friend Mr. Valentino, and I have a bridge game with Elizabeth, Monty, and Mr. Selznick."

"Mr. . . . You know David O. Selznick?"

"Indeed I do, but it's his father, Lewis, who is our fourth in bridge. He was in the motion picture business, too, you know."

Billie's ghost blows me a kiss and starts to fade away like fog. Then Lois's ghost waves and begins to disappear as well.

"But . . . Wait!"

Lois's disintegration arrests itself. "What is it, Felix?"

"My daughter? Aliza?"

"Yes, what about her?"

"Is she okay?"

"I should imagine so. Why?"

"Because I'm . . . I mean, if I'm . . . Where is she?"

"I suspect she's at work, writing the article she's been assigned. Isn't that what you suggested she do? Work diligently in silence and let her writing make the noise?"

"Yes but . . . Are you *sure* I'm not dead? Because she'd be . . . And, well, you know. I've always imagined that when and if she gets married, I'd walk her down—"

"Relax, Felix. You're alive and well and your daughter has no reason to grieve your loss. Now if I were you, I'd stop worrying and start viewing your films. No one knows better than we of the shaded realm that one's time as a living is not to be squandered. I may stop back from time to time to offer a little direction if necessary, but other than that, you're on your own. And so, I bid you *adieu*."

"Stop! I have one more question."

"Yes?"

"Why have *I* been chosen to . . . These films you want me to see. Didn't you say it's only the dead who . . . Why has an exception been made for me? Is it because you want me to write that book about you?"

"Well, that would certainly be self-serving of me, wouldn't it? It would be lovely if you took on such a project, but no. This opportunity is not an attempt to bribe you, dear boy. You've been selected because you've been deemed educable."

"You mean edu*cated*? Because I have a doctorate?"

She throws back her head and laughs. "Good heavens no. Your academic pedigree is beside the point. You've been chosen because you grew up with sisters, Felix, and because you are the father of a young woman who has entered the fray of modern life. We feel you have great potential."

"Who's we? Potential for what?"

Instead of answering me, she says she hopes that I have an illuminating and fruitful experience. And with that, she fades away to nothing.

THREE

I stare at the spot where, a minute before, both ghosts had been. Or *hadn't* been, more likely. Communing with the spirit world, Funicello? Really? . . . But if they were nothing more than pipe dreams, then how the hell did . . . ? And hey, Steve and Maura saw ghosts, too. We can't all be nuts. That coffee I drank: it *had* to have been laced with something. Because whatever I *thought* I saw—whoever I *thought* I was talking to . . . You know what? I need to get the hell out of this theater. Go home and sleep off whatever this is. Am I okay to drive? I *feel* okay. A little agitated maybe, but under the circumstances, why wouldn't I be? Maybe I should get some blood drawn first. Have it analyzed and sue the pants off Dunkin' Donuts if—

Ow! Goddamned son of a bitch!

I look at what my knee's just slammed against: those stacks of film canisters. I rap my knuckles against the metal. The ghosts may have been vaporous, but these things feel and sound solid. So maybe the films she was talking about . . . Okay, I guess there's only one way to find out. "Funicello, F. 1959," this one says. I open the canister and count the reels inside. Four of them. I grab the one marked "July–Aug–Sept" and lug it up the stairs to the balcony. Unlocking the door at the back, I climb up the narrow steel steps to the projection room. Take out reels one and two, unspool a foot or so from each, and hold the celluloid to the light to make sure there's something there. There is, and as luck would have it, neither reel is "tails out." Whoever ran these reels through a machine before believed in "Be kind. Rewind."

I load the first reel onto projector number one and the second onto projector number two. Hit the On switch and kill the lights. On the big screen downstairs, the grainy countdown begins: 10, 9, 8, 7 . . . I do the math.

In the summer of 1959, I had just turned six years old. The countdown finishes, the title comes up: *The Life of Felix Funicello: July–August 1959*. And then . . .

Wow! It's the downtown New London of my childhood. The three-decker parking garage they put up across from the train station in the mid-seventies doesn't exist yet. Instead, the bus depot is back, undemolished. Inside was where my father made our family's living. I look around to see if Lois and Billie are back. Nope. It's just me and this inexplicable film of the past. *My* past. It's strange, surreal . . . but so astonishingly cool.

Lots of coming and going the day this was filmed. A train's arriving from New York, a Greyhound bus is pulling away from the depot on its way to Boston. Good god, look at the size of the cars everyone drove back then. That eight-cylinder lavender showboat with the gold fins is a Plymouth Fury. And there goes Chevy's answer to the Volkswagen Beetle: the "sporty" rear-engine Corvair that, five or six years from now, Ralph Nader's going to warn is "unsafe at any speed." My mother's not going to want to hear *that*. She loved that Corvair Pop bought her.

Oh man! Check out that red convertible with the vertical front grille in the showroom window at Fontanella Ford. The infamous Edsel. That banner proclaims it's Ford's "car of tomorrow, *today*!" Ha! It's about to become one of the biggest flops in the industry. Gas guzzlers, all these models. But at that Esso station up the hill, they're pumping gas for twenty-five cents a gallon and that's *with* an oil check, plus a windshield washing courtesy of a paid employee in a uniform, not some homeless guy with a squeegee and a crack addiction. But to be fair, none of these drivers has heard of hydrofluorocarbons or greenhouse gases yet. So put the pedal to the metal, daddy-o. America is invincible and ignorance is bliss.

Okay, the camera's going inside the depot. I hope Pop's around. And maybe Uncle Iggy. He hung around the lunch counter quite a bit after he and Pop buried the hatchet. I might even see Ma. She used to make my sisters babysit for me so she could go down there and do the books, pay the bills. I'm excited to see my folks as they once were, but a little hesitant, too. I know how things are going to end and it's not pretty. I was with both of them when they passed—Pop in 2001, Ma four years later. Neither had it easy during their long last years of dementia (Ma) and physical diminishment (Pop).

Parenting my parents against their will was rough. That time I insisted Pop hand over his driver's license and he burst into tears? Man, I felt like a total heel.

Thwocka-thwocka-thwocka-thwocka . . . Now there's a sound you don't hear much anymore: the rickety rotation of those old ceiling fans. Air-conditioning was already around, I remember, but it wasn't ubiquitous yet. You could enjoy "refrigerated air" at the movies or in your home if you could afford the 300-pound monster and stand the noise. But in the car, you still rolled down the windows on a hot day. And in public buildings like the depot, your best bet was to stand under one of these ceiling fans and catch a breeze as the blades above you sliced the warm air.

There's Blanche in the ticket booth. Her walking was pretty compromised even with those braces she wore—not that you'd notice once she was stationed at her window. I was told that Blanche contracted polio when she was a kid. I remember her struggling down those bus steps when she came to work. Makes me think about the time my sisters and I stood in line at that United Workers clinic to get our polio shots and I kept whining about how it was going to hurt. Ma finally got fed up and said, "You'd better thank your lucky stars that you can *get* a shot, Felix. How would you like to have to walk like poor Blanche? Or be forced to breathe with an iron lung?" Not realizing she was talking about a ventilator, I pictured them cracking open my rib cage and installing some heavy machine I'd have to lug around in my chest for the rest of my life. So Ma's mission was accomplished: I shut up. And although I may have had a quivering lip and tears in my eyes when we got to the front of the line and they stuck me with that needle, you couldn't really call it crying.

But I'm tearing up a little now, to tell you the truth, because here's the lunch counter just as I remember it. There's Albie Molinaro at the grill, but where's Pop? He was usually out here in front, too. Oh, hold on. The wall clock says it's 2:46, so he could have been over at Whaling City Savings making a deposit. Banker's hours back then; no ATMs. If you showed up at 3:01, you'd be shit out of luck.

Albie started working here after he quit high school a month shy of graduation to join the army. When they rejected him because of his flat feet, Pop hired him as a favor to Albie's uncle, Frido Molinaro, who he played cribbage with down at the Italian Club. "Useless": that was my father's nickname for Albie. Pop used to fire him periodically, then feel guilty and hire him back. Funny thing is, Albie and his younger brother, Chino, eventually bought the business after Pop let go of the fantasy that I was going to take it over from him. The Molinaro brothers pretty much ran things into the ground, which didn't really matter because the city seized the depot by eminent domain, demolished it, and put up that parking garage. As for what's happening on the screen, though, Albie's frying burgers for those two sailors parked on the stools. They must have been stationed at the sub base across the river in Groton. According to the prices posted on the wall, those "anchor clankers" had to cough up seventy-five cents each for their burgers, eighty-five if they ordered cheeseburgers, or a buck and a quarter if they got the deluxe platter that came with french fries, a beverage, and a scoop of ice cream or a piece of pie for dessert.

Albie's flipped the burgers and he's cutting a few slices off that block of Velveeta, so I guess those sailors sprang for the cheeseburgers. Oh god, look at that! The camera's just gone to a wide shot and there, at the other end of the counter, is one of the lunch counter regulars, Cindy Kowalski. She was a salesgirl at the S&H Green Stamp redemption store. Or was it the Plaid Stamp store? The First National gave out Green Stamps with your grocery purchases and the A&P had Plaid Stamps. Ma traded at both places, depending on which store had better specials that week, so she collected both. Cindy had a crush on Albie, I remember. Look at the way her eyes follow his every move. But he's obviously not interested, probably because Cindy's what my mother used to describe as "pleasingly plump."

Funny thing is, although Albie pretty much ignores Cindy now, in another five years, he's probably going to be one of the guys who'll be paying a cover charge to see her dance at the Hootenanny Hoot over on Route 1. Cindy became something of a local celebrity around here. Sad story, really. She packed on another hundred pounds and reinvented herself as Cindi Creamcheese, dancing the jerk and the Watusi on the bar in a shimmy dress, taking tips and catcalls without ever fully realizing that the clientele was making fun of her. Her overworked heart gave out in the middle of a performance and she tumbled off the bar, crash-landed, and was dead by the time the ambulance got there. Such is the not-so-humorous underbelly of irony, I guess. But on the summer afternoon when this film was shot, she's on lunch break from the stamp redemption store, enjoying a grilled hot dog, a vanilla milkshake, and some sneak peeks at Albie's ass as he slides those cheeseburgers onto a couple of toasted, buttered buns.

No Pop yet. Maybe he went to place a bet with his bookie, Tootsie Utley. Ma was never too thrilled that Pop played the ponies, but he worked from 5 a.m. until eight at night, with or without catching a midday catnap in the back when Albie was on. Gambling and smoking were my father's only vices, so Ma didn't say too much. She would have squawked a lot more if he'd had a drinking problem—*or* if she knew how much those two packs of cancer sticks a day were screwing with his health. But Pop was true blue, far as I know, and limited himself to a couple of Rheingolds on the weekend and a little anisette in his coffee on holidays. Back when they filmed this thing, the tobacco companies were still squelching the information that cigarettes could kill you; the surgeon general's report wouldn't be published for another five or six years. On the gambling front, it would be another three decades before the Wequonnoc, Mohegan, and Pequot tribes opened their casinos, making this area a destination area for gamblers of all stripes. Once those places were up and running, everyone with get-rich-quick dreams was down there, pulling on the one-armed bandits, shooting craps, playing roulette—plus buying stacks of tickets from the state lottery. The Tootsie Utleys of the era I'm looking at were put out of business when the State of Connecticut became the bookie.

The term "gambling addiction" wasn't even in the lexicon around here back in 1959, but it's woven into the fabric of our area now. Not long after the casinos opened, a lot of the elderly began gambling away their retirement funds. Accountants and comptrollers started embezzling from the companies and towns that employed them, always with the intention of paying it all back once they hit it big. Then there was the story about some poor desperado who, unable to stay away from the roulette tables, lost his savings, his family, and his house. He checked out by checking into the casino's high-rise hotel with a suitcase filled with bricks. He hurled said suitcase through the window of his room on the twenty-sixth floor, then followed it down. It made the national news.

Speaking of which, the camera's panning the news rack. Wow, look at how many different papers there were back then. Hard to believe that in another fifty years, most of these venerable rags will have gone digital or gone bust. The mastheads on all those front pages say it's August 14, 1959. Check out the headlines: IKE PROCLAIMS HAWAII 50TH STATE . . . ARKANSAS GOVERNOR SUBMITS; FIVE BLACK STUDENTS INTEGRATE LITTLE ROCK SCHOOL . . . POLL SAYS 94% OF WHITE AMERICANS OPPOSE INTERRACIAL MARRIAGE. Good god. But that was the way it was back then, in the North as well as the South. I remember Uncle Iggy's theory that the NAACP and Martin Luther King were just out to cause trouble, and that the Communists were behind it.

Sports Illustrated has the White Sox shortstop Luis Aparicio on the cover; he was as good a base-stealer back then as Ellsbury and Rajai Davis are today. If I have my dates straight, Chicago went on to win the pennant that year. . . . Looks like Nixon's made the cover of *Time*. This must have been right around the time of that "Kitchen Debate" he had with Khrushchev. The cover headline says he's the front-runner to be the Republican nominee next year. Well, we know how that one's going to turn out. He'll lose the election to Kennedy from Massachusetts. A couple of election cycles later, he'll win against Hubert Humphrey in a squeaker, then get reelected in a landslide against George McGovern. Strange how neither Kennedy nor Nixon ended out their respective terms in office—one in his first because he was assassinated, the other in his second because he resigned in disgrace.

There's Pop! He's just come out from the back. I'm . . . oh god, he looks so young. He was born in 1917, so he was in his early forties when this was filmed. It's tricky, watching this. Look at him, going about his business, innocent of what's coming. He starts mixing up a batch of his signature ham and pickle salad. Stops to light up one of the Kools that will eventually kill him. Atherosclerosis: heart, not cancer. Must be a Friday because the dinner special he's just posted is fish and chips. (Catholics hadn't yet been given the good news that eating a burger on Friday wouldn't send them to hell after all.) My mother must have been in the back, because Pop's just called to her, "Hey, Marie? You want something to drink?" She does, she says: a Coke. It's strange to hear her voice again. Pop puts down the tub of ham salad, puts his Kool in the ashtray, and grabs a glass. Slides it under the syrup dispenser and hits the button. At the lunch counter, sodas are still made the old-fashioned way: syrup on the bottom, then add seltzer and stir. One time, my sister Frances got in big trouble when Pop caught her sticking her face under the spigot, hitting the button, and filling her mouth with Coke syrup. Ma said it served her right when, the next time Frances went to the dentist, she had to get four new fillings.

"Yoo-hoo, Albie?" Cindy says. "Why don't you play us some music?" She slides a quarter to the end of the counter. He asks her what she wants to hear. "Anything," she coos. "Something *you* like." He nods, grabs the coin, and heads over to the jukebox. Ten to one, he's about to play something by Bobby Darin. He was Albie's idol, I remember, ever since the day Bobby missed his train back to Manhattan, got a thirty-five-cent cup of coffee at the lunch counter while he was waiting for the next one, and left a five-dollar tip.

Wow, the old jukebox—look at that baby. It was a Seeburg G Select-o-matic 100: polished chrome, light-up purple pilasters. I saw one of these vintage beauties on eBay a while back and the asking price was 5K. The cinematographer's got the juke in close-up to show the way the player glides back and forth until it finds the record, drops it into place, and plays it sideways.

Splish splash, I was takin' a bath
Long about a Saturday night . . .

Ha! Just like I thought: Bobby Darin. I read a biography about him a while back. Poor guy: he'd had rheumatic fever as a kid and was still in his thirties when he died of heart complications. And before that, life gave him a triple wallop. First, his marriage to his movie star wife, Sandra Dee, went bust. Then he found out his parents were really his *grand*-parents and his sister was really his *mother*. And as if that wasn't enough to mess with his head, he was on-site at the Ambassador Hotel in L.A. when Bobby Kennedy, the presidential candidate he'd been campaigning for, was assassinated. Tough stuff. But sing on, Bobby. It's 1959, you're a big star and a generous tipper, and none of the bad stuff has happened yet.

Well, it was a good thing those sailors didn't order the deluxe platters because they're just polishing off their cheeseburgers when the Greyhound bound for Springfield chugs up to the station and honks. They slap their money on the counter and grab their duffels. "Later, alligator," Albie says. They wave and head out the door.

The film stops abruptly. When I turn toward the projector to see what's wrong, there's Lois's ghost.

"Good god, don't do that!"

"Do what, Felix?"

"Appear out of nowhere and scare me like that!"

"Oh, fiddle-faddle. What would you have me do—send you a calling card via your butler? Now, the camera is about to follow those two bell-bottoms outside and onto the bus. As you may recall, it passed through your hometown of Three Rivers, which is your film's next destination."

If I go for that psych eval, I'd better get a physical, too. These spooks must be raising holy hell with my blood pressure. My pulse is racing like cars at the Indy 500.

"The technique you're about to see employed is the split screen, which, incidentally, was pioneered by yours truly."

"Yeah, you told me," I mumble.

"Did I? Well, there you have it. You will see, in side-by-side screens, the point of view from both the left and right windows of the bus."

"Yeah, but . . ."

"Yes?"

"I haven't seen my mother yet. Let's stay with the lunch counter scene until—"

"Who's directing this experience, Felix? You or I?"

"You are, but—"

"That's correct. *I* direct. *You* take direction. Now I want you to go downstairs to the loge. Billie will be joining us in a moment, *en costume*, and what I should like you to do is narrate what you see along the way, as if you're explaining the sights as they were back then to a young woman living in today's world. Your daughter, for instance, or one of her contemporaries."

"Yeah, hold on a second." Her mention of Aliza has gotten me worried again about her safety. Illogical? Sure. But this whole goddamned experience is illogical. So, okay, I'm being a helicopter parent. Guilty as charged. Be that as it may, I pull out my cell and speed-dial my daughter to make sure she's still okay.

"Hello?"

"Oh, hey, kiddo. Guess I must have just butt-dialed you, heh-heh. You okay?"

"Yup. Hey, you were right. This Miss Rheingold stuff is pretty cool."

When I glance over at ghost-Lois, she looks peeved. "Is it? Okay, great. Well, I'll let you go then. Talk to you soon."

"Are *you* okay, Daddy? You sound a little off."

"No, no. I'm fine. Excuse the interruption."

"Sure. No problem. Love you."

"Love you more."

The palm of Lois's see-through hand appears over my right shoulder. Against my better judgment, I surrender my cell phone, which, for some reason, sits there instead of falling through to the floor. It dawns on me that I've just given away my option of calling 911 should things get any freakier, if *that's* even possible.

"Ah, here's Billie now," Lois says. "Hurry down there and join her."

When I see "the American Beauty," I do a double take. The Roaring Twenties glamour is gone. She's wearing a Death Cab for Cutie concert T, leather pants, and stilettos. I guess she's supposed to be outfitted as the "young person living in today's world" I'm supposed to be explaining things to. She sits down next to me and Lois shouts "Action!" The film resumes.

It's a split screen, like she said. In the view out the left window, a woman drives past in an army green Nash, her unseatbelted kids bouncing around in the backseat. Out the right window, a white-uniformed Good Humor guy pulls a Popsicle out of the side of his truck and hands it to a red-haired girl with braids. I can all but taste the Toasted Almond bar I'd get if I were in that line. The bus pulls away from the depot and heads north toward Route 32.

"A*hem*," Lois says from somewhere behind me.

Oh yeah, she wants me to narrate. "So that's the Coast Guard Academy on the right," I tell twenty-first-century Billie. She's shifting distractedly in her seat; I don't think leather pants are her thing. "And across the road on the left is Connecticut College, where my daughter went—or, where she's *going* to go, I guess I should say. It's still a women's college at this point, which means housemothers, parietal hours, and propriety. No men in the dorm rooms upstairs, no slacks in the dining room or, god forbid, if you've been invited to take tea with the dean. And most of all, no premarital sex. Carnal knowledge is *not* on the syllabus, so college girls enjoy the presumption of innocence.

"But nature is nature, right? If someone's sneaking out to 'do the deed' with a townie or a cadet from across the road, those two had better use a rubber or the rhythm method. Backroom abortions carry legal risks as well as medical ones, and the Pill is against the law even for married couples. Fifty years from now, abortion will be legal, the morning-after pill will be one of several birth control options, and women's colleges like this one will be coed. Open and affirming, too—no need for 'sewing circles' or 'lavender marriages' on college campuses."

Billie bats her eyes, giving a convincing performance of naïveté.

"And changing sexual mores will be nothing compared to the way technology's going to shake things up. But this being 1959, nobody's heard of iPhones, iPads, or iPods yet. They won't be around for another several decades. Hey, Steve Jobs isn't even a kindergartener yet."

On the right screen, the bus passes the vacant building that, once upon a time, was Longo's Inn. "That's where my parents had their wedding reception."

Billie cocks her head. She seems engaged, so I go on.

"They got married right after Pop came back from the war. According to the story that used to get trotted out at family get-togethers, Pop's brother, my Uncle Iggy, had just returned from San Francisco and, while he was out there, he'd become fond of this 'tiki drink' called the Mai Tai. So at Ma and Pop's reception, he has a few too many Mai Tais and forgets to make his hands behave themselves while he's dancing with Bruno DiGiorgi's wife, Ida, who, according to my father, was 'a real tomato.' Next thing you know, Bruno punches Iggy in the face, busts his nose, and poor Pop spends his honeymoon night in the ER with his brother."

Billie points to the view on the left screen as the bus passes by the drive-in. According to the marquee, *Ben-Hur* is playing there. "That's the one with Charlton Heston, not the silent film," I tell Billie's ghost. "My folks took my sisters and me to see it that summer, but they made me wear my pajamas in case I fell asleep—which I did. For the next several weeks, my sister Frances needled me about having missed Jesus' resurrection and, even worse, the chariot race. Ma didn't make her shut up about it until I started crying. This drive-in's going to close in the 1980s, after everyone starts buying VCRs and renting videos. Then the state's going to buy the property, tear down the screen, yank the speaker poles out of the ground, and put up a super-max men's prison. Like every other prison in this country, the majority of inmates will be black and Latino. No big surprise there. In 2008, we'll be patting ourselves on the back for electing a half-black president. Declaring that we're now a *post*-racial society, which is a bunch of bullsh—horsefeathers. Racism will still be as alive and well; it'll just be hiding out in prison. Progress, right?"

Billie gives me a silent sigh.

"Oh, that's the harbor. Pretty, isn't it? We're heading into downtown Three Rivers now. Looks busy. Shoppers, city workers, a couple of grocery markets, two different movie houses. After the mall gets built on the outskirts of town and the state hospital starts busing mental patients down here—dropping them off for the day with nothing to do but loiter—this will start to resemble a ghost town. All that idle hanging around coupled with all the shoppers' fear and misunderstanding about who psych patients are and aren't: it'll be sad. But that won't happen for another decade or so. Right now, the downtown's all hustle and bustle."

The bus chugs to a stop in Franklin Square alongside the five-and-ten. People get off the bus, get on. One of those two sailors who boarded in New London hops off and buys a pack of smokes at that newsstand. Lights up and gets back on board. Most of the other passengers are smoking, too; the air is thick with fumes and carcinogens. Bus starts moving again. Takes a turn and heads up Broadway.

"Okay, that's the Wauregan Hotel on the right. Abe Lincoln once spent the night there—when he was campaigning,

I think. . . . Ah, I forgot about this pet store. The guy who runs it wears a patch. Lost his eye in the war. Plenty of those 'greatest generation' warriors around at this point, and even some World War I vets. They didn't have it easy, the guys who fought in those wars, but at least they had tangible enemies they could aim a rifle or lob a grenade at. It will be a different kind of war after 2001 when the mission will be to destroy an abstraction like terror.

"That building up ahead is City Hall. Impressive, isn't it? Second Empire architecture: a French style that was popular back in 1870 when they built it. Three Rivers was a wealthy town back then, from textile manufacturing mainly. Ponemah, Three Rivers Woolen, Blackstone Linen: those were just a few of the mills in and around town. Here in New England, we like to assume that slavery was an evil we had nothing to do with, but we were complicit. All that cotton they grew in the South during the eighteenth and nineteenth centuries may have been picked by slaves, but then it was shipped up here, manufactured into cloth, and sent off to other parts of the country and to Europe.

"Okay, top of the hill on the right: that's Saint Aloysius Gonzaga Cathedral, where my mother, sisters, and I go to Mass every Sunday. My father doesn't go to church with us, except on Christmas and Easter. Most of the stores close down on Sunday because of the Connecticut Blue Laws, but Pop has to keep the lunch counter open for the travelers. That building next to the church is the parochial school where my sisters go, and where I'll be going, too, in a few weeks. I'll be a first grader. Inside, the janitors are probably getting things ready for the coming school year. Waxing the wooden floors, cleaning the glass on the framed portraits of President Eisenhower and Pope John XXIII that hang on the classroom walls, replacing the American flags that only have forty-eight stars with ones that have fifty. Alaska became a state this year, too, about nine months before Hawaii. I'm excited about—"

"Cut!"

The film freezes again. Ghost-Billie has disappeared; her T-shirt, pants, and stilettos are in a pile on her seat. Lois's ghost approaches from behind, speaking in an imperious tone. "I need you to go downstairs to the orchestra section now, Felix. Step onto the stage with your back to the orchestra seats, and when I call for action, place your palms against the screen. You'll be traveling back in time at a rapid rate so your ears may pop and you will have the sensation that you are dropping rapidly. You may feel a twinge of queasiness, but that will dissipate as you come closer and closer and land, once again, on terra firma. Then—"

Overcome by another wave of what-the-hell-*is*-this, I tell her to hold on. "If you don't mind, I'd rather just—"

"Come, come, dear boy. We have a schedule to keep. Now as soon as you've grounded yourself in the scene, you will be a child again, inside your home on Herbert Hoover Avenue, directed by your six-year-old brain."

"Will my parents be alive?"

"Yes, but they're down at the lunch counter. Remember? You're being cared for by your sisters. Now hurry down and do as you're told. I shall see you on the other side of the scene, when you step back into the now."

I stare at her for several seconds, then turn and start down the stairs.

"That's it, dear," she calls to me. "*Now* you're on the trolley!"

FOUR

Looking back at Lois up there in the balcony, I mount the stage from the side, step by hesitant step. What's that she's holding? A megaphone? She puts it to her mouth and calls down in an authoritative voice that carries across the auditorium. "Action!"

I turn my back to her and, fingers splayed, put my palms to the screen. It begins to flap and buckle like a giant window shade being jostled by a strong wind. Keeping my hands flat against the screen, I close my eyes and hear moving water—falling rain at first that becomes the sound of a rushing brook that, in turn, intensifies into a roar as loud as Niagara Falls. When I open my eyes again, I am face to face with a wall of falling water. I'm pulled into it and carried down and down, although, strangely, I remain dry. As the falling sensation ends, I'm carried along by a fast-moving river. Then a whirlpool spins me in circles against the current. Dizzy and disoriented, I let go of the screen and cover my eyes. The sound of the water slows to a trickle and stops. I take my hands from my eyes. I'm stationary now but the spinning sensation remains. I stagger across . . . across . . .

Oh! It's the worn checkerboard linoleum floor of our kitchen on Herbert Hoover Avenue. There's our old Caloric gas stove with the pilot light that was always having to be relit. There's the teapot wall clock, the clown cookie jar on the counter. I stumble toward one of our green kitchen chairs and sit. Look down. I'm wearing my old Buster Brown shoes. How the hell are my size 12 feet fitting into . . .

My busquito bites are itching me like crazy! I got them last night when we were playing hide-and-seek. Simone's friend JoBeth Shishmanian was over at our house and when she was "it," I couldn't run in cause she's such a goal-sticker. So the busquitos just kept biting me and biting me. If I had a machine gun, I would shoot all the busquitos in the whole world and then no one would get bit any more because of me.

Last night JoBeth kept saying her family and her have a big secret that they can't tell anyone yet, but pretty soon they can. Frances says maybe someone like that rich guy on *The Millionaire* is giving them a bunch of money. Simone says nobody would do that in real life, only on TV. She thinks maybe they're getting a puppy or an in-the-ground swimming pool. And if it's a pool, JoBeth might have a pool party before school starts. I asked Simone if she thought JoBeth would invite me to her pool party, and Frances laughed so hard she started choking on her M&M's.

Simone is my oldest big sister. She's going into seventh grade once summer gets over. Frances is my other big sister and she's going into fifth. I don't have any little sisters, just big ones. I'm the only boy in our family, not counting my father, cause he's a man, not a boy. Ma says I'm her baby, but that just means I'm the youngest. Cause I'm big. Next month I'm going into first grade at the school where my sisters go to already. Last year in kindergarten, I rode the bus, but now I'm gonna be a walker. Simone says I better not dawdle on the way cause the nuns get mad if you're late and you have to stay after school. And Frances says I better hope Sister Agrippina isn't teaching first grade. "If you get her, Felix, which you probably will, you should just jump off the Empire State Building instead." Ma said I shouldn't listen to Frances cause she loves to exaggerate. That's kind of like lying but not really.

Simone and Frances are babysitting me today on account of my mother is down at our lunch counter helping Pop with the books. Ma is good at arithmetic and Poppy's a good cook. Plus he knows how to hang a spoon off his nose and it just stays there and doesn't fall off. Uncle Iggy can do it, too, and so can Frances. Uncle Iggy is Poppy's brother and he has a crooked thumb that's kinda flat. Cause he got it caught in an old-fashioned washing machine a long time ago before I was born.

I wish Ma was home so she could squirt Bactine on my bites and not make me wait like Simone. I'm not allowed to squirt myself cause Bactine is medicine. Plus I might waste it like the time I wasted a whole roll of Scotch tape trying to give myself Japan eyes like Mr. Moto. He's this wrestler I like. Pop says Mr. Moto probably has a tag on him that says "Made in Japan" like everything else does these days. I like

Bobo Brazil for a wrestler, too. My worst wrestler is Killer Kowalski. He's a dirty fighter. One time I seen him kick Bobo Brazil in that place where if you're a boy, it really, really hurts. Midge Rosenblatt hit me down there once when the kids on our street were playing dodgeball and I started crying in front of all the other kids. Then I quit and went in the house. Later on, Simone said the ball hitting me there was an accident and that Midge felt real bad. Frances said yeah, but everyone else thought it was funny and even Midge was laughing too.

"For real?" I asked Simone.

She said a few kids might have been laughing a little. She doesn't remember.

Simone likes JoBeth Shishmanian cause they're best friends, but Frances thinks JoBeth is stuck-up on account of her big sister, Shirley, is a model. We seen her once on *Queen for a Day.* And when this sad-looking lady with glasses got to be the queen cause she needed a wheelchair for her crippled kid, Shirley gave her a giant bouquet of roses and a cape that had fur on it. Ma said Shirley Shishmanian babysitted my sisters and me once—a long time ago when I was just a baby. And she was a *terrible*, *terrible* babysitter cause she spilled soda on our kitchen floor and didn't clean it up good so the floor was all sticky. Plus, she fell asleep on the couch and wouldn't wake up even after Ma and Poppy got home and kept going, "Shirley? Yoo-hoo." And after that, she never got to babysit us again. Simone says her name isn't Shirley Shishmanian anymore. She had to get a fake name on account of she's a model. I bet Killer Kowalski's got a fake name, too, cause it wouldn't be very nice if you named your baby Killer. Frances is always going that wrestling is stupid and fake, but I tell her, "No, it's not—*you're* stupid and fake." Sometimes Pop watches wrestling with me. He likes Lou Albano on account of Lou's Italian and so are we. And when Lou is fighting, Pop goes, "Come on, *paesano*! Knock his block off! Clobber him!"

Oops, I'm scratching again and one of my bites is *bleeding*. "Simone! Can you please, please, *please* squirt me? I'm bleeding to death."

"As soon as the story's over."

"When's it gonna be over?"

"Five more minutes," she says. "Are you remembering not to scratch?" Her and Frances are both eating their lunch on TV trays in the parlor cause they're watching *Search for Tomorrow.* I tell her I'm *trying* not to scratch, but I can't help it.

Frances goes, "Well, I hope you like scars then." She knows this girl in her class that got flea bites from her cat. And she kept scratching them until they turned into scabs. Then the scabs turned into scars. And even when she's an old lady, that girl's legs are still gonna have those ugly scars on account of she kept scratching. Sometimes Pop calls Frances Little Miss Know It All and she gets mad. I get happy, though, cause how does *she* like getting picked on? When I forget and pick my nose, she calls me Mr. Picky Nose. Or Stanley Wierzbicki. He's this weird kid on our street that eats his nose junk. Him and Frances use to be in the same grade together, but Stanley stayed back so now they're in different grades. Sometimes when he's out playing in his yard, we joke around and say, "Uh-oh, we better get a cootie shot."

I have to eat lunch in the kitchen cause it's Lipton chicken noodle soup and I might spill it on our new rug that's called a *braided* rug. We got it at Sears cause our old rug was cruddy and a little bit smelly from our cat, Winky. So Pop rolled it up like a big, giant cigar. And when him and me brought it to the dump, I saw two rats and a hundred million seagulls. . . . I don't get why it's *chicken* noodle soup. All's I see are noodles and little green things that Simone says is parsley, not bugs. I just put a saltine on top of my soup. And one of Frances's pop-it beads on top of the saltine. Cause the saltine is a raft and the pop-it bead is this guy who can't swim. And when the raft gets mushy, it's gonna sink and the pop-it guy might drown unless I save him with my spoon. . . .

Sometimes Frances and me play this game where she spins the globe in her and Simone's bedroom and I have to close my eyes and put my finger on it. And wherever it stops, that's where I'm going to live when I'm a grown-up. One time I got Switzerland and this other time I got the Pacific Ocean. And Frances went, "Ha-ha. Nice knowing you. You just drowned." Last time we played the globe game, I got Japan. That time when I used all the Scotch tape trying to get Japan eyes like Mr. Moto? After I pulled the tape off, there was a hole in my Pledge of Allegiance eyebrow. That means my *right* eyebrow. Cause your right hand is what you say the Pledge of Allegiance with. So that's how I remember my right and my left. When I used to be in kindergarten, we always said the Pledge of Allegiance and the Our Father first thing after we put our coats in the cloakroom and sat down at our desks. It's called morning exercises, but they're not exercises like the kind that Ma does in the parlor when Debbie Drake is on TV. At school? When we say the Our Father? I'm not 'posed to say the "for thine is the kingdom and the glory" part cause us Catholics don't say that part. Just Protestants do. And maybe Jewish kids. I'm not sure. I'm glad I'm Catholic cause we get guardian angels. You can't see them, but they're always right behind you, keeping you safe. Like, if you forgot to look before you crossed the street and a car was coming? Your guardian angel would save you. Sometimes I look back real quick to see if I can see mine, but I haven't yet.

Frances and Simone don't know it, but I'm watching *Search for Tomorrow* from the kitchen even though I'm not 'posed to cause I'm too young for those kinds of stories. So ha-ha for them. Yesterday? Joanne Tate's friend Lisa was crying cause she thinks her husband's got a girlfriend. And he does, too, cause I seen him kissing this other lady at his work. And Lisa's having a baby so she doesn't want to get a divorce. Oh good, here's a commercial.

"Simone! *Please* can you squirt me now?"

"Can't! I just painted my fingernails and they're not dry!"

So I go, "You better not spill nail polish on our new rug!"

Then Frances has to put her big nose in it. "You should talk, Felix! You spill stuff all the time!"

"I do not!"

"You do so!"

Simone tells me she'll get the Bactine after her nails get dry and there's another commercial. On TV right now, this lady's cleaning a toilet and singing, *There's less toil with Lestoil. It's so easy when you use Lestoil.* I know lots of commercials. Like *You get a lot to like with a Marlboro. Filter, flavor, flip-top box.* And *Rice-A-Roni, the San Francisco treat. Rice-A-Roni, everybody's got the beat.* Now this other lady's waxing her floor with Johnson's Glo-Coat. Ma uses that. First her and Simone carry the table and chairs out of the kitchen. Then Ma washes and waxes our floor. And after it dries but before they bring the table and chairs back, it's real slippery. You can wear just your socks and pretend you're ice skating.

Oh no. Here comes stupid Frances into the kitchen. I ask

her what's for dessert and she goes, "Nothing if you don't eat your—*hey!* Get my pop-it bead out of there." She grabs it and puts it under the faucet. "What are you playing with pop-it beads for anyway? Are you a little girl or something?"

And I go, "No. Are you a big smelly baboon?"

"Yup," she says, and she starts monkey-walking and going, "Ooo-oo-ooo. Me want banana." I don't want to laugh, but I can't help it. Out of my two sisters, she's the funny one. And out of Pop and Uncle Iggy, Uncle Iggy is the funny brother but Pop's kinda funny, too.

Frances takes the jug of spring water out of the icebox. Then she gets the Zarex out of the cabinet. Frances makes Zarex better than Ma cause she puts in way more syrup and it tastes nice and sweet.

"Can I have some?" I ask. She shakes her head. "Why not?"

"Because you haven't even drank your milk yet."

"Then can I make chocolate milk?" She says no. "Why not?"

"Because I said so. Now shut up and eat your soup."

When I tell her she's not my mother, she goes that's a relief because I sure was an ugly baby. "You're mean!" I say.

"You're mean," she says back.

"Plus, you're a brat!" I tell her.

"Plus you're a brat."

"I know you are, but what am I?"

"I know you are, but what am I?"

Ma says that when Frances starts copying me, I should ignore her cause she's just trying to get my goat. Which means make me mad. The first time Ma said, "Don't let her get your goat, Felix," I went "Huh?" Cause all's I could think of was the goats up at Wequonnoc Park that eat out of your hand if your mother gives you a nickel to buy some pellets from this machine that looks like a gumball machine.

"Ha-ha, Frances," I go. "You're not even getting my goat."

And she goes, "Ha-ha, Frances. You're not even getting my goat."

"Shut up, copycat!"

From the parlor, Simone tells me to stop screaming. She tells Frances that whatever she's doing, to stop egging me on. And that the commercial's over and their show's back on.

"Shut up, copycat," Frances says, 'cept she doesn't yell it. She whispers it, and that *really* makes me mad. Plus my busquito bites are itching worse than ever. Frances takes a big gulp of her stupid Zarex and says, "Ahh, dee-*lish*!" After she goes back to the parlor, I take her whole stupid pop-it bracelet and throw it in the garbage under some icky scrambled eggs from breakfast that I didn't eat. Then I start watching *Search for Tomorrow* again.

I wish Ma would get home. Or else I wish I was down at the lunch counter where her and Pop are. At the lunch counter, we got stools that you can spin around on. And when you get off, you're dizzy and it makes you walk like you're Lush Magoon. He's this drunk guy who lives in the apartment house across the street from us. One time he fell off the sidewalk into the gutter in front of our house and just stayed there. And my mother had to call the cops so he wouldn't get runned over and squashed to death. One time I had a bad dream where Lush Magoon was chasing me and I kept trying to yell "Help! Help!" but no sound would come out. When I woke up, I was still scared so I went to Ma and Pop's room and woke up Pop. And he went, "To what do we owe *this* honor?" Then he walked me back to my room and sat on my bed. He said I didn't have to be scared of Lush cause he was harmless. And that he felt sorry for him cause Lush has a fake leg from being in World War Two. And after he came home again, his wife didn't want to stay married to him anymore. And that was why he always got drunk: cause he had to get a fake leg *and* a divorce. So then I didn't feel scared anymore, except I still did a little bit cause I kept thinking about the bloody stump where his leg used to be.

Before Ma left, I asked her what we were having for supper and she said beans and hot dogs. I was happy cause that and English muffin pizzas are my two best things to have for supper. My worst thing to eat for supper is Mrs. Paul's fish sticks on Friday cause we can't eat meat. Fish makes the house stink when you cook it. Or when you have a goldfish but don't clean out his bowl as much as you should. The water gets stinky from fish poop. I had a goldfish named Skippy once. So one time I thought, hey, if his name is Skippy, I bet he likes peanut butter. So I put some in his bowl and he died. Ma said he woulda died anyway, but Frances kept calling me Goldfish Killer. Ma made her go to her room and think about other people's feelings. And when she came out, she had to apologize. Then me and her buried Skippy in the backyard and made him a Popsicle-stick cross. Some families, if their goldfish dies, they just flush him down the toilet. But not us. We bury ours.

Yippee! Here comes the Bactine. I stick out my arms and Simone squirts them. "Close your eyes," she says, and when I do, she squirts the two on my neck.

"Don't forget my earglobe," I remind her.

She laughs. "Ear*lobe*," she says. "Felix, you're so funny."

Frances comes in carrying her TV tray and she goes, "Yeah,

funny *peculiar*." Simone's nice most of the time. Frances is nice sometimes, like when she plays with me, but sometimes she's snotty. I like them both the same, but not when Frances is mean to me. Then I just like Simone.

They start doing the dishes. Simone always washes and Frances always dries. Sometimes I help Ma get supper ready. I'm the napkin folder and the fork and spoon putter-outer. Simone says I should finish my lunch so I can go out and play. But I don't want to cause our street is so boring. 'Cept for Stanley Wierzbicki and me, our whole neighborhood is girls, girls, girls: Midge Rosenblatt, Pinky Jenkins, DeeDee Abercrombie. Oh, and there's this other, older girl who may even be a woman that lives around the corner on Freedom Street. Her name is Roxy Rajewski and she's a tomboy. She spits in the gutter and kinda has a mustache. And when you're jumping rope and she takes an end? She yells "Hot pepper!" and starts turning it so fast it's almost like a *whip*! My mother said Roxy should put some Nair on her mustache cause it's so noticeable, but that she better not shave it cause then it would grow in thicker. This summer Ma let Simone shave her legs cause they were getting hairy. And you know something else? Some people call Roxy this bad name which, I'm not 'posed to say it but I'll whisper it. Roxy Rotten Crotch.

One time me and Frances were making a snowman and Stanley hit me in the face with a snowball on purpose and I got a bloody nose. And this other time, he pulled down his pants and went to the bathroom right in his front yard while cars were driving by! Frances says he was such a dumb bunny when he was in her grade that he couldn't even say the *easy* multiplication tables. And last night? He wanted to play hide-and-seek with us, and Simone said no and told him he had to go home. But he wouldn't. And when Pinky started counting "One Mississippi, two Mississippi," Stanley hid behind our car, *even though we weren't even letting him play!* Then Frances said if he didn't get off our property, she was going in and getting our father to come out and kick him out of our yard. But then Stanley's big brother, Brad, who's a teenager, came out and went, "Hey, nimrod! Get the H-E-double-toothpick in here! Supper!" 'Cept he said the whole word, not just the letters.

There's something I don't get about swearing. One time I asked Frances if I could have a bite of her Popsicle, and she said, "Yeah, as soon as hell freezes over."

And I said, "Uh-oh, you just said a swear."

And she went, "No I didn't, cause I was talking about hell *the place*, not saying it like, 'What the H do you think you're doing?'" But I kind of don't get the difference cause this other time Frances was being a brat and calling me names. And I went, "Go to hell, Frances the Talking Mule." And Ma heard me. So I told her I meant hell the *place*. She said it didn't make any difference, and I had to sit on the kitchen stool until I heard the stove timer ding. . . .

Some teenagers are nice and some are hoody. Brad Wierzbicki's hoody. Simone said she seen Brad in front of New Breed Auto Club where all the hoody boys go to fix their cars and hang out. And he was smoking and spitting in the gutter, which is a dirty habit. Spitting, I mean. Not smoking. Smoking's okay as long as you're a boy. The only girls that smoke are hoody girls.

My pop smokes Kools and Uncle Iggy smokes Old Golds. Their real names are Salvatore and Ignazio. I wish I had a brother like Poppy does. On my this year's birthday, that was my wish. I blew out all the candles, too, but I got a Mr. Potato Head instead of a brother. On my next year's birthday, I'm going to wish for a Lionel train instead. You can only wish for one thing, my mother said, cause you don't want to be greedy. I seen that train set at this store over near where my Nonna and Nonno Pucci live that's called Mister Big's. My mother is Nonna and Nonno's daughter and her name used to be Marie Pucci. Now it's Marie Funicello cause she and Pop got married. Before Poppy went into the army, he used to live with Nonno and Nonna Funicello plus Uncle Iggy.

One time? Pop and Uncle Iggy had this big fight where they were fighting each other *for real*, not just horsing around. I wasn't even born yet so I don't remember it. Pop got Uncle Iggy in a headlock, and when Uncle Iggy tried gettin' out of it, he kicked over our coffee table and it broke and so did our lamp. Before that fight, him and Pop used to run our lunch counter together. But then Uncle Iggy started working at this other place called Electric Boat that makes submarines. Now him and Poppy are friends again. The only person who ever calls Uncle Iggy "Ignazio" is my Nonna Funicello. She's Poppy's mother and Uncle Iggy's mother. Uncle Iggy still lives at Nonna Funicello's house on account of he never got married. I think maybe no lady wants to marry him cause he has that flat, crooked thumb. Sometimes Pop calls Uncle Iggy his numbnuts brother, and I think it's cause Uncle Iggy has this fake can of salted nuts that, when he says, "Want some?" and you open up the can, these fake snakes come flying out. And there's not really any nuts in there. One time when we had company, Ma bought a real can of mixed nuts, and Frances got in trouble for eating most of the good ones before the company even got here. And all that was left practically was peanuts and Brazil nuts. Frances was 'posed to stay in her room, but she kept coming out and having to go to the bathroom cause all those nuts gave her the runs.

Simone and Frances finish the dishes and go out to the front hall to call Ma. They want to find out when she's coming home on account of they want to walk downtown and see some dumb Elvis Presley movie.

Oh, look. Here comes Winky. She's a girl cat and she's got a broken purrer that Uncle Iggy says sounds like an old jalopy that's trying to start up in winter. I'm not 'posed to feed her from the table, but sometimes I do. "Here, Winky. Want some soup?" Yup, she does. She's sitting in my lap and has her front paws on the table, and I'm letting her lick soup from my bowl. Frances told me cats' mouths are cleaner than people's mouths. Plus, cats always land on their feet. Even if they fell off the top of the Empire State Building, they wouldn't get hurt cause they'd land on their feet. For real.

Out in the front hall, I hear Frances's whiny voice. I go to the doorway so's I can listen better. "But Ma, can't you come back here *before* you go grocery shopping? We've been stuck with him all morning. And anyway, he'd get bored watching that movie. Then he'd start being pesty and bothering us."

"Let *me* talk to her," Simone says. Ma must be saying a bunch of stuff on the other end, cause Simone just keeps going, "Yeah, but . . . I know, but . . . But Ma, that movie's just for *little* kids."

After she hangs up, Simone tells Frances they can go downtown to the show, but it has to be *Pinocchio* cause they have to take me. "But she says we can take the money that's in the coffee can and, after the movie, use what's left over for spending money."

I ask Simone do I get spending money, too, but Frances butts in and goes, "Why should *you* get any when it's *us* who get stuck babysitting you all the time? And anyways, you get to see *your* stupid movie and we can't see ours."

And I go, "So?"

And she goes, "So why do you always have to wreck everything? The *baby*! The *boy*! Mommy and Poppy's little *pet*!"

Simone tells Frances to cut it out. Then she says she's going upstairs to change cause if we're going downtown, she might see some kids she knows. When it's just Frances and me, she keeps staring at me with her mad face and her nose holes going in and out. And I get a little bit scared cause sometimes when she gets this mad at me, she gives me zammo punches on the arm with her knuckles. That's what she calls them, and they hurt and give me black-and-blue marks. Only right now, Frances isn't punching me. She's just saying mean stuff to hurt my feelings. "You know something, Felix? Everything used to be good around here until *you* came along. Why don't you just go back where you came from?"

And I go, "How could I do that when I'm way too big to fit in Ma's tummy?"

And she says, "Ha! You're so stupid you don't even know you're *adopted*."

"No I'm not!"

"You are so. Simone and I are Poppy and Mommy's real kids, but *you* aren't. You were so ugly and pathetic, your real parents didn't want you. So we took you because we felt sorry for you."

I tell her she's lying.

"No I'm not." She raises her hand. "I swear on a stack of Bibles."

"Shut up, you liar!"

"Okay, *don't* believe me. What do I care? Oh, by the way. Poppy and Mommy can still give you back to your real parents if they want to. They're thinking about it."

"They are not!"

"No? Then how come I heard them talking about it last night? And you know who your real parents are? Lush Magoon and Roxy Rotten Crotch."

"No sir!"

"Yes sir. Aw, look. Tiny Tears is crying now."

"I'm not Tiny Tears!"

"Oh, that's right. You're Betsy Wetsy." She laughs this shrieky laugh and starts upstairs. I pull off my shoe and throw it at her, but it misses. After she reaches the top and goes out of sight, I yell up after her, "I don't care what you say! I did *not* get adopted. Poppy's my real father and my real mother is Ma!"

And I'm pretty sure they are.

Aren't they?

FIVE

Felix?"

Lois is seated on a canvas director's chair, left aisle, by the rear orchestra seats.

"Yes?"

"Be careful up there. You look a bit dazed, and you're awfully close to the front of the stage. I don't want you to fall and hurt yourself."

"Oh." I take a step backward.

"That's better. Why did you exit the scene just now?"

"I . . . needed to take a time-out."

"Because?"

"I don't know. It's just so strange to be back there—to be both *of* that long-gone childhood and apart from it, too. Temporally apart from it, I mean—not emotionally. I didn't expect that it would be so . . ."

"Revealing?"

I shake my head. "Painful."

"Well, good heavens, she was attacking you at a very primal level. Trying to convince you that you didn't belong? That you were pitied rather than wanted?"

"But that was over fifty years ago. Shouldn't the statute of limitations have run out by now?"

"Temporally, perhaps. But as you've noted, not emotionally."

It's odd having a personal conversation with a ghost who's starting to sound more like a therapist. And where's her sidekick? Billie Dove seems to have flown the coop. Why has this whole weird experience come down to "the directress" and me?

"Look, I should be able to let it go because I know things now. Things I *couldn't* have known back then."

"Because you were so young?"

"That, and because things were being withheld from me. Withheld from Frances, too. The bottom line is that she zeroed in on me because she was so insecure."

"About what?"

"Who she was, who she wasn't. She was afraid that our parents didn't love her as much as they loved Simone and me. So she passed her fear to me like we were playing a game of hot potato. That's what was at the heart of it. Looks-wise, she was never going to compete with Simone. She was just the chubby, mouthy younger sister. Then I come along, and as Frances said, I was the boy, the baby. I mean, I *get* that. So why doesn't that give me the wherewithal to let it go?"

Lois smiles but says nothing.

"Look, let me ask you something. Before? When you said I was educable? What did you mean by that?" Okay, that smile of hers is getting annoying. She's a spook, not a sphinx. "Hey! Answer me!"

Her smile fades. "It's not for me to reckon with the film of your life, Felix. That's your job. Are you ready to go back again?"

I shake my head. "I'll watch, but I'm not reentering it."

"Very well," she says. "Come down off the stage then and take a seat." She turns and looks up at the empty projection booth, raises her hand and snaps her fingers. The film resumes and, from my seat in the second row, I watch my oversized past play out up there on the big screen. . . .

Looks like my sisters and I are getting ready to leave the house now. I'm the first one outside, and from the way I'm dancing around, I'd say I'm pretty excited about seeing *Pinocchio*. Frances lets the cat out and, true to form, Winky heads right for Pop's garden on the side of the house. It's her favorite napping spot, possibly because she enjoys flopping down on the cucumbers and chewing the vines in case Pop hasn't yet gotten the message about her contempt for him. Of course, if she's still there when Pop gets home, he'll engage equally in their *pas de deux* by aiming the garden hose at her. Funny thing is, when Winky gets hit by a car a few years from now, it's Pop who will stay up all night with her, attending to her slow and laborious dying. I'll wake up the next morning to the sound of spade hitting earth and stone. When I look out my bedroom window, I will see my father tenderly placing his feline nemesis, shrouded in one of our checkered dish towels, into the ground.

"Hurry up, Simone!" I yell through the screen door. "We're gonna be late."

"Since when can *you* tell time?"

"Shut up, Frances. Who's talking to you?"

"I'm telling Mommy you said shut up."

"Then I'm telling Poppy you smoked one of his cigarettes."

Ha! *That* shut her up. When Simone comes out, she locks the front door. Hides the key beneath the metal milk box, one of the first places a burglar would look. My sisters and I start down the front sidewalk.

For some reason, I remember those clothes Frances and Simone have changed into: outfits they made at that Saturday morning sewing school they attended. The more talented seamstress, Simone is wearing her *señorita* blouse and toreador pants. In her tent-like sack dress, Frances looks like a life-size orange Popsicle. I used to moan and groan about having to go with them to those sewing classes. Pop was working and Ma, a member of the St. Aloysius Gonzaga Rosary Society, had to spend Saturday mornings helping to decorate the altar for Sunday Mass. Ah, the injustice of having to spend Saturday mornings among sewing machines and juvenile seamstresses when all the good cartoons were on, plus the live-action kids' western *Fury*. The titular character of that show was a kind of equine Lassie—an unbroken stallion who somehow always managed to assist young Joey and his adoptive father, Jim, in prevailing over that week's villains. Unlike *Fury*, my sisters' sewing school was devoid of drama, except for the time when one of their contemporaries became distracted and accidentally stuck her finger under a jabbing machine needle. It went through her cuticle and out the other side, causing her to scream, jump up, and pass out cold. I had never seen anyone faint before, and until Mrs. McCune resurrected her by calling her name and slapping her cheeks, I'd assumed the sewing machine had killed her.

Simone gives me permission to walk on other people's walls on our way down to the movies as long as I'm careful. I loved wall-walking, which made me taller than both my sisters. "Hello down there, you midgets," my younger self says, but they just ignore me. Frances informs Simone that she forgot to take the Scotch tape off her bangs before we left. Simone says no she didn't—that it's so humid out, she's keeping them taped until we get closer to downtown so they won't frizz up before we're inside with the air-conditioning. Simone hated frizzy hair so much that one time during this era she knelt down on the kitchen floor in front of the ironing board and scorched her hair trying to press away the frizz. "P*U*," I kept saying until she chased me outside. The only other time I can recall Simone getting *that* mad at me was when she and I went to the corner store to buy bread and Jerome Spears, a classmate of Simone's for whom she'd been harboring a secret crush, was at the store, too. When the three of us arrived simultaneously at the front counter, I disclosed to Jerome the reason why the hair on Simone's arms was orange: because she bleached it with peroxide so that she would look less hairy. When we got home, Simone told Ma how I'd humiliated her. That made Ma mad, too. "I don't *care* if it's the truth, Felix. Some things are *private*. Now you go to your room until I tell you you can come out. And after your time is up, I want you to apologize to your poor sister." When I did so, Simone said, "That's okay. From now on, I'll just wear a bag over my head in public."

Walking along those walls, I keep picking dead dandelions

from people's lawns. Hiding them behind my back, I come down from a wall. Looks like I'm about to make Frances my victim. "Here's a beautiful bouquet for you, my darling girl," I tell her, holding the dandelion puffs up to her face and blowing hard. But a breeze foils my plan and most of the fuzz comes back at me. Frances starts snort-laughing. "You've got fluff stuck to your eyebrows, you stupid idiot," she says. Try as I might, I could never quite get the best of my tormenting sister.

"When we get to the show, can I buy some popcorn?" I ask Simone.

"No!" Frances says. Ever the mediator, Simone tells us we'll get one box and share it. No, I *can't* hold the box, she says. She'll sit in the middle and hold it. When I ask if I can get a soda, Frances nixes that idea, too, but Simone says we'll see. It will depend on my behavior. "Guess you're gonna be thirsty then," Frances says. When I stick my tongue out at her, she sticks hers out at me, curling it for an extra taunt. Frances could curl her tongue, a skill which, try as I might, I never could master.

Frances turns around and looks behind us. "Oh no," she groans. "Look who's coming." The camera follows her gaze and there he is, in a long shot: our pesty neighbor, Stanley Wierzbicki.

"Hey!" he calls.

"Hay is for horses!" I call back. Simone says to just ignore him and keep walking. Frances says she wishes she brought her cootie spray.

"Where you goin'?" Stanley wants to know.

Frances calls back, "Crazy. Wanna come?"

"Go home, Stanley," Simone tells him. She reminds me not

to look back at him because that will just encourage him. But as I recall, Stanley was not easily *dis*couraged.

"Guess what?" he calls. When we don't answer, he says, "You know that dog food that makes its own gravy?"

"Yeah, genius. It's called *Gravy* Train." Frances says it *sotto voce* so that we can hear her but Stanley can't.

"My mom got a bag of it for Taffy. And guess what. I *ate* some of it."

Forgetting my instructions to pay him no attention, I stop short and look back at him, wide-eyed. "You *did*? What did it taste like?"

"Kinda like caca. The gravy was good, though, after I put salt on it."

That's enough for Simone. She turns and faces him, points, and orders him to go home. Stanley reminds her that she's not the boss of him.

"You better stop bothering us, or we're gonna tell the cops!" Frances shouts.

"Go ahead, Fat Chunks," he shouts back. "I *want* you to."

"Or the guys in the white coats! So they can take you to the loony bin!"

"You're so fat you should be the fat lady at the carnival!"

"And you're so dumb you probably *still* don't know your times tables!"

"I do so!"

"Okay then. What's eight times seven?"

A close-up of Stanley reveals that he has no idea. "Who doesn't know that?"

"Okay, what is it then?"

"You're fatter than a hippopotamus!"

"Have you learned your *one* times table yet? Here's a tough one for you. What's one times one?" When he answers that it's two, Frances's laughter is raucous.

Simone tells her to stop it—that he'll follow us all the way downtown if she keeps it up. So she stops. Clearly, however, Stanley has struck at Frances's Achilles' heel. She's rubbing her wet eyes with her fists.

"I bet you a hundred dollars I know where you're going," Stanley says. "You're walking down to Treat's to get sundaes. Can I come? I got my own money."

"No! Go home and eat more dog food!" Frances screams.

"Frances, would you *stop*?" Simone pleads.

Then, just like the night before during hide-and-seek, Stanley's brother Brad saves the day. His souped-up purple Chevy Bel Air convertible with its whitewall tires and Hollywood muffler comes roaring around the corner and slows to a crawl. "Howdy, neighbors," he says, speaking solely to Simone. She must have pulled the Scotch tape off her bangs when she heard him coming, because the film reveals a hairy ball of tape in the grasp of her right hand. "Is the nimrod bugging you?"

"Yes!" Frances declares.

"Plus, he ate Gravy Train," I add. "And he called my sister Fat Chunks." Frances reaches over and gives me one of her signature zammo punches.

Brad yells at Stanley to turn around and "get the fuck back home." I can tell from the way my eyes bug out that I'm as shocked by Brad's language as I was by his brother's revelation that he'd eaten dog food.

"Psst," I whisper to Frances. "Brad just said the F-word."

"Oh really?" she whispers back. "Gee, I wish *I* had ears like you."

When Stanley asks his brother if he can have a ride back,

Brad tells him to beat it before he gets out of his car and pounds him to a bloody pulp. "Okay, okay," Stanley says. My mouth drops open as I watch him cross the street. "You didn't look both ways!" I call after him.

My sisters and I resume our trek toward the movie theater. A long shot reveals that Brad's got his head out the window. He's checking out Simone from the back. "Wish I had that swing in *my* backyard," he calls. Simone smiles a little and touches the back of her neck. Her enjoyment of this attention from an older boy ends abruptly, however, courtesy of her little brother. "Uh-oh, Simone. Your bangs are frizzing up," I tell her.

"Keep walking, Felix," she says.

We pass the National Guard armory, the Civil Defense lady's house, the local A.M.E. Zion—which, back then, we called "the colored people's church." My sisters and I are silent; it looks like we're lost in our own long-ago thoughts. Then Frances asks Simone if her sack dress makes her look fat. Simone says no, that that style is very flattering on her and Stanley Wierzbicki is just a little jerk who doesn't know what he's talking about.

Frances says, "But if you were a complete stranger and you walked by, would you think I was fat or regular. Be honest."

"Regular," Simone says.

"And anyways, Stanley shouldn't talk," I chime in. "When he runs, he has a jiggly stomach." For a second or two, Frances seems to appreciate my observation. Then she remembers it's me who said it.

The film captures Herbert Hoover Avenue as it once was, bringing back a flood of long-forgotten memories. We pass old Mrs. Popple's house. We shared a party line with her back in the day. If the phone rang once, it was for her, two quick rings in a row signaled that someone was calling us. Aliza's generation spends most of their waking hours phoning, texting, tweeting, and Snapchatting. If I mentioned party lines to a room full of millennials, they would draw a collective blank. And if I described what was available to consumers back when I was a kid, I'd come off like a cave-dwelling troglodyte. Well, so be it. Time marches on and technology gallops ahead. I suppose that's a troglodyte's viewpoint, too. I remember back in the late seventies, when microwaves started becoming standard kitchen equipment, my father boasting that he'd just ordered one of those new "microphone ovens" from Sears, Roebuck. "Delivery in seven business days *or under*," he added. "Man oh man, that's one company that's got their act together." Today, Amazon can get customers' purchases to them within twenty-four hours, and from what I read, not long from now their stuff will arrive by drone an hour or two after you've placed your order. But back to 1959. . . .

"Your pettipants are showing beneath your dress," Simone informs our sister.

"I *told* her I didn't need that size," Frances laments. "Her" must be Ma, the bane of Frances's existence back then. Simone says it's no big deal. She can just roll them up at the waistband.

"How am I supposed to do that out here in *public*?" Frances wants to know. Simone tells her to go down the alley and fix them while she stands guard so that nobody looks.

When Frances emerges from the alley a few minutes later, her pettipants aren't showing anymore but she's still mad at our mother. "They keep falling because they're too loose since I lost weight."

"You did?" Simone says. "How much?"

"Almost two pounds. And I could lose a lot more if she'd let me buy Metrecal *with my own money.* Why *can't* I take it out of the bank? I don't even know if I *want* to go to college. And how come she says I can't shave my legs until eighth grade when you already got to and you're only going into seventh."

"Because your legs aren't as hairy as mine," Simone says. "You're lucky."

"That's not the point. The point is you're her favorite, he's her little pet, and I'm just the one in the middle who she always says no to because she hates my guts."

"Oh, Frances, that's not true."

"It is *so* true! And I'm shaving my legs in seventh whether she likes it or not." (I have to smile at Frances's defiant assertion. In college, she embraced feminism so wholeheartedly that she made a political statement by refusing to shave her legs and underarms. Aliza's diehard feminist mom retired her Lady Schick and went *au naturel* for a while as well.)

Insinuating myself into this conversation, I tell Frances that Simone is right. Ma loves the three of us the same.

"Pfft. What do you know, dummy?"

I respond to her put-down in verse: "I see London, I see France / I can see your pettipants." She checks, sees that it's untrue, and suggests that I go play in traffic. Simone tells her she shouldn't say things like that, even if she's kidding.

"Maybe I'm *not* kidding," Frances says. When I threaten to tell our parents what she just said, she laughs. "Not if you play in traffic you won't. Splat!"

"If you two don't stop, we're just going to forget about the movie and go home," Simone threatens. Frances and I dummy up, sticking our tongues out at each other as we walk behind our unsuspecting older sister. But the camera reveals that Frances's pettipants have in truth come back into view beneath the hem of her sack dress. I watch my younger self notice this but remain uncharacteristically discreet—probably so as not to risk a U-turn back toward our house should Simone make good on her threat or jeopardize my getting a soda once we get to the show. And so, *Pinocchio*, here we come!

In a bumpy tracking shot (handheld, no doubt; the Steadicam wasn't even around back then), the camera follows us as we reach the end of Herbert Hoover Avenue and proceed onto Franklin Street. Those mosquito bites I got the night before must be bothering me again because I'm scratching myself without seeming to notice. Simone notices, though. She pulls the Bactine out of her purse and gives me another several squirts.

Then the camera goes full-frame and, from the left side of the shot, who comes staggering into drunken view and heads right toward us but none other than Lush Magoon! I have vivid recall of this incident—the sight of him, the smell—and my body tenses up the way it must have that day. Lush's fly is down and there's a big dark spot on the front of his pants where he must have pissed himself. Simone says we'd better cross the street *now*. The problem is: traffic's going both ways, and fast. So we just stop. Lush comes up to us and he stops, too, staring at us.

I had never seen him this close before, and the camera's extreme close-up mimics what my six-year-old eyes were looking at: the horror of Lush's alcohol-damaged face—his pockmarked nose and red-rimmed eyes, the burst purple veins on his cheeks. I have no recollection of having done this, but my childhood self somehow gets the courage to speak to him. "The post office is open," I say. Sitting here at the Garde, I'm just as confused by my remark as Lush appears to be. Then the neurons in my brain fire off another memory: Uncle Iggy telling me that *if a fella needs to tell another fella that he forgot to zip up, he says the post office is open. It's like a private message that girls and ladies won't understand.* But Lush ignores my message. He puts his face in front of Frances's and says "Boo!" She stands there, frozen, in lockjawed defiance.

Lush moves on to Simone. "Who wansa dance? Whaddabout you, cupcake?" She shakes her head and says, "No thank you," but he grabs her by the wrist anyway and starts trying to engage her in a sidewalk waltz. When I begin to whimper, Frances takes my hand and gives it a reassuring squeeze.

"Please let go of me," Simone says, but Lush keeps holding onto her and trying to make her dance.

"Jesus Christ, *relax*," he says. "You dance worse than a goddamned broom."

Frances yanks back her hand and sticks it inside Simone's purse, rummaging for something. When she pulls out the Bactine, she starts squirting Lush in his eyes! Uttering a string of curses, he lets go of Simone and we start running. I keep looking back to see if he's chasing us, but we're in luck.

After we get out of breath (Frances, mostly), we slow down to a fast walk. "Is he gonna go blind now?" I ask. Frances shakes her head. She says his eyes are just gonna sting for a while.

"Oh. You were brave."

"Pfft," she says. But the camera catches the trace of a smile. "Thanks."

When we reach the heart of the downtown area, my sisters stop to look at the windows of the LaFrance Dress Shop, the Bostonian, the House of Tee—stores that closed decades ago after the mall was built on the outskirts of town. At the newsstand, Simone and Frances stop again, this time to browse through the movie magazines and read things aloud to each other. "Tab Hunter: Cool Cat or Squaresville?" . . . "Homesick Private Presley Scrubs Latrines, Hopes Fans Won't Forget Him" . . . "Will Liz Break Eddie's Heart Like He Broke Debbie's?"

"Come *on*," I whine, pointing to the blinking lights that outline the Midtown Theater's marquee. But when we get as far as Melady's Package Store, our progress is arrested yet again. "Fran, look!" Simone says. "The new Rheingold girls!"

A full-frame shot shows the three of us from the back as my sisters study the cardboard picture of the six Rheingold girls propped in the front window; they're dressed in identical powder blue dresses, waving their white-gloved hands. Inside the store, life-size head shots of the same six women are strung up near the ceiling. Collectively, they declare, "Our Beer Is Rheingold the Dry Beer!" Two of the women are blondes, there's a redhead and three brunettes. All six have bright red lipstick and dazzling white teeth.

"I'm either voting for Olga Grogan or Flo-Ann Cobb," Simone says.

"Not me," Frances tells her. "They both look stuck-up. I want Rita Regan. She looks a little like that singer Anna Maria Alberghetti."

"Mitzi O'Neill's pretty, too," Simone says.

Frances sticks out her tongue. "Yuck. I wouldn't vote for her in a dog show. She might get it, though. The best one never wins."

"Are they sisters?" I ask.

"Models," Simone says. "It's a contest. You vote for who

you want, and the one that gets the most votes wins Miss Rheingold."

"Rheingold like the beer Pop drinks?" I ask.

"Yeah."

I start singing the TV jingle. *My beer is Rheingold, the dry beer / Think of Rheingold whenever you buy beer.* Then I call in to the package store proprietor, whom we knew from church. "Hi, Mr. Melady!" He waves back. When Frances asks him can we come inside and vote, he says sorry but children can't enter a liquor store without their parents. Frances makes the argument that she and Simone aren't really children and that I can wait outside. Mr. Melady says we should vote over at the First National because grocery stores sell beer and kids can go into them on their own.

Simone checks her watch and says we'd better vote *after* the movie. Then she says, "So who are *you* voting for, Felix?" I point to the lady on the end and ask what her name is. She says it's Dulcet Tone.

"Ha! There's no way she's gonna win with *that* corny hairdo," Frances scoffs. "And why doesn't she try plucking her eyebrows?" After which, she gasps and grabs onto Simone's arm. "Oh my god! Oh my god, Simone! Look who it is!" Simone squints at the hanging head shots inside the store and realizes what has just dawned on Frances: that Dulcet Tone is none other than JoBeth Shishmanian's sister, Shirley. Frances and Simone grab each other by the shoulders and start jumping up and down, squealing in the same way that, five years later, girls will squeal for John, Paul, George, and Ringo. Mr. Melady looks out at them and shakes his head. Then he looks over at me and shrugs. I shrug back. Simone and Frances keep squealing.

In the ticket line at the Midtown, my sisters are still yapping about Shirley Shishmanian. Frances notes that the only other famous person who ever came from Three Rivers was Benedict Arnold. I'm ignored when I ask who that was. "This was the exciting thing JoBeth couldn't tell us about before," Simone says. When I ask if the Shishmanians are still getting a puppy or a swimming pool, Frances shakes her head. "This is better," she says. "*Way* better. If she wins, Miss Rheingold will be someone who used to *babysit* us!"

When we get to the front of the line, Simone tells the ticket lady that we need three children's tickets. (I remember that old crab; she had that job forever and seemed to exist to hassle moviegoers—kids, especially.) "Don't you mean two children and one adult?" the ticket lady says. "What are you? Fourteen? Fifteen?" Simone tells her no, she's twelve. The ticket lady says she doesn't believe her.

"She is *so* twelve," Frances chimes in. "She's going into seventh grade at St. Aloysius. I swear on a stack of Bibles."

The ticket lady says she doesn't care what Frances swears on because she knows a high school kid when she sees one.

Frances tries another approach. "You better sell us our three children's tickets or we're going home and getting our father."

"You do that," she says, pointing her thumb at Simone. "And have him bring her birth certificate while he's at it because if she's twelve, then I'm Zsa Zsa Gabor."

"Hey, what's the holdup?" some father behind us complains.

Visibly mortified, Simone succumbs. "Okay, fine. Two children's tickets and one adult." She pushes the money through the slot and we get our tickets.

Frances leaves the ticket lady with a parting shot. "I hope you know our babysitter's running for Miss Rheingold!"

"Oh really? Well, let me know if she catches her. Next customer!"

One sister's huffy, the other's chagrined, but I'm too excited to be either. We push open the big glass doors and walk the mosaic-floored corridor to the inner sanctum. A uniformed usher rips our tickets in half at the entrance to the lobby (decorated in Art Deco style, I realize now; back then, I just thought of it as fancy). At the concession counter, we get our popcorn. Simone renders her decision about my behavior and says I can get a soda despite Frances's prosecutorial objections. We enter the auditorium and find seats near the front. The houselights dim and the previews begin: *North by Northwest, Rio Bravo, The Diary of Anne Frank, Journey to the Center of the Earth*—vintage 1959 films that I will later see and study, but that have yet to be released.

When the houselights go from dim to dark, Jiminy Cricket croons "When You Wish Upon a Star" as he struggles to open a giant storybook. I can see from the close-up of my shadowy face—eyes gone wide, mouth dropped open—that I have tuned out my sisters' excited whispering about Miss Rheingold, having fallen quickly and deeply into the narrative on the big screen: the Blue Fairy's glittery descent from the night sky for the purpose of granting the kindly woodcarver his wish; Jiminy's appointment as the puppet-boy's conscience; Pinocchio's kidnapping by a puppeteer more terrifying than Lush Magoon; Geppetto's imprisonment in the belly of a hostile and voracious whale. I have forgotten all about eating my fair share from the popcorn bag in Simone's lap and that I'm holding my cup of orange soda. My face conveys the shock I feel at Pinocchio's errant behavior after his transport to Pleasure Island. He has smoked cigars, told lies, swilled beer until he was tipsy. When he sprouts jackass ears as a result of his transgressions, I am so horrified that I spill soda all over myself.

As an avid moviegoer, and later, a scholar and professor of film, I have screened, studied, lectured on, and written about thousands of movies. Yet I cannot recall a more satisfying ending than the one I viewed on that memorable afternoon when the Blue Fairy, heard only now in voice-over, turns Pinocchio into a flesh-and-blood boy—a flawed but triumphant kindred spirit to the captivated child who sat between his two older sisters, not the least bit focused on his mosquito bites or his soda-soaked clothing. Was I ever again as emotionally engaged by a film as on that August afternoon when I sat watching what, several decades and an education later, I recognize as the mythic journey of Joseph Campbell's prototypical hero from self-interest to social responsibility? Was this when I began my lifelong love affair with the movies? Was this where and why?

Emerging from the theater, my sisters and I squint as we walk out into the ambient light of mid-afternoon. Simone says she enjoyed watching *Pinocchio* again and Frances says, "Yeah, it wasn't *that* bad." When I declare that "this was the best movie out of all the movies I've ever seen in my whole life," Frances says, "And how many have you seen? Three? And no fair counting *Ben-Hur* because you *slept* through most of that." I tell her to shut up, and she says, "No, *you* shut up." Simone groans and says our next stop is the five-and-ten so that she and Frances can spend their babysitting money.

The camera tracks us en route and then inside the store. At the candy counter, Frances buys a pair of wax lips, a strip of penny candy, and an oversized Sugar Daddy that she says she's going to bring home and hold over the burner on our gas stove so it will turn soft and gooey and be even more delicious. In the record department, Simone buys a 45 rpm record: Frankie Avalon's "Bobby Sox to Stockings." She says she could have gotten *two* 45s if she didn't have to buy an adult ticket at the show. With the change that's left, Simone tells me I can buy a bottle of bubble stuff. "And here," Frances says. She tears off some of her penny candy and hands it to me. I pull the colorful little bumps of hardened sugar away from the paper, pop them all into my mouth, crunch down, and smile.

Next we cross the street and walk to the First National so that we can vote for Miss Rheingold. Strictly business, Frances approaches a worker stocking shelves. "Where's the beer at?" she asks him. With a smirk, he tells her the *root* beer and the *birch* beer are in aisle 6. We finally locate the ballot box atop a waist-high tower of Rheingold six-packs. Simone demonstrates how to vote for Dulcet Tone and I do the same. Bolder than the two of us, Frances tears a thick wad of ballots from the pad, checks off Dulcet's name on each one of them, and jams them through the slot in the box. Simone says she's lucky she didn't get yelled at.

I'm blowing bubbles and walking back home behind my sisters when the miracle happens. The film I'm watching captures beautifully how I remember it. The soundtrack becomes cacophonous with tooting horns. Cars traveling in both directions pull to the curb as if for an approaching ambulance. Pedestrians stop and stare, pointing at the three gleaming white convertibles coming toward us. On the backs of the cars' rear seats sit six beautiful women, two per car—visions not unlike the winged fairy who appears to Pinocchio at the beginning of the film and, at story's end, orchestrates his transmutation from wood to flesh.

It is the Rheingold girls, transmutated from cardboard to flesh, as three-dimensional as life itself, or something you'd see inside your View-Master. As they pass us, the six women wave their white-gloved hands identically. They wear identical dresses the same shade as the Blue Fairy's shimmery blue gown. Their red-lipstick smiles are as fixed as dolls' smiles.

"Hey, Shirley! We just voted for you!" Frances shouts. She grabs Simone by the arm, raises it, and yells, "Her and your sister JoBeth are best friends! She comes over to our house all the time!" Simone yanks her arm back and tells her to keep quiet, but Frances runs out into the road and starts jogging alongside Shirley's convertible. "Our last name's Funicello! We're cousins with *Annette* Funicello! Remember when you used to babysit us?" The Rheingold girl seated beside Shirley says something to her. Shirley laughs and nods. Then she turns away from Frances, waving to the crowd on the opposite side of the street. Frances stops, staring after her, until a cop tells her to get back on the sidewalk. When she walks back to Simone and me, out of breath, she shrugs. "It's so noisy she couldn't even hear me," she says. Her pettipants are hanging a good three inches below the hem of her sack dress.

SIX

My ghost-director seems to have vanished—at least for the time being. I look up at the screen, staring at the arrested image of Frances, hands on her hips, staring at the backs of the Rheingold girls in their retreating convertibles.

In the years that followed, I heard many analyses from my sisters about how our former babysitter had orchestrated her self-transmogrification from ho-hum Shirley Shishmanian to glamorous Dulcet Tone—how she had, in effect, been her own wish-granting Blue Fairy. There was the pseudonym, of course—the denial of her ethnicity. But in addition there were theories about eye-color-changing contact lenses, falsies and faddish diets, a dye job, a nose bob. (The last of these was verified by a reliable source, Shirley's sister, JoBeth.) Having forsaken her past identity for her new one as she rode triumphantly through her hometown, Shirley was clearly snubbing my sister that afternoon. However, this did not lessen Frances's rapture or dissuade her from swinging into action on Dulcet's behalf. If one of our own could rename herself, move to Manhattan, become a fashion model, and then, with luck and loyalty from her hometown, reign as Miss Rheingold, then anything could happen. Anything! Frances's future had just lit up with the fireworks of possibility. In response, she did everything in her power to get Dulcet Tone elected.

On the morning after the Rheingold girls' surprise appearance in Three Rivers, Frances more or less appointed herself Dulcet's precinct captain and made me her deputy. We traipsed down to Melady's Package Store and, since we could not step inside without a parent, Frances called Mr. Melady out onto the sidewalk. She used her powers of persuasion to get him to agree to our borrowing of the Miss R ballot box so that we might ring doorbells, canvass the neighborhood, and secure as many votes as possible for the hometown favorite.

"Would you like to vote for Miss Rheingold?" she would ask, pushing the box at whoever answered a door or emerged from a car.

"I'm kind of busy."

"It will only take two seconds of your time. This one comes from Three Rivers. She used to be our babysitter. If you don't want to think about it, just vote for her."

"Well, all right."

"Care to vote for Miss Rheingold?"

"Sure. Now let's see. I guess I like this blond one—Flo-Ann Cobb."

"Really? She's never gonna win. What about Dulcet Tone?"

"Hmm. She's pretty, too. All right. I'll vote for her."

We were like secular Jehovah's Witnesses, armed with paper ballots rather than pamphlets, but energized nonetheless with missionary zeal. And by "we," I mean my sister.

We usually campaigned until noon. After we ate lunch, we would return the ballot box to Mr. Melady—but not before Frances popped open the back, removed the ballots, and separated them into piles. If Dulcet Tone was not way ahead, she would adjust the returns by filling out several more ballots and instructing me to do the same. "I bet you and me vote more times than anybody else," I told her.

She nodded. "If she gets Miss Rheingold, she probably has *us* to thank."

We canvassed for the next two weeks. One morning, we rang doorbells on Boswell Avenue, the street where the Shishmanians lived. When Mrs. Shishmanian answered the door, she said JoBeth was over at her cousin's house. Would we like to come in and have some refreshments? Frances and I nodded like bobbleheads, all but speechless in the presence of the woman who had birthed a Rheingold girl.

We waited in the parlor while Mrs. Shishmanian went out to the kitchen.

"Psst. Look," Frances whispered, pointing to a framed picture atop the Shishmanians' piano. "That's *her*."

"Who?"

"Who do you *think*?" The girl in the photo resembled JoBeth, except she was older. I shrugged. "What are you, a moron?" Frances said, tapping her index finger against Dulcet Tone's face on the ballot box.

I saw not the slightest resemblance. "No sir," I said.

"Yes sir," she insisted. "It must be her high school graduation picture."

I stared in disbelief at this pre-Dulcet Dulcet until Mrs. Shishmanian came back with two glasses of pink lemonade and a plate of Lorna Doones. When she invited us to have a seat, Frances and I sat next to each other on their sofa. Mrs. Shishmanian sat across from us on a cushioned chair. She kept looking at us—at me, mostly—and smiling. "Next time I talk to Shirley on the telephone, I'm going to tell her how a certain adorable little boy in the neighborhood has been working hard to get her elected," she said.

"And my sister too," I reminded her.

"And your sister too."

When we got back outside, Frances started mimicking Mrs. Shishmanian. "A certain adorable little boy." I braced myself for a zammo punch; she sounded angry enough to deliver a doozy. "And his sister, too, Miss Nobody, who doesn't even count. Typical. I do all the work and Little Mr. Adorable gets all the credit." Clutching the ballot box against her chest with one hand, she grabbed me by the arm with the other. "Come on!"

I reminded her that we'd already been to those houses toward which she was pulling me. Didn't we have to go the other way? She shook her head and said there was something on Division Street I needed to see. Her fingers felt tourniquet-tight against my upper arm as we rushed toward what she wanted to show me, but I knew not to protest when she was in a mood like this.

We came to an abrupt halt when we arrived at an ugly institutional-looking gray building with peeling paint. I asked her what the sign by the front door said and she read it to me. "'The Esther Clark Spain Children's Home.' Follow me." She led me around to the back where, instead of a yard it had an asphalt . . . what? Was it a parking lot? A playground? Cars were parked there and motor oil stained the paved ground. But there was a swing set, too, with two good swings and two broken ones. Someone had drawn a grid on the ground for a game of hopscotch. On the opposite side of the fence from where we stood, I saw a dirty Raggedy Ann doll, faceup in litter and dead leaves, stabbed in the heart with a broken pencil.

"What is this place?" I asked. "A school?"

"An orphanage," Frances said. "This is where we got you from when you were a baby. The lady who runs it called us and said your real parents didn't want you and would we please take you because everyone else she asked said no. Poppy and Mommy felt sorry for you, so they said they would. That's why you're in our family. You didn't believe me before when I said you were adopted. So here's the proof."

I shook my head. "Simone said I *wasn't* adopted."

"Because she didn't want you to feel bad."

"Yeah, but—" A bell blaring inside the building cut me off. A side door banged open and a bunch of loud, skinny kids came outside, both boys and girls. Some of them started playing and some stared back at Frances and me as we watched them from the other side of the fence.

"They're like zoo animals," Frances said. "But not really, because everyone loves zoo animals. Nobody loves these kids, not even their parents."

From that long-ago day to this, I can picture with near-cinematic clarity the boy who came running toward us from the opposite side of the fence. Up close, I could see that he had two different-colored eyes and a bald patch on the side of his head. He was too skinny for his pants; they were all bunched up under his belt. He didn't look at Frances, just me. When he smiled, I could see the cavities eating away at his front teeth. "You know what? I smoked a cigar once," he said.

"Oh," I go. "You did?"

"Yup. What's your name?"

"Felix. What's yours?"

Without answering, he ran over to the swing set. "Hey, boy! Watch this!" he called back to me. Grabbing onto the chain from one of the broken swings, he shimmied up, then climbed onto the crossbar at the top. Hooking the backs of his knees around it, he let go and hung upside down like a monkey. When he waved to me, I waved back.

"Just think, Felix," Frances said. "Mommy and Poppy and Simone and me could have picked *that* boy instead of you. See what a lucky duck you are? Come on. We better get the ballot box back to Mr. Melady."

As we headed toward Franklin Street, I decided that Frances, not Simone, must be the one who was telling me the truth about my origin. Hadn't she just shown me the place where my real parents had dropped me off when they gave me away?

"Come on. Let's cross," Frances said. Halfway across the street, without realizing I was about to do it, I reared back and, hard as I could, punched her in the stomach. She doubled over and cried out in pain, dropping the ballot box. I thought she was about to retaliate, but instead she staggered the rest of the way across the street, crying. Then I was crying, too. Then a car drove by and ran over the Rheingold girls. The box had been squashed flat, popping open the back. A breeze caught the spilled ballots and sent them dancing down the street.

When we returned the ruined box Mr. Melady yelled, "Is this how you two take care of something that doesn't belong to you?" I looked away from the tire mark across Rita Regan's and Mitzi O'Neill's faces. Even if he could get a replacement from the salesman next time he came around, Mr. Melady said, we would not be allowed to borrow it anymore. Maybe the next time someone lent us something, we wouldn't be so careless with it.

Walking back to our house, Frances offered me a deal: she wouldn't say anything about my having punched her if I didn't tell anyone about her having shown me the orphanage where I'd come from. I agreed. "And who cares if he won't let us borrow that stupid ballot box anymore?" she said. "I don't even want to, and I hope stupid Shirley Shishmanian loses." She said she was pretty sure Shirley had heard her that day when they rode by in their white cars but pretended she hadn't because she was so stuck-up and fake. She told me that now she hoped Flo-Ann Cobb won Miss Rheingold instead of Ugly Face Shishmanian.

"Yeah," I said. "Me too."

Good god, these memories and movies of my past, these ghosts: it's all so vivid and so confusing. What does it mean? I get up from my seat, walk to the foot of the stage, and pace. Then, for no particular reason, I climb the side stairs, walk to the center of the stage, and gaze out at the rows and rows of empty seats.

"Felix? What are you doing up there?"

Aha, my mentor from the shaded realm returns. I see her, vaguely, at the back of the auditorium. But as she approaches, I realize it's *not* Lois's ghost who's just spoken. It's Jeannie, one of the theater managers.

"Oh, hey. I'm . . ." In a panic, I look over my shoulder to see if that frozen image of Frances and the Rheingold girls is still up on the screen. It's not. "It's nothing, really. Occurred to me that, as many years as I've been coming to this theater, I've never seen the view from up here on the stage. So I . . ."

"Oh, okay," she says. "Because if you were thinking about breaking into vaudeville, you're seventy or eighty years too late."

"Vaudeville? Oh, ha-ha, no. Can't sing, can't tap-dance." I can hear the nervousness in my laughter. But okay, she's bought the bluff.

Maybe I should just tell her what's been going on. After all, Steve and Maura have seen ghosts here, too. Still, a sighting is different from a full-scale exchange, with paranormal movies thrown in. And as real as it's all seemed, I'm still not a hundred percent sure that I'm *not* cracking up. I mean, *recalling* things from childhood: sure. Who can't do that? But watching your past play out on a movie screen? Dropping back *into* your life back then? If I spilled all this to Jeannie, I'd probably get tranquilized and carried out of here, headed for the psych ward.

I come down off the stage and walk up the aisle toward her. "So what are you doing here on your day off? Can't stay away from the place, eh?"

She says she's got some paperwork she needs to catch up on and a grant application to write. "So are you all set up for your movie club tonight?"

"Uh-huh. So I guess I'll take off now." I start toward the exit doors.

Oh shit! What about those film canisters up there in the

mezzanine? How am I supposed to explain where *those* came from and why they've got my name on them? I'm halfway up the stairs to the mez when I realize she's watching me. "Just checking something first," I tell her.

She nods, but there's a puzzled look on her face. "Are you feeling okay, Felix?"

"Me? Yeah. Never better. Yup. Maybe a little too much coffee today. Makes me jumpy, you know?"

"Yeah, me too. Well, I'd better get to my office and make some headway. Nice to see you, Felix."

"You too. Later, then. Say hi to Steve for me."

At the top of the stairs, I'm relieved to see that all those cans of film are gone. But I'm confused as well—and disappointed that they've disappeared.

Driving home from the theater, I look at my face in the rearview mirror. "Who are *you* to dismiss the possibility that ghosts exist?" I ask it. "Or that paranormal experiences are just something you'd see on the Syfy channel? Isn't it a little grandiose to assume that the dimension *we* inhabit is the only one that exists?" In other words, maybe I'm *not* cracking up.

Back home, I flop face-first onto my bed, hoping to grab a nap. My body's exhausted, but my mind keeps racing with moving images—the ones I watched up there on the screen and the ones that kicked in from memory after the film froze. . . .

It had been a baffling summer, to say the least. Puppets became boys, cardboard women became real ones. Most confusing of all was that my sister Frances could be both protective and cruel—that she could squeeze my hand one day to reassure me that I was safe, and the next day jab at my security like a lance-wielding picador by taking me by the hand and leading me to a broken-down building that housed a bedraggled orphan boy who was far scarier than Lush Magoon.

It's clear to me now that Frances's campaign on behalf of Shirley Shishmanian was really a campaign for her own legitimacy. Caterpillars become butterflies, right? Ugly ducklings transform into graceful swans. So maybe a chubby, insecure little girl in a homemade sack dress needed to project herself as some future Cinderella. But then that mean streak of hers had kicked in and, to undermine and frighten me, she'd dragged me to that orphanage. And I *had been* frightened, too, which was why I'd landed that surprise punch to her gut. And then a car drove by and flattened the ballot box, and Frances's fantasy along with it. Cinderella's castle walls came crashing down all around her. What I didn't know at the time—couldn't have known—was that Frances's own insecurity provoked her effort to convince me that I was once unwanted and abandoned, the implication being that I had better watch my step because that braided rug in our living room on Herbert Hoover Avenue could be yanked out from under me at any time and I'd be sent tumbling back to the Esther Clark Spain Children's Home to live the life of that unclaimed no-name boy and all the other kids nobody wanted. . . .

Tossing and turning rather than falling asleep, I see, once again, that strange boy on the other side of the rusty fence: his ill-fitting pants, his mismatched eyes and rotten teeth. What became of him? Did he fall victim to some disease? Rise up from his bleak beginnings and become someone in the world who mattered? Maybe he had entered the military and become a hero—or a casualty of war.

I *hadn't* been adopted. Frances's lie was disproven several times over. But each of the half dozen or so times I have screened, for my students or myself, that vintage 1938 film *Boys Town*, in which Spencer Tracy rescues Mickey Rooney from juvenile delinquency, my illogical fear of being an unwanted orphan has been reignited. Recently, I did an Internet search of Nebraska's *actual* Boys Town, the basis for that sentimental film of the same name, and was surprised to learn that it's still in existence—still in the business of saving disturbed and deprived youth, and that it boasts generations of success stories. Among its alumni it counts real estate moguls, college professors, and captains of industry. But then again, Charles Manson had lived there, too.

SEVEN

Hooray for Hollywood! That screwy ballyhooey Hollywood . . .

"Well, well. The prodigal daughter finally calleth. I was wondering when I was going to hear from you."

"Sorry, Daddy. I was balls-to-the-wall all weekend trying to finish my Miss Rheingold piece."

Now there's a curious phenomenon I've been noticing lately: testicles seem to have become gender non-specific. The other day on the radio, I heard that radio shrink Dr. Laura advise a caller that she should "grow a pair" and kick her philandering husband to the curb. Later that same day, while reading something in the *New York Times*, I came across the term "gender fluidity." By and large, I'm cool with all this, with the exception of having to stand in line now to use restrooms that have gone unisex. Biologically speaking, we who were already equipped with a pair didn't used to have to do that.

"—and you know, Daddy, you can get with the twenty-first century and text like everyone else in the world does."

"Honey, I've got big hands and sixty-year-old eyes. The couple of times I've tried it, it felt like typing through a fog with oven mitts on. And those tiny letters? They're smaller than the bottom line on the optometrist's chart."

"Excuses, excuses. You're just afraid to try anything that takes you out of your comfort zone."

"Yeah, I guess I need to grow a pair, huh?"

"Okay, Daddy. That was just plain weird." Apparently, there's some nuance involved when invoking the testicular metaphor. "Hey, can Jason and I come up this *coming* weekend? Jason's still up for some movie-watching if you are."

"Sounds good. By a stroke of luck, my social calendar is empty."

"And whose fault is that?"

"Uh-oh. You're not going to make another pitch for those online dating sites, are you? Can't I just start texting instead?"

"So you had a couple of bad experiences. That doesn't mean—"

"Three, actually. The weepy divorcée, the woman whose grammar I kept wanting to correct, and the one who told me, with unnerving delight, that I was the same age as her father. *You* don't have any daddy issues, do you?"

"Nah. Mom can drive me nuts sometimes, but you and I are good. You just need to refine your search a little. When I come up this weekend, we can check out some sites that have more mature women."

"Meaning what? That I'll be able to hook up with some nonagenarian who's looking for a young buck like me?"

"Stop speaking PhD, Dr. Funicello. What's a nonagenarian?"

"A piece of ass in her nineties. Is that un-PhD enough for you?"

"Daddy, don't be gross."

"Okay. Change of subject. Did you get your article finished?"

"I hope so. I emailed it to my editor yesterday. He hasn't gotten back to me yet. Wish me luck."

"I do, not that you need it. You're a talented writer, kiddo. That last *Invincible Grrrl* post you put up on Tumblr was brilliant."

"Brilliant, huh? And it's not like *you're* subjective, right? Too bad blogging doesn't pay the bills."

"Well, like I told you before, you never can tell when one thing's going to lead to another. But anyway, send me your Miss Rheingold article. I'd love to read it."

"Thanks, Daddy."

"You bet. By the way, did you ever get ahold of Shirley Shishmanian?"

"Oh yeah, I meant to tell you! Aunt Simone is still friends with her sister, so she got me Shirley's number. Did you know she sells real estate out in California? Or that she's on her fourth husband?"

"I did not. Wow."

"She was fun to talk to, and I got some awesome quotes. She told me she dated that creepy lawyer Roy Cohn when she was in the contest."

"Joe McCarthy's and J. Edgar Hoover's buddy? Really?"

"Uh-huh. I had never heard of him, but then I looked him up. What a motherfucking hypocrite he was, huh?"

I wince once more at my little girl using that kind of language—her New Yorkese, as she puts it—but concur that Cohn was indeed a motherfucker.

"Anyway, thanks for the lead."

"You're welcome. Oh, wait. Forgot you were still in the millennial demographic. What I meant to say was, 'No worries.'"

"Oh, Daddy. You're starting to sound like an old fuddy-duddy. So what are you up to today? You must be going down to the Garde, right?"

I flinch at the question. It's been a week now, and I haven't told anyone about what happened there. Or didn't happen. But probably did. Maybe. "The Garde? Why are you asking about that?"

"Because it's Monday. Isn't Monday the day your movie club meets?"

"Uh, yeah. Yes it is."

"And you go down earlier in the day to set things up. Right?"

"Why are you asking about . . . ?" Recover, damnit. Don't sound so defensive. "No, that's right. I do. In fact, I was just getting ready to leave."

"Daddy? Is something wrong?"

"No, no. Not at all." Don't put this ghost stuff on her. She'll start worrying about you, calling her mother or her aunts to see if you're okay. "Uh-oh. Someone's at the door, Aliza. Guess I'd better go."

"Okay. Love you, Daddy."

"Love you more."

"Hey, Daddy?"

"What?"

"No, never mind."

"Aliza, I'm *fine*."

"It's not about that. I may have some news, but I'm not sure yet."

"Some news about what?" She's not pregnant, is she?

"Nothing. It can wait."

"Then just tell me. Is it good news or bad news?"

"Go answer the door, Daddy. It can wait. I'll send you my article. But be honest about it, okay? Don't tell me how brilliant it is if it sucks."

"Deal. But I already know it doesn't suck. See you."

"See you. Have fun at the Garde."

"Yup." *Click.* Again she mentions it? But no, last time I said something about ghost sightings down there, she pooh-pooh'd it. And what's her news? What's that about? Should I call Kat? Maybe she knows something.

I'm about to head off to the theater when my laptop pings that I've gotten a new email. It's from Aliza, subject line "Read It and Weep." Her article's in an attachment. I put down my car keys and open it. The Garde can wait. And the ghosts, too, if there are any. Or if there ever were . . .

MISS RHEINGOLD REDUX

How a Jewish Beer Maker's "Shiksa Fantasy" Became a Marketing Bonanza

by Aliza Funicello

My beer is Rheingold, the dry beer
Think of Rheingold whenever you buy beer
It's not bitter, not sweet, it's the extra dry treat
Why not try extra dry Rheingold beer?

For millions of East Coast baby boomers, the Rheingold beer jingle is one of those "ear worms" that will forever circulate in their collective memory. And chances are, if you recall that little ditty, you may also remember voting for your favorite among the six "Rheingold girls" in what was touted as "America's *second*-largest election." The Miss Rheingold contest—a perfect storm of democracy, consumerism, and demure sex appeal—became one of the most successful marketing campaigns of the twentieth century. That catchy jingle helped, of course, but it was the public's yearly exhortation to choose the new Miss Rheingold that shot the "extra dry" beer to the top of the sales charts in the Northeast, a position it held through the reigns of twenty-five Miss Rheingolds.

The Rheingold story reaches back to nineteenth-century Germany. Samuel Liebmann was a successful *Braumeister* whose inn was a popular watering hole for the royal soldiers of the Kingdom of Württemberg until he fell into political disfavor for espousing personal freedoms over subservience to the monarchy. When an irate King Wilhelm forbade his soldiers to drink Liebmann's beer or frequent his tavern, business dropped off dramatically. But rather than censor himself, the brewmaster cast his eyes westward. With his wife and six children, Sam Liebmann emigrated to the U.S. in 1854.

The family settled in the Bushwick section of Brooklyn and Liebmann and his sons opened a brewery plant at the corner of Forest and Bremen Streets. Progressive, civic-minded leadership, and an embrace of such industry innovations as artificial refrigeration and packaging in "modern cans," kept the company in the black through the early years of the twentieth century. Then the U.S. entered World War I against Germany.

As anti-German backlash spread across the United States, S. Liebmann's Sons experienced a sizable drop in market share. Nor did the business recover when, shortly after the armistice, Prohibition became the law of the land. At a reduced rate of production, the plant survived by manufacturing lemonade and "near beer."

Following the repeal of Prohibition in 1933, the brewery rebounded and expanded, adding plants in the Bronx and Orange, New Jersey. Ironically, Hitler's rise to power further fueled the company's success. The Third Reich had begun to harass German-Jewish businessmen, among them Dr. Hermann Schülein, the brilliant manager of Germany's world-famous Löwenbräu brewing plant. When the Nazi persecutions turned deadly, Schülein escaped to the U.S. and Löwenbräu's loss became Liebmann's gain. Named the plant's general manager, Dr. Schülein proved a valuable steward. Together with Philip Liebmann, founder Samuel's great-grandson, he developed a dry, golden-colored lager they branded as "Brooklyn's Rheingold." Originally, Rheingold had been conceived as a special brew to commemorate a Metropolitan Opera Company's production of *Das Rheingold* by German composer Richard Wagner, an avowed anti-Semite. Rheingold proved so popular with the public, however, that it became the company's leading brand.

Rheingold was marketed as a down-to-earth working-class beer. From the start, sales were healthy, but it wasn't until Miss Rheingold that they became phenomenal. Using photographs of pretty women to sell products had not been an advertising industry standard until the mid-1920s, when it came about as the result of a labor strike by commercial artists. It's hard to believe, but prior to this, advertisers had relied on illustrators to draw the imagery that promoted their clients' wares. But a desperate mail-order company preparing a spring catalog needed pictures pronto. And so, comely chorus girls were borrowed from Broadway and photographed. Their halftone images replaced the hand-drawn illustrations that had been the norm and sales improved significantly. As a result, a new Manhattan-based industry—professional modeling—was born.

Barcelona-born Eugenia "Jinx" Falkenburg, arguably America's original "supermodel," was the first Miss Rheingold—and she was selected, not elected, via a bit of chicanery. Philip Liebmann, an aficionado of pretty ladies (he later married Hollywood glamour queen Linda Darnell), asked Paul Hesse, Hollywood's persnickety "photographer for the stars," to show him a number of models' photos. From these, he would choose the Rheingold Girl of 1940. Intent on ensuring that the photogenic Falkenberg would be selected, Hesse tricked Liebmann by presenting only pictures of *his* model of choice in different costumes and wigs. No surprise, then, that Liebmann picked Falkenburg to be the star of print ads and store displays in which she declared that *her* beer was Rheingold, the *dry* beer.

The decision to tie the brew to the face of a beautiful spokeswoman was strategic. Rheingold had already captured blue-collar guys as customers, but market research revealed that more women than men purchased the six-packs that sat in New Yorkers' family fridges. Thus, Rheingold was targeting a demographic that included homemakers and working women. Ads featured an attractive woman with the well-scrubbed "American look," who by example could coach her less glamorous female brethren in the techniques and trade secrets of feminine desirability. Fashionable and female-friendly, Falkenburg was an instant hit with both consumers and the company's bottom line. Jinx made sales jump!

The following year, Jinx Falkenburg made it clear to Liebmann executives that she and her now-famous face were on their way to Hollywood. And so, the barkeeps and package store proprietors who sold Rheingold were invited to choose Falkenburg's successor. They selected raven-haired Ruth Ownbey, who was named the Rheingold Girl of 1941. As Ownbey's reign wound down and she, too, packed her bags for Tinsel Town, the "Mad Men" who handled the Liebmann account hit upon a stroke of promotional genius. Rheingold, after all, was a populist beer. Why not invite the public to choose the company's next spokesmodel?

Along with photographer Paul Hesse, Manhattan's top modeling agents, John Robert Powers and Harry Conover, narrowed the field to six lovely ladies, who were photographed and prepped for the coming campaign. Newspaper and magazine ads featured head shots of the six hopefuls and posed the question, "Want to give a pretty girl a great big break?" Signs announcing "Board of Rheingold Voters Meets Here" were placed in no fewer than 30,000 tavern and storefront windows. Inside, customers were greeted by "festoons"—life-size posters of the six smiling Miss Rheingold finalists strung from the rafters. Collectively, they proclaimed, "Our Beer Is Rheingold, the Dry Beer!" A cardboard ballot box with headshots of each "candidate" was placed next to the cash register. Customers could vote by tearing a ballot from the pad, checking off a contestant's name with the little pencil tethered to the box, and dropping said ballot into the slot. Or *several* ballots for those who were particularly partisan. Ballot box stuffing was allowed—this was, after all, Tammany Hall country—

and no age requirement precluded children from registering their choice, too. After 200,000 votes were tabulated, brunette commercial artist Nancy Drake emerged victorious as the first publicly elected Miss Rheingold, beating out runner-up Elyse Knox, a blond cover girl who lost the contest but won the photographer. Hesse and his bride returned to Hollywood and Elyse became a starlet. (Later, she divorced Hesse to marry football star and World War II fighter pilot Tom Harmon, with whom she had three children, including actor Mark Harmon of the popular television series *NCIS*.) Meanwhile, back in Rheingold country, the public election proved worth all the hoopla and expense. Beer sales blasted through the roof and the contest became an annual event, which grew in size each year. Those 200,000 votes cast during the first contest eventually became 25 million—so many that, instead of counting the ballots, Rheingold's election supervisors had them sorted into barrels and bins and weighed on the plant's loading docks. The new Miss Rheingold would be the girl with the most paper poundage.

Vote, vote for Miss Rheingold—Miss Rheingold 1961
Vote, vote for Miss Rheingold—step right up and join the fun!
Time to vote for your selection in our annual election
Time to choose the name of the gal you'll send to fame!
Don't wait! Choose a candidate! And vote!

So sang dancing husband-and-wife movie stars Marge and Gower Champion in the five-minute TV commercial that introduced the public to the six finalists vying to be the twenty-second Miss Rheingold. The Miss R promotion was at its peak of popularity, fueled by a massive and now well-oiled publicity campaign. The Rheingold girls were everywhere: on television and radio; in full-page, full-color newspaper and magazine ads; on billboards and subway car cards; in die-cut displays propped up in storefront windows that invited customers to come inside, vote for their favorite, and, while they were at it, pick up a six-pack or two. For six late-summer weeks, the contestants traveled nonstop with their sharp-eyed chaperone and their company drivers—two finalists to each gleaming white Pontiac convertible. They made personal appearances at parades and policemen's benevolent association picnics, roller rinks and supermarket openings, county fairs and Knights of Columbus carnivals. They smiled for the local press, waved to the crowds, and then rode on to the next gig, often having to reapply their makeup and change their outfits in the car en route. The schedule was exhausting, but the Rheingold girls' ubiquity translated into millions of votes and, more importantly, phenomenal sales that, year after year, topped themselves. The company climbed from number six to number one in the greater New York market.

Here's how it all worked. Each May, cover girls and college homecoming queens, housewives and Hollywood hopefuls, secretaries, socialites, stewardesses—virtually any pretty girl with her eyes on the prizes—up to $50,000 in cash, modeling fees, travel, wide visibility, and, in the early years, war bonds—would converge on New York's Waldorf-Astoria Hotel. Portfolios in hand, they were paraded before a panel of celebrity judges who chatted with them (Rosalind Russell, Joan Fontaine, Art Linkletter) or flirted with them (Tony

Randall, Fernando Lamas, Tallulah Bankhead). The hordes were thinned and herded into three groups—brunettes, blondes, and redheads—then winnowed down to a sextet of finalists. Before they were introduced to the public, the lucky six were fitted for identical outfits, photographed, and investigated by private detectives. Miss Rheingold was, perennially, a girl-next-door type of a higher order, devoid of the "va-va-voom" of the Vargas girls, the overt sexiness of film icons Marilyn Monroe and Jayne Mansfield, or, god forbid, the bare-breasted cheesecake of free-spirited Bettie Page. She could be pretty, beautiful even, but because the high-stakes contest was inextricably linked to the company's bottom line, scandal had to be avoided at all costs. A Rheingold girl with a tawdry past could sink the ship. One finalist was shown the door after she was photographed at the Stork Club with a reputed mafioso. Another was abruptly dropped after an investigator reported that her Greenwich Village roommate was a lesbian poet. A third finalist, German-born Hildegarde "Hillie" Merritt, was cleared after it was determined that she had no Nazi skeletons in her family closet. She went on to win, becoming Miss Rheingold of 1956—even though, in private life, she was both a Mrs. and a mom. Marriage and motherhood did not exclude women from the competition, but pity the Miss R who became pregnant during her twelve-month reign. It happened a couple of times, and photographer Hesse—by all reports a demanding perfectionist—could get testy about having to pose Miss Rheingold and her baby bump behind flower carts, rumpus room bars, or prizewinning pumpkins at the harvest fair.

So much for how it worked. But *why* did it work—so effectively that it is considered by many to be *the* most successful advertising campaign of the twentieth century? Filmmaker Anne Newman, herself a finalist in the running to become Miss Rheingold of 1960, explores this question in her documentary about the contest's impact, *Beauty and the Beer.* Answers emerge in Newman's interviews with past winners, culture critics, and fans of the yearly ritual. Novelist Esther Cohen likens the candidates to human paper dolls, recalling that "as a kid it was really nice to have these beautiful women in the world that you could have a relationship with just by voting." Advertising executive Jerry Della Femina concurs. "You had a choice," he says. "I'd never had a choice about anything. I equate Miss Rheingold with rooting for your favorite baseball team." Former Miss Rheingold Emily Banks observes that each year's winner was reliably "clean, lovely, graceful."

"But not sexy," notes playwright Ilene Beckerman.

"Virgins all," quips Della Femina, who gets no argument from filmmaker-finalist Newman. "Women [of that bygone era] didn't even expect to have orgasms. They had sex but weren't necessarily supposed to enjoy it. That would have been unladylike—and, perhaps, sweaty."

Miss Rheingold was a mid-century myth, "a triumph of style over substance," notes Celeste Yarnall, Miss Rheingold of 1964.

Shirley Greenglass, a 1959 finalist, shed her Armenian surname, Shishmanian, and ran for Miss Rheingold under the pseudonym Dulcet Tone. "The biggest reward wasn't the title or the lucrative contract that went with it," she says. "What we were really competing for was the best prospective husband, meaning a guy who'd wine and dine you, buy you nice jewelry and a beautiful home, father your children, and if the marriage didn't work out, set you up with a generous divorce settlement and monthly alimony in the four-figures range." She recalls the brief period in 1959 when she dated attorney Roy Cohn, whose clients later included John Gotti, Donald Trump, and the Roman Catholic Archdiocese of New York. "Roy was famous for his roles in the Rosenberg trials and the McCarthy hearings. He took me to the Copa, the Latin Quarter, El Morocco—the kinds of places where we'd be noticed and written about in the gossip columns. Photographed for the tabloids, too. He was a short, bug-eyed man. I towered over him, so he always insisted the photographer take our picture sitting down. He wasn't interested in me, personally. It was about the fact that I was one of the finalists. We were interchangeable. A Rheingold girl made for good copy and good eye candy. I had no idea at the time that the little toad was in the closet, but I should have guessed. He was a lousy kisser."

The six finalists were, indeed, interchangeable. Each wore red lipstick, white gloves, identical powder blue shirtwaist dresses with Peter Pan collars, and matching powder blue pumps. They carried hatboxes with their names emblazoned on them and distributed campaign cards with their pictures on one side, their bios, height, and weight on the other. (No breast, waist, and hips measurements, thank you.) Unlike Miss America contestants, the Rheingold girls were not required to sashay down runways in bathing suits and high heels, wear lame costumes that pegged them as representatives of the Beehive State or the Hawkeye State, demonstrate their talent for tap dancing or baton twirling, or give "Kumbaya"-like answers to interview questions posed by Miss America's perennial master of ceremonies, Bert Parks. They merely had to look lovely, exude charm, and be photogenic—and, during that grueling six-week campaign, try to convince the public that they were the *most* lovely, the *most* charming, the *most* photogenic of that year's six, so that in December after the votes were in, they could be declared the winner and climb on to the Miss Rheingold pedestal for the next twelve months' worth of photo shoots, ribbon cuttings, and fashion shows.

Speaking of fashion, is it mere coincidence that in 1959 at the pinnacle of Miss R's popularity, the Mattel toy company introduced Barbie, its mute fashion doll with the perfect figure, the demure sidelong stare, and the dozens of chic outfits, beneath which was the absence of a vagina? Did Miss Rheingold beget Barbie? That first year, the doll was available as a blonde or a brunette (buyer's choice; you voted with cash). Like Rheingold beer itself, Barbie even had a Teutonic lineage. A voluptuous, narrow-waisted German doll named Bild Lilli was designer Ruth Handler's template for her bestselling Barbie—and, perhaps as well, for Miss R, whom Esther Cohen wryly notes was "Philip Liebmann's shiksa fantasy."

Of the twenty-five Miss Rheingold titleholders, sixteen were brunettes, six were blondes, and three were redheads. They had perky first names like Pat, Kathy, Nancy, and Margie, and Anglo-Saxon surnames like Austin, Banks, Woodruff, Bain—not a Finkelstein or Faragosa or Flores in the bunch. Rheingold's monthly ads in the *New Yorker*, *Gourmet*, *Playbill*, and the *New York Times* depicted them as active women who hunted, skied, golfed, bowled, square-danced, and gardened. Year after year, they were established as animal lovers who cuddled with puppies, kittens, baby chicks, miniature ponies. Miss Rheingold of 1953 even played with a pair of bear cubs, and in one memorable 1947 ad, Miss Rheingold goes for a Coney Island roller coaster ride with her Scottish terrier. Occasionally, a Miss Rheingold ad would give a nod to current events. Miss R of 1943 posed as Rosie the Riveter. During the presidential campaign between John F. Kennedy and Richard Nixon, Miss R of 1960 led a marching band flanked diplomatically by a baby elephant on one side, a donkey on the other. When the New York Mets came into existence, Miss R of 1962 posed with the team's curmudgeonly manager, Casey Stengel. (Liebmann Breweries was a major Mets sponsor.) More typically, however, Rheingold's "super saleswoman" was depicted at the center of fun: poolside parties, picnics at the beach, backyard barbecues, hay rides. They were cowgirls one month, hostesses in couture the next. In the ads and on the billboards, they never smoked, never frowned, never looked lustfully at the innocuous male models who occasionally showed up in the ads. Indeed, Miss R was so fashionably prim that she never chugged or even took polite sips of the beer she perennially served and proclaimed was *hers*.

Oh, and one more thing: Miss Rheingold was always white.

If the perfect storm of democracy, consumerism, and sophisticated sex appeal had created the Miss Rheingold phenomenon in the early 1940s, a perfect storm of a different kind unraveled it in the mid-1960s, namely the rising tide of racial unrest, the gathering winds of feminism, the growing market share of national brands, and the sudden crack of rifle fire in Dallas.

By 1963, the civil rights movement had reached a fever pitch and put Liebmann Breweries in a difficult position. For many years, Rheingold had been appeasing its customers of color—a large and important market—with print ads that featured celebrities like Louis Armstrong, Dorothy Dandridge, Carmen Miranda, and Jackie Robinson. Significantly, Rheingold also stepped up as a regional sponsor of *The Nat King Cole Show*, television's first variety show to feature a black entertainer as host, when no national sponsor could be convinced to underwrite the program. (Said Cole, "Madison Avenue is afraid of the dark.") But African-Americans and Latinos took note that none of their own had ever made it to the finals of the Miss Rheingold contest. (The closest to ethnic diversity the contest had come was finalist Audrey Garcia, a Hawaiian native who competed the year Hawaii was to become the fiftieth state.) Rheingold executives feared a fierce backlash from white consumers—its dominant customer base—if it accommodated its minority customers with a black or Hispanic candidate. The adage "No publicity is *bad* publicity" had not yet been embraced by Madison Avenue. Miss Rheingold was about fun, after all, not controversy.

As the admen responsible for the Rheingold account wrestled with racial politics, feminist Betty Friedan published her watershed book about women's roles, *The Feminine Mystique*. Friedan's treatise pulled no punches. "The feminine mystique has succeeded in burying millions of American women alive," she argued. At this, the dawn of feminism's second wave, Miss Rheingold began to be regarded by some as a quaint, semi-insulting, or even dangerous stereotype—one that endorsed the male chauvinist value of beauty over brains, objectification of "the fairer sex" over a woman's true worth. Contestants were, after all, women. Why were they referred to as the Rheingold *girls*?

Meanwhile, as the nation's newspapers ran front-page stories of the latest race riots, and editorials about the empowerment of women, the financial pages reported that national brands like Anheuser-Busch had begun to eat away like termites at the sustainability of regional brews like Rheingold. A decade earlier, the Liebmann company had tried and failed to make a foray into the California beer market. But if the Northeast was loyal to the "extra dry" lager, the rest of the nation made it clear that they preferred Schlitz, "the beer that made Milwaukee famous"; Miller, "the champagne of bottled beer"; Schaefer, "the one beer to have when you're having more than one"; and Budweiser, the beer that "said it all." Rheingold's aging plants were facing costly overhauls and its labor force had begun demanding more concessions and threatening to strike. And then those shots rained down on Dealey Plaza, a president was mortally wounded, and his charming and photogenic first lady was covered in his blood.

Celeste Yarnall, the last of the traditionally elected Miss Rheingolds, recalls, "The day I was notified that I had garnered twenty million votes and won it all was the day before John F. Kennedy was shot. This happy new nineteen-year-old Miss Rheingold went from joy to sorrow in twenty-four little hours as I was a kid fresh from that Camelot 'fantasyland' and Jackie Kennedy was my idol. I had the dark hair cut in the flip, the white gloves and the pearls. My heart was broken when I flew into New York to pose for the photos that would announce my having won." The rest of the country had had their hearts broken as well, of course, and a nation's grieving, added to the racial controversy, Liebmann Breweries' falling profits, and the new thinking about a woman's place in the world, drove a stake into the heart of the Miss Rheingold contest. Sharon Vaughn, Miss Rheingold of 1965, was appointed rather than elected, just as the original titleholder, Jinx Falkenburg, had been. Gone now were the lavish magazine and billboard ads, the eye-catching store displays, the TV and radio commercials. Vaughn, a decidedly downsized Miss R, made public appearances at events like the Polish fair and the firemen's muster and gradually just faded away—as did the venerable and storied Liebmann Breweries. The company was sold to PepsiCo and limped along for a decade or so until the first day of February 1974, when the Brooklyn plant's remaining 1,500 workers were handed their pink slips. A hundred thousand gallons of Rheingold were dumped into the East River and the factory doors were closed and locked for good.

Well, so much for the beer. But what became of those twenty-five victorious beauties? A number of Miss Rs became the arm candy, and then the wives, of wealthy men, among them famous actors, athletes, and executives. Opting off the modeling merry-go-round, these women raised children and enjoyed well-heeled private lives and, perhaps from time to time, could now indulge in *dessert*. But many Rheingold "girls" became successful career women: television producers, political activists, professional photographers, and company heads. Celeste Yarnall earned a PhD in nutrition and authored books on holistic health care for cats and dogs while maintaining an acting career on TV (*Star Trek*, *Bonanza*) and in films (Elvis Presley's *Live a Little, Love a Little*, Roger Corman's *The Velvet Vampire*). Among those contestants who sought to parlay their Rheingold girl cachet into big-screen film careers, the losers fared better than the winners. Rheingold runners-up Hope Lange, Diane Baker, and Tippi Hedren went on to successful acting careers. Grace Kelly, the biggest movie star of the bunch, had failed to even qualify as one of the six finalists. Too thin, the Rheingold judges concluded.

Monaco's Prince Rainier thought otherwise. He made Kelly his Cinderella bride in a televised spectacle broadcast around the globe. Ironically, the couple's 1956 nuptials were covered on American television by none other than Jinx Falkenburg, now a small-screen "personality."

The Miss Rheingold contest is long gone, of course—a nearly forgotten footnote from Madison Avenue's checkered and colorful past. Miss R is buried in advertising's graveyard along with those glossy-haired Breck shampoo girls and subterranean New York's Miss Subways. Still, vestiges of Miss Rheingold's influence survive, as do many of the actual titleholders. Nancy Drake, who won that first public election way back in 1942, is the oldest surviving Miss R. A well-heeled widow now in her nineties (who declined to be interviewed for this article), she splits her time between Palm Beach and Watch Hill, a tony Rhode Island enclave, where her neighbor is Taylor Swift, the Barbie doll–like pop superstar. (With her wholesome image, adorable smile, and red carpet fashion sense, who *wouldn't* have voted for Swift if her face had appeared on a ballot box during that earlier era?) Barbie herself is still going strong; sales of Mattel's statuesque fashion doll are as robust as ever.

Here are two curious footnotes to the Miss Rheingold story.

First, Kevin McCrary, a "son of privilege" whose mother was Miss Rheingold *numero uno*, Jinx Falkenburg, was the subject of a 2011 episode of A&E TV's series *Hoarders*. McCrary later faced eviction from the rent-stabilized walk-up on Manhattan's Upper East Side where, for thirty years, he had resided among his various and sundry "collections."

Second, zombie-like, as if from a crypt in advertising's aforementioned graveyard, Miss R rose again at the dawn of the twenty-first century, alas briefly and unsuccessfully. In 2003, the Rheingold brand reemerged, marketed now as an "authentic" local craft beer for New York City's young hipsters. The company brought back a "six-pack" of Miss Rheingold contenders for beer drinkers of a decidedly different era. The contestants now were sexy bartenders with snug-fitting "wife beater" T-shirts and skimpy jean cutoffs, augmented breasts, come-hither looks, and pierced belly buttons. Voting was online now, or in the bars where the women poured, shook, and stirred alcohol for their ogling clientele. In this new incarnation, a tongue-in-cheek talent component was added. Kate Duyn danced on the bar to become Miss Rheingold of 2003. On the oversized, in-your-face billboards erected on buildings in SoHo and the East Village, this bad-ass twenty-first-century Miss R glared over her shoulder at passersby as she sat naked in a tub full of Rheingold, the bathroom floor littered with dozens of empties. Dani Marco succeeded Duyn as Miss Rheingold of 2004, having flamenco-danced her way to victory over her competitors: sleeve-tattooed Erin; fanny-jiggling Raquel; Carmel, who demonstrated the takedown of a male customer in the talent competition; raunchy Kim, whose talent was pouring Rheingold over her T-shirt front and tongue-kissing another woman; and six-foot-plus opera singer Shequida. Interestingly, Shequida was the first Rheingold girl who was, biologically speaking, a Rheingold *boy*—a female impersonator who, at the conclusion of her aria, snatched off her long blond wig to reveal his close-cropped Afro. At long last, the Miss Rheingold contest had an African-American contestant, albeit one with a penis. No surprise, though, that the white girl won—another brunette.

OKAY, DON'T EXPECT *me* to be objective, but in her old man's humble opinion, Aliza nailed it. This piece just may give her enough clout so that she gets to do the stories she wants instead of pitching them and then seeing them go to someone else.

And who knows? Maybe writing about this subject helped her to better appreciate the rocky road her mother and other feminists had to travel back then when they'd been raised with the message that the ultimate symbols of a woman's worth were a tiara, a dozen long-stemmed roses, and a marriage certificate. "There she is, your ideal," the host would croon whenever the new Miss America took her first walk down the runway in Atlantic City. Miss Rheingold, Miss Universe, Miss America: the titles may have differed but they were all "*your* ideal." But who was the *you*? Impressionable young women with Cinderella fantasies? Young men looking for a marriageable girl they could take home to their mothers? Donald Trump's predecessor, mogul and marketing mastermind Philip Liebmann?

But it was all a pose, wasn't it? A myth? I remember when one of the Miss Americas from the 1950s wrote a book years later about how she'd been incested by her father throughout her childhood. And another winner who came out about getting beaten up by her pro football player boyfriend. How many trips to the altar did Aliza say Shirley Shishmanian had made? Four? Well, at least she hadn't married Roy Cohn.

EIGHT

On the drive to New London from Three Rivers, I pull up to the same Dunkin' Donuts drive-thru as I did the week before. Tell the talking speaker that I want a medium hot coffee, one cream, *no sugar*. When I get up to the window, there he is again: that same sketchy guy who may have drugged my coffee the last time. When I pull back onto the road, I take a tentative sip. No sugar. I catch myself feeling a little disappointed—I mean, it *was* an awesome experience: returning to my childhood, communing with ghosts from Old Hollywood. I wonder what a film scholar like Jeanine Basinger at Wesleyan or a writer like the *New Yorker*'s Anthony Lane would give to have a conversation with a celluloid pioneer like Lois Weber. . . . But I guess I'm relieved, too, because it was freaky as hell to be tripping like that, if that's what I was doing. At any rate, if I see any ghosts today when I get to the Garde, I guess I can rule out acid-laced coffee as the cause.

No good parking space out in front this week. I circle the block twice before I find a space. Get out of the car and head up the hill to the theater, key in hand.

Inside, I scan the lobby. Look down the hall to where the offices are. No lights, no action. I open one of the doors to the auditorium and gaze down at the stage. The ghost lamp's lit; the curtain's down. I cup my hands around my mouth. "Hello?" No answer. "Anyone here?" Okay then. We're back to normal for a Monday—no one else here, living or dead. I head up the grand staircase to the projection room. I'll get tonight's film set up for my group, then get out of here until this evening. I'm still a little jumpy, but whatever happened last week is *not* going to happen again.

No, check that.

There they are: those film canisters. And here *she* is—Lois's ghost, blurry at first, then coming into sharp-edged focus. "I was beginning to wonder if we'd see you today, Felix. Or if, perhaps, you had decided you were afraid of ghosts."

There's a trace of sarcasm in her tone. She's outfitted differently than the week before—dressed more like a woman from the 1930s than the twenties. She's using a cane now and her translucent hair has gone gray. Do ghosts age?

"No Billie Dove this time?" I ask.

While it's still a jolt to commune with a spirit who knows so much about my past—has it on film, no less!—at least this time I know I'm not dead.

"Miss Dove sends her regrets. She has a tennis match with her doubles partner, Jinx Falkenburg. They're hoping to upset the reigning doubles champs, the two Vivs."

"The two Vivs?"

"Vivian Vance and Vivien Leigh. They're favored to win three-to-one among the bettors in our ranks, but one never knows."

"Ethel Mertz and Scarlett O'Hara are tennis partners? Wow. And there's betting where you are? For money?"

"Not the kind of legal tender I imagine you're thinking of, but there are many kinds of currencies, dear boy. Now let's get down to the business at hand. I've brought along another member of our realm to assist us today, an actress from Hollywood's Golden Age whom you will no doubt recognize."

And indeed I do. Materializing before me is *Casablanca*'s Ilsa Lund and Hitchcock's female lead in both *Spellbound* and *Notorious*. Yet she is costumed in the nun's habit she wore as the feisty but tubercular Sister Benedict, Bing Crosby's costar in the top-grossing film of 1945, *The Bells of St. Mary's*. "It's an honor to meet you, Miss Bergman," I tell her, bowing before her. She is, after all, Hollywood royalty.

She laughs at the gesture and offers me her see-through hand. I can't feel it, but kiss it nonetheless. "Now let's dispense with the formality, shall we?" she says. "Lois tells me you're a professor of film history. Yes?"

I nod. "And an admirer of your work. I screened *Gaslight* for my college students last semester and *Anastasia* for the little film club I run here at the Garde."

"Ah, my two Best Actress roles. They were bookends, in a sense. I won the Oscar for *Gaslight* when my virtuous image was intact, and for *Anastasia* when Hollywood decided to forgive me after all for my love affair with Rossellini. During the intervening years, as you may know, I was maligned in the American press and boycotted by the studio for having strayed from my marriage. One of your ridiculous politicians went so far as to condemn me on the Senate floor for being 'a powerful influence for evil.' Thank goodness the Italians were not so provincial. The five pictures I made with Roberto during my exile did quite well in Italy, thank you." She turns to Weber's ghost. "Of course, you, too, felt the lash when you were a 'living,' Lois. How dare you film a woman in her natural state!"

"Ah, yes. They were happy to undermine the career of a woman who dared to play by the same rules as the men in the business and, worst of all, succeed."

"I suppose the exception was Hitler's fair-haired filmmaker, Miss Riefenstahl," Bergman's ghost muses. "He was her patron, she was his muse. Of course, she was making propaganda, not art."

"Yes, but it was artful propaganda. I'll give Leni that much. She pioneered the tracking shot in *Olympia* and did impressive work with her slow-motion shots as well. As a director, she was quite technically adroit."

"Indeed. Nevertheless, you cannot overlook the fact that she was complicit in the atrocities being orchestrated inside the camps, despite her insistence that she was ignorant of those horrors. I saw her just last week at the MGM reunion, and she was *still* proclaiming her innocence. It's really quite tiresome."

"And not at all convincing," Lois adds. "Leni's directorial skills far exceeded her skills as an actress playing the role of the wide-eyed naïf."

Wow! I could listen to their banter for hours, but Lois taps her cane against the floor. "Well, down to business," she says. "Perhaps, Felix, you are wondering why I have asked Ingrid to reprise her role as Sister Benedict for your edification. My thinking is that, since you were taught by nuns as a child and since Ingrid played one in *The Bells of St. Mary's*, it would be appropriate to have her give you the following presentation."

I look from one ghost to the other. "What kind of presentation?"

"Well, today you will revisit your life in the year 1965. And so, I thought it might be fruitful to offer you some context: what was happening in the news at the time, and in the popular culture—that sort of thing. After which, we shall examine some specifics in the life of twelve-year-old Felix Funicello. Shall we begin?"

"I guess." Something tells me I don't really have a choice.

"Splendid. Please proceed then, Sister Benedict."

"With pleasure." Bergman's ghost steps behind a podium that has somehow materialized. Downstairs, the curtain rises, the screen descends, and images begin flickering. The houselights dim and the screen fills with newsreel shots: frenzy on the floor of the New York Stock Exchange, a joint session of Congress, elderly people at some sort of clinic.

"It's autumn—the first of November, to be exact," Bergman says. "When economists look back on this year, they will regard it as one of the country's best in terms of inflation-free growth and economic equity. Politically speaking, this is an era when Congress gets things accomplished through bipartisan cooperation. Medicare and Medicaid were signed into law earlier this year. And congressional cooperation has forced the tobacco industry to begin printing warnings on cigarette packs about the hazards of smoking. But in terms of world politics, there is trouble."

The film cuts abruptly to a rice paddy being strafed with machine gun fire, American soldiers tramping along a jungle path, a village of thatched huts in flames.

"The U.S.'s effort to contain Communism in Vietnam is reaching the boiling point, and the protest movement is gaining momentum in response to President Johnson's order that an additional fifty thousand American troops are to be sent into what will later be seen as a political quagmire. Some veterans of this divisive war will return unscathed. Others will suffer psychological and physical disabilities, from having witnessed or participated in traumatic events to having ingested Agent Orange. The unluckiest will end up as homeless drug addicts, MIAs, or names carved into that black wall of sorrow down there in Washington," she says. As if on cue, the film shows somber visitors at the Vietnam Veterans Memorial. I have to catch my breath when the camera zooms in for a close-up of one of those names on the wall: Stanley T. Wierzbicki. My mind flashes back to our former neighbor, running after my sisters and me as we walk down Herbert Hoover Avenue, begging to be included.

The film shifts to black-and-white footage of the civil rights struggle. "Betty Shabazz's heart was broken in February when her husband, Malcolm X, was shot dead at a speaking event in Harlem. The assassination was followed by rioting and looting. But there have been victories as well as setbacks this year. The Selma-to-Montgomery marches convince LBJ to ask Congress to pass a sweeping voting rights bill. '*We* shall overcome,' the president says, and with that first-person plural pronoun, he aligns himself with the cause of justice. The Voting Rights Act becomes law in August."

From behind me, I hear the tapping of a cane. Ever the directress, Lois is still in charge. Sister Benedict looks past me, nods, and clears her throat. "This presentation will now conclude with a silent montage depicting popular culture," she says. On the screen, in rapid succession, the great Sandy Koufax winds up for a pitch, the Celtics' Bill Russell sinks one from downtown, Gale Sayers scores a touchdown for the Bears, and Cassius Clay KOs Sonny Liston. I catch glimpses of popular TV shows (*The Munsters*, *The Beverly Hillbillies*, *The Man from U.N.C.L.E.*) and long-forgotten commercials (Mr. Whipple squeezing the Charmin, Josephine the Plumber hawking Comet). The Beatles fly by, the Rolling Stones, Bob Dylan. The screen flashes scenes from that year's biggest films: *Dr. Zhivago*, *Thunderball*, *The Sound of Music*.

"Hey, even my parents went to see that last one," I tell Bergman's ghost. "Ma kept hounding Pop to take her until he finally surrendered. When they got home, he said the next time she wanted to see a bunch of screech-owl nuns singing, he'd take her to High Mass at St. Aloysius."

Sister Benedict puts her hands on her hips, feigning insult at this swipe against nuns. Then she laughs and looks back at her director. "Is that a wrap?"

"Yes, thanks ever so much, my dear," Lois tells her. "You're free to return now."

Bergman's ghost waves goodbye and begins to fade. "Great to meet you!" I call to her diminishing figure. She smiles. Curtsies. And then she's gone.

Lois approaches. "So there's your *macro*-tutorial of 1965, Felix. Now tell me who *you* were then."

"Who *I* was? I don't know. There's not that much to tell."

She frowns. "That's not an answer. It's an evasion."

Sheesh, here she goes with the therapist talk again. "Well, let me think. I was twelve. Still tying double knots in my shoelaces, if I recall." I smile; she doesn't. "And, let's see. As you know, I was in parochial school. Our class was getting ready to make our confirmation that year so that, according to the nuns, we could become 'soldiers in Christ's army.' Which was a pretty truculent way of putting it, now that I think about it. I mean, they were also telling us that Jesus was the Prince of Peace."

"What else can you tell me about that time in your life, Felix?"

I shrug. "Are you looking for something specific?" She shrugs back. "Well, I collected baseball cards. I had a signed card from Ron Swoboda. He played left field for the Mets. . . . And, uh, I watched a lot of TV back then."

She looks unimpressed. "What about books? Were you a reader?"

"Not especially. Oh. There was this one book I liked so much that I read it twice: *Dune* by Frank Herbert. I tried picking it for a book report, but Sister Godberta frowned at the cover and nixed that idea. Looked too subversive, I guess. So, instead, I recycled my last year's book report on *The Yearling*. Got away with it, too, although I had to copy it over because my fifth-grade teacher, Madame Frechette, had scrawled '*Magnifique, Monsieur!*' across the top. Madame was French-Canadian. Didn't last too long at Aloysius Gonzaga. I got the feeling that the nuns found her not quite acceptable. It was probably that beret she wore, and the patterned stockings. And the fact that she doused herself with perfume."

"What about socially? Were you outgoing? Shy? Any sweethearts back then, Felix?"

"Girlfriends? No way. I was already pretty self-conscious about being the shortest kid in my class. Then, one by one, the sixth-grade girls started transforming themselves into sequoias with breasts. And it wasn't as if my parents or the good sisters of St. Aloysius Gonzaga were lining up to teach me about human sexual development. So that left me with my buddy Lonny Flood as my main source of information. Lonny had stayed back twice and, at thirteen, was ahead of the curve, developmentally. His voice was cracking all over the place and his upper lip looked like it needed dusting. One afternoon while we were riding our bikes, he confided that he'd had a wet dream that felt 'weird but bitchin'.' I was confused about why *that* was; to me it sounded like a variation on bed-wetting, which only felt hot, uncomfortable, and itchy. I didn't get my growth spurt until ninth grade, which was when I got *my* first wet dream and started getting interested in girls."

She observes that she was asking me about romance and I went right to sex.

"So noted. But as long as we're on that subject, can I ask you something? Do you ghosts have sex lives? I mean, since you're dead, I assume you can't procreate. But what about recreational . . ."

Instead of answering me, she points at the screen and says, "Felix, look. Is that you?" *Now* which of us is guilty of evasion? But it's me, all right. A tracking shot follows me walking down Otis Street, wearing my St. Aloysius uniform and lugging a stack of books. "Heading home after school," I tell Lois. On the screen, I turn onto the street where we lived. "That was our house up on the left—the gray one with the green shutters. But be forewarned: 33 Herbert Hoover Avenue was a war zone back then."

"Oh? What was this war about?"

"Not what. Who. My sister Frances."

"With whom was she at war?"

"The rest of us. My parents, my other sister, me. But mostly she was at war with herself. And her body was the battlefield."

NINE

The camera follows me into the house. There's our old sofa and the cabinet-model TV we used to have—the one that exploded and scorched the wall behind it. Speaking of that wall, my sisters' and my framed high school graduation photos are missing, which makes sense; it's 1965 so none of us has graduated yet. There's Winky curled up on the couch, probably dreaming up new ways to torture my father. God, this is as weird as the last time: seeing our home the way it was back then. For some reason, it makes me feel . . . claustrophobic.

Ma's in the kitchen—young again, and healthy. No strokes yet, no dementia. Her hair hasn't even gone gray. Why did I think back then that she was old?

"How was school today, Felix?"

"Good."

"What did you do?"

"Nothing."

"Really? That must have been pretty boring. Would Sister agree with that summary of your day?"

I shrug. Simone enters the room. "Ma, can I talk to you about something?" she says. "It's kind of important."

I go over to the stove to see what's cooking on the front burner. When I lift the pot lid, the camera goes in for a close-up of Ma's meatballs simmering in sauce. After my parents died, the job of emptying out the house and getting it ready to sell fell to me. I brought most of the kitchen stuff over to Goodwill, but for sentimental reasons, I kept Ma's saucepot—the one shown here. I make a decent *ragú*, but it doesn't come close to Marie Funicello's.

I turn to my ghostly companion. "Too bad this movie doesn't have Smell-O-Vision," I tell her. "The aroma would put your salivary glands into overdrive."

"If I had them anymore," Lois sighs. No salivary glands? That must mean no sex glands either. Mystery solved.

On the screen, I head over to the breadbox. "Hey, Ma, can I make myself a sandwich?"

"No. Those meatballs are for supper. And don't interrupt."

I put my hands together like I'm praying to her. "Please, Ma. I'm *starving*."

She shakes her head. No means no. "You can rip off the heel of that loaf of Italian bread and dunk it in the sauce, but no meatballs."

"Can I have one of those ice cream sandwiches in the freezer then?"

"They're for dessert. Have an apple."

"I don't want an apple."

"Then you must not be very hungry after all."

"Felix, do you *mind*?" Simone says. "We're trying to have a conversation."

I grab an apple, polish it against my pant leg, take a bite, and shift into eavesdropping mode. This was mostly how I gathered information when I was a kid. It wasn't like anyone was going to confide in me. So I listened, as unobtrusively as possible.

Simone tells Ma that her assistant manager at the grocery store where she's a checkout girl has been bumping up against her accidentally-on-purpose and staring at her chest when he speaks to her. "Some of the things he says make me feel uncomfortable and . . . I don't know. Dirty or something."

I stop eating my apple. This is starting to sound interesting, and the crunching might remind them that I'm still here. Ma tells Simone to give her a "for instance."

"Yesterday he started talking about how great I must look in a bikini. And how I'm so voluptuous that I could pose for *Playboy*."

"Maybe you should tell your father," Ma suggests.

"And then what? He goes over there and causes a stink so that I get fired? Ma, *please* don't tell Poppy." Simone turns her attention to me. "And don't you say anything either, Mr. Big Ears."

"About what?" I ask. "I'm not even listening."

Lois chuckles. "That was pretty convincing just now," she ribs. "Maybe you should have considered a career in front of the camera."

"Well, honey, men are men," my mother tells Simone. "Shapely girls like you just have to put up with stuff like that in the working world. Or else quit. Those are your choices."

"But I don't want to quit, Ma. I like my job other than that. And I like making my own money."

"Then just try to ignore it. Or laugh it off. If you let him see that it gets your goat when he says things like that, he'll do it more. And if you complain to *his* superior, he might turn against you and make your life miserable."

Jerking forward in my seat, I address the screen. "Ignore it, Ma? Shut her mouth and put up with it? That's *terrible* advice."

"Perhaps," Lois's ghost says. "But that's what women have always had to do. And in fairness, you can't apply today's standards to what was or wasn't acceptable fifty years ago. It was even worse during my era. By the time the Nineteenth Amendment was passed and I was allowed to cast my first vote for president, I had already written and directed more than seventy-five motion picture plays. I was forty-one years old."

"Point taken. By the way, who did you vote for? Harding?"

"I most certainly did not! Those matinee idol looks of his didn't fool me. Judging a person's character by what his face told me—that was a skill I developed casting my films. I could tell just by looking at him that Warren G. Harding was a philanderer and a scoundrel. I voted for James M. Cox and his running mate, Franklin D. Roosevelt. Now, I should like you to return to the business at hand. Please direct your attention to your film and tell me what you see."

"Okay, well, I'm going into the living room." On the screen, I put down the half-eaten apple and pull our bulky dictionary off the bookshelf. "Looks like I'm starting my homework."

"Voluptuous, voluptuous . . ." my juvenile self mumbles.

I have to laugh. "Or not."

We watch as I flip through the tissue-paper pages at the back of the book. An extreme close-up of my finger going down columns of V-words shows that I've incorrectly assumed that "voluptuous" begins with either *vul* or *vel*. When I finally find it, I read the definition out loud. "'Ripe; fleshy; devoted to the luxury of sensual pleasures.'" Then I flip back to the S's in search of the word "sensual."

I tell Lois's ghost that the vocab words I picked up while eavesdropping were far more interesting than the ones Sister Godberta gave us. But the directress is distracted by something else on the screen. Or rather, some*one*.

"Good heavens," she says. "Who's *that*?"

And there she is, at her worst. I have to take a breath before answering her. All these years later, it's still painful to see her this way.

"My sister Frances."

"Is it cancer?" I shake my head. "Then what's wrong with her?"

"That was what *we* wanted to know. Our whole family was baffled about why she was doing this to herself. Frances would only say that she was tired of being the family hippo and was finally doing something about it."

"Aha," she says. "Then it's anorexia nervosa."

"Right, but how—?"

"It didn't yet have a name when I was a living, but the condition certainly existed. Many starlets were afflicted, and some of the young male actors as well."

"I looked it up a while back. It was already in the books by 1965—specifically, the DSM-I, but—"

"The what?"

"The *Diagnostic and Statistical Manual of Mental Disorders*, first edition. It's the go-to guide for shrinks. So it had been identified by the experts, but it wasn't on the radar in mainstream America yet. Karen Carpenter's death was what made anorexia a household word, but that was almost two decades later."

"Ah yes, I remember when Miss Carpenter crossed over. A sweet girl, but she was so shy and withdrawn initially. She's better now. She's a vocalist in a trio that plays for us from time to time."

"She played the drums, too, I'm pretty sure."

"Oh yes, she plays them still. As does her friend, Mr. Moon."

"*Keith* Moon? Drummer for The Who?"

Lois says she's not sure—that so many rock 'n' rollers crossed over because of their various excesses that she can't keep them all straight. "But tell me, Felix, how did you and your parents and Simone respond to Frances's illness?"

"It was confusing," I tell her. "Isolating. I think we all felt ashamed and alone with what we assumed was a problem only *we* were facing: the voluntary starvation of one of our own."

Lois nods. "The poor thing looks so strange with those bulbous eyes and collapsed cheeks," she says. "But her body looks almost bloated."

"Because she was dressing in layers of clothes to throw people off. Look at the way her hair was thinning out. She started wearing hats to hide her bald patches. When people asked her if she was sick, she'd say she was getting over a bad stomach flu. Frances was 'getting over a stomach flu' for months, ever since she'd started dieting and doing a daily calorie-burning regimen that ratcheted up to a thousand jumping jacks, two hundred sit-ups, and, if neither of our parents was home to stop her, forty-five minutes' worth of manic running up and down the basement stairs.

"If my mother was up to doing battle with Frances before school, she could get her to eat the top half of a hard-boiled egg and a few nibbles of unbuttered toast. My sisters had the same lunch period at school, so Ma enlisted Simone to spy on Frances. Simone would report back that Fran did, in fact, buy lunch as she swore she did: soup and crackers most days. Simone would sometimes lose track of the conversation at the table where she sat with her girlfriends because she was so busy counting the spoonfuls of soup Frances put in her mouth: on average, four or five. She never ate the crackers, Simone said.

"One time in the middle of all this, I remember barging into our bathroom, assuming it was empty and that I was the only one home. And there was Frances, who had mistakenly assumed that *she* was the only one home. She was standing on the scale in just her underwear. 'Get out, you idiot!' she screamed, and I backed away from the wild-eyed witch who seemed, almost, to have stolen the identity of my real sister. I ran down the stairs and out the front door, I remember, then wandered the neighborhood, kicking stones into culverts and trying to unsee what I had seen. Despite Frances's frequent campaigns to belittle me, I loved her and was afraid of what was happening—which is not to say that I understood what that was. When I got back home after my confused wandering up and down our street, I tried watching TV, but the benign images on the screen were no match for the image of my sister's protruding ribs and pelvic bones, her pencil-thin arms and knitting-needle legs. To eradicate what I had seen in the bathroom the hour before, I attempted to picture other female bodies: the golden James Bond girl on that *Life* magazine cover; our shapely cousin Annette in her white two-piece swimsuit on the poster above the fryolator at Pop's lunch counter; the buxom, pucker-mouthed women spilling out of their tops on the covers of the *Police Gazettes* and *Sir!*, the magazines I peeked at while waiting for my haircut at the barbershop. It didn't work.

"That evening when my parents got home, I didn't tell them about what I had walked in on and seen. Frances tried to get herself excused from supper, pleading the need to study for an upcoming test, but Pop insisted she join us. When she sat down at the table, I couldn't look at her so I did not know if she was able to look at me. Pop said grace as usual, turning pointedly in Frances's direction when he spoke the words 'from Thy bounty.'

"After the blessing ended with our amens, my mother said she had a special request: could we all just enjoy a peaceful meal together? Our last several suppers had been stressful, she noted, as if any of us needed a reminder. I nodded in agreement and, seated across from Simone, saw that she nodded, too. 'Sounds good,' Pop said.

"I piled *braciole*, peas, and salad onto my plate—enough for two people—and, without looking up, started shoveling food into my mouth. No one spoke. I kept listening for the clink of silverware on Frances's dinner plate but heard nothing. I was three-quarters done with my huge meal when Pop threw up his hands and ordered Frances to stop moving her food around and *eat* it, goddamnit! 'And don't try that trick where you hold it in your mouth, then go spit it out in the toilet. We're onto that one. This foolishness is over, as of *right now*. Starving yourself in an *Italian* home? Jesus Christ, I make my living *feeding* people! Why in the goddamned hell would you even *want* to do this to yourself? Do you think it looks good? Because it doesn't. You look like you've just been freed from a concentration camp. Well, like I said, it stops here and now. Your mother and I have had it. You're going to eat like a normal person from now on. No, you're going to *be* a normal person. You hear me?'

"No doubt she *did* hear him; he was shouting. But despite Pop's decree, it did not stop there and then. Ma's peaceful, stress-free meal proved unattainable. Faces turned red, tears fell, a chair tipped over, food was flung to the floor, a plate broke in half. When Pop grabbed Frances as she tried to escape the chaos she had triggered, I was afraid he might snap her bony arm in half.

"Later that evening, Pop appeared at my bedroom door while I was staring at, rather than reading, the first page of the social studies chapter I had been assigned earlier that day. 'Look, Felix,' he said. 'We're going through a little bit of a tough patch with your sister right now, but don't worry. It's gonna get better. Okay?' Nodding, I kept looking down at my book instead of up at him. 'And in the meantime, I just want to remind you that what goes on in this house stays in this house. Because it's nobody else's business. Understand?' The print on the page in front of me went blurry, but of course I understood—instinctively if not yet intellectually. Silence, discretion, distrust of non-blood relatives: it was our family's code of honor, ingrained in me although it was only much later that I would learn why. Our forebears were Southern Italian—Sicilian, specifically—and the island of Sicily had been attacked so often by so many foreign aggressors that *omertà* had developed as a survival tool. The code of silence had traveled across the Atlantic in my grandparents' psyches and been instilled in my parents, who, in turn, had instilled it in my sisters and me.

"And so, I lugged our family's secret turmoil to school each day like a backpack filled with rocks and, each afternoon at the dismissal bell, lugged it back home again. Rather than trust myself not to blurt out what was happening, I began to isolate. I kept telling Lonny I didn't feel like doing whatever he suggested we do, so much that the suggestions stopped and he started hanging around with Monte Montoya instead. I quit Junior Midshipmen and Saturday basketball at the Y. Too distracted to do all the memorizing that led to 100s on Sister Godberta's tests and quizzes, I withdrew from the competition. Let Rosalie Twerski be the top sixth-grade student. What did I care? And let Rosalie or one of the Kubiak twins stay after school and do all those charitable deeds so that they could receive the Good Citizenship medal or get elected to be our class's representative to the mock UN. What *I* elected to do was walk back to our unhappy home, watch TV with the volume turned low, and eavesdrop on the tearful arguments between my exasperated parents and my walking skeleton of a sister who, once upon a time, had had a secret stash of Ring Dings, Rolos, and Royal Crown cola but now thought even water and carrots would make her fat. I needed to be there, on duty, in case something terrible happened—Pop hurting Frances in anger, say, or Frances tumbling down the stairs during her crazy exercise routine. She might need me. Any one of them might, but what good would I be if I was somewhere else than at my post, watching and listening? *You gonna eat that yourself or do I have to force it down your gullet? . . . Stop running up and down those stairs, Frances! You're scaring me to death. . . . I only saw her eat four spoonfuls today, Ma. And none of the crackers. . . . Whose life is it—mine or yours? Would you people get off my fucking back! . . . Don't you dare use language like that in this house! . . . No? Why the fuck not? . . . Frances, what's happening? What's wrong with you? . . . You are, Mommy! All of you!*

"Like alcoholics and drug addicts, anorexics become talented manipulators. To avoid having to disrobe in front of her classmates, Fran had forged a doctor's excuse to convince her gym teacher that she needed to take partial showers because of her erratic periods. (In truth, because of her condition, she had stopped menstruating.) Nevertheless, she pushed herself to play rigorously during gym, the better to burn more calories. And then one day, during a game of volleyball, she collapsed in a heap onto the hard gym floor. The school nurse was called, and then an ambulance arrived. As the other girls in her class sat on the bleachers and watched, she was put on a stretcher, carried out of the building, and rushed to the emergency room of Baxter Memorial Hospital. The diagnosis was dehydration, malnourishment, and acute exhaustion. A psychiatrist was consulted and that was when the term 'anorexia nervosa' first became part of the Funicello family's lexicon. Despite Frances's fierce and tearful objections, a feeding tube was inserted into her abdomen. She was weighed three times a day.

"She stayed in the hospital for a couple of weeks. Simone quit her after-school job so that she could visit her every afternoon and bring the homework assignments she'd collected from Fran's teachers. My parents took the evening shift (six to eight p.m.). 'Do you want to come with us or stay home?' Ma would ask me before slapping together a sandwich for my supper. 'Stay home,' I'd say. My excuse was always that I had too much homework. 'Okay then.' Home from the lunch counter, Pop would pull into the driveway and honk. My mother would blow a kiss in my direction and rush out the door. 'Frances says hi,' Simone would tell me each day when she got back from the hospital. 'Yeah? Tell her I said hi back.' 'Do you want to come with me tomorrow? I could pick you up at school.' 'Nah, that's okay. I have to work on this big report Sister assigned us.' There was no such report.

"I asked neither Simone nor my parents if Frances was improving—if she was regaining weight and acting less crazy. I wasn't angry with her, exactly, but I was resentful. Even from her hospital bed on the other side of Three Rivers, she seemed to be upending all of our lives. The family secret I was obliged to keep, the dinner table battles, the indelible image of her body that day when I'd barged into the bathroom: these had exhausted me. During Frances's hospital stay, I would get home from school, go up to my room, flop facedown on my bed, and fall into a deep sleep for an hour or two. These extended naps would lead to middle-of-the-night bouts of insomnia, during which I would worry that Frances was getting worse. Still, I was unable to ask if she was getting any better or force myself to go to the hospital in order to find out for myself.

"After Frances had been stabilized and gained back a little weight, she was discharged from Baxter Memorial. To my unspoken relief, she did not come home. Instead, she was transferred to the Institute of Living, a venerable psychiatric hospital in Hartford where Manhattan sophisticates, Hollywood celebrities, and pedophile priests had undergone the 'rest cure' before reengaging with the social calendar, the camera, or a new pastoral assignment. The DSM-I described anorexia as 'a psycho-physiological reaction.' But what was Frances's bizarre behavior a reaction *to*? The Institute of Living was where this mystery was revealed.

"Neither Simone nor I was present at the session during which Dr. Darda, the psychotherapist Frances was working with, explained to my parents that their daughter's disease was the manifestation of a long-standing subconscious fear that now had been brought into the open. As it was reported to me years later, Dr. Darda then turned to her and invited her to ask my mother and father the question she needed them to answer. 'Am I adopted?' At first, neither of my parents spoke. Pop looked over at Ma, then back at Frances. It was my mother who finally spoke. 'Yes.'

"Later that same week, Ma, Pop, Simone, and I were summoned to a family session with Frances and Dr. Darda. Our parents had not yet shared with Simone and me what had been revealed during the earlier session and so, it was in the car en route to Hartford that Simone and I, side by side in the backseat, learned that our sister had started out life as our cousin. 'She was an infant when we took her,' Ma explained. 'Simone, you were little yourself and, of course, you weren't even around yet, Felix.' Pop was driving and, perhaps, too uncomfortable to glance in the rearview mirror to see how we were taking the news. Ma was not looking back at us either, but I could hear from the way she kept snapping her pocketbook clasp open and shut that she was nervous. It was a strange thing to get this shocking information delivered from the backs of my parents' heads. 'I have always loved your sister as if I bore her,' my mother assured us. 'Which is why I can't understand why she is . . .' She didn't or couldn't finish her sentence.

"'So if you're not her mother, is Pop still her father?' I asked. Ma jerked her head around, her eyes flashing outrage. 'Of course he's not! Why would you even *think* such a thing, Felix?' I didn't know why; I just wondered and thought I'd ask. Ma turned back toward the road ahead and sighed audibly. 'We had the best intentions when we decided to keep it from her, and from you two,' she said. 'We never, ever imagined it would come to *this*.' Simone reached over and squeezed my shoulder when, unbeknownst to my parents, I began to cry. For the rest of that ride, all was silent except for the songs coming from the radio."

"It was such a long time ago. Why is it still so hard?" I'm in tears again.

Lois's ghost asks her questions gently. "Did she die?"

I shake my head. Watch her hand reach over and grab my shoulder the way Simone had. I appreciate the gesture; I just wish I could feel it.

"Are you all right?" she asks.

Am I? Looking ahead at nothing, I shrug.

"It's time to go back now, Felix. Time for you to relive it, not just watch it."

"I don't want to," I tell her. "It's too painful."

"Pain is part of the process, I'm afraid. It's unavoidable."

"What *process*? Why am I being put through all this?"

Instead of answering me, she directs me to go downstairs, climb onto the stage, and touch the screen.

And so I do.

The wind-whipped screen, the thundering water, the sensation of falling, the whirlpool: it's as strange as the last time, but not as scary. What's *more* frightening than the way I've gotten here is what's happening now that I've arrived. But for better or worse, here I am again: Felix Funicello, a twelve-year-old who's confused, angry, and quietly terrified by all that I don't understand.

TEN

Dr. Darda has a potbelly and a big wen on his forehead. It's uncomfortable to look at, but hard to keep my eyes off of. Me and Simone get introduced. Frances has been called down from the ward and, while we wait for her to get here, Ma asks Dr. Darda a bunch of questions: How is she doing? Is she maintaining the weight she's gained? Has she gained any more? Does she seem any less angry? I look over at Simone and she looks back at me. We just found out that our sister isn't really our sister. What about how *we're* doing?

When Frances enters the room, she doesn't look at Simone or me. Or Pop. All she's looking at is Ma and I recognize that look: she's gunning for her. Dr. Darda says, Why doesn't

Frances start? Now that she's had a few days to reflect on what she's found out, does she have anything she'd like to ask?

She nods, smirking now as she addresses Ma. "So tell me. Whose bright idea was it to keep it from me all these years?"

Ma and Pop look at each other. Pop opens his mouth to say something, but Ma beats him to it. "It was mine," she says. "Poppy wasn't sure what we should do, but I thought it would be better for you if you didn't know."

Frances's laugh is snotty. "You're pathetic," she says. She turns to Pop. "You both are. And so is he."

He? Does she mean Dr. Darda? Me? If you ask me, *she's* the pathetic one. Except no one's asking me. I'm not even sure why me and Simone are here. And why is Pop talking about Uncle Iggy? What's *he* got to do with anything?

Dr. Darda asks Ma if she can explain what their reasoning was when she and Pop decided to withhold the information from Frances and her siblings.

"They're *not* my siblings," Frances says. She turns to Simone. "Did you know we aren't really sisters?" Simone shakes her head. Frances is looking only at her, so I guess it doesn't matter to her that I'm not really her brother. Simone says she and I just found out, too.

Ma starts to answer Dr. Darda's question. "Well, as we discussed last time, the circumstances weren't the best and—"

"Mrs. Funicello?" Dr. Darda says. "Why don't you address Frances?"

"Oh. Yes, certainly. Sweetheart, you have to understand how difficult the circumstances were. The police had to be called in. There was an investigation."

What? The police? Why?

"We thought—*I* thought—it would be easier for you if you

didn't know. I thought, well, maybe when she's twenty-one and better able to handle . . . And now I realize it was a mistake to keep it from you. I mean, look what it's led to. But it's not like we could see into the future. We were just trying to shield you from . . . We were just trying to protect you from the ugly truth."

Dr. Darda turns to Frances. "Can I tell you what I heard in what your mother just told you?"

"Go ahead. You're going to tell me anyway. Knock yourself out."

One of our vocabulary words last week was "flippancy." I got points taken off in the quiz because I couldn't use it in a sentence. Now I could, though. *Frances's flippancy is very rude.*

"I hear maternal instinct," Dr. Darda says. "Mothers will do anything to protect their young."

"Right. She'd do anything to protect *those* two." She points her chin at Simone and me. "Her beautiful real daughter and her precious little boy. But she played by different rules when it came to me. The fat one, the kid who wasn't really her kid." She glances at Pop. "Him too. They both treated me different."

"That's malarkey," Pop tells her. "We treated you three all the same. And that's why we kept it from your sister and brother, too. Because we didn't want them to treat you any different, either."

"So if everything was always even-steven, Poppy, then why was I the one you were always teasing and making fun of?" She points her finger at Ma. "And why was she always playing favorites? Whenever I asked her if I could do something, it was always no. But if the little prince or the perfect daughter asked, it was always . . . You can stop shaking your head over there, Simone, because you know I'm right."

Dr. Darda asks Simone if she'd like to say something. She shakes her head again. Well, I would. I'd like to say that none of what she's claiming is true, and that Frances is just being her regular whiny self. But no one wants to know what I think.

"Well, for your information, all your lying didn't work because a part of me always knew I didn't belong to you people," Frances says.

She did? Then why was she always telling me that *I* was adopted? Why did she take me to that orphanage and say it was where they got me from? Was that where *she* came from? Or did we both come from there? Have they been lying to me all this time, too? Am I adopted? This is all so mixed up.

Ma says, "Honey, we're not 'you people.' We're your family."

"Ha! So now that you've finally stopped lying to me, what should I call you? Auntie Marie? Mrs. Bullshitter?"

"That's enough," Pop says. "Show your mother some respect."

"How can I do that?" Frances snaps back. "She's *dead.*"

She is? Who is she? *Was* she? This is like being in a race where you can't catch up because everyone else has a big head start.

"You know damn well what I mean," Pop says. "Cut it out."

Frances turns to Dr. Darda and asks what the new rules are. "I mean, if he's not my real father, I don't have to obey him anymore. Right?"

Ordinarily, Pop would not put up with this kind of smart-ass from one of his kids. He would yell. Give her a punishment, maybe. But here in this windowless office with its gloomy gray walls, he just puffs up his cheeks, then lets out the air.

"Sweetheart, you should call me what you've always called me," Ma tells Fran. She's in tears now. "You're our legally adopted *daughter.* Poppy and I feel the exact same way about you as we do your sister and brother. You are *loved.*"

"Nice try, Marie," Frances says. Her cheeks are sunken in and her eyes are bulgy. I can make out the skull underneath her tissue-paper skin. Her teased hair is lighter than Simone's and mine. In some of the pictures of her when she was little, she had reddish blond hair. I guess that should have been a clue that she was someone else's kid. How did her real mother die? Why were the cops—

"Look, kiddo," Pop says. He's glaring at Frances but pointing his finger at Ma. "You oughta thank your lucky stars you ended up with *her* for a mother. You could've been stuck in some foster home someplace. And anyway, your situation's not even all that different. You're still a Funicello, aren't you?"

So Pop really *is* her father? Why did Ma say he wasn't?

"Well, whoop-de-do," Frances snickers. "My so-called parents are impostors. My real mother copped out by dying. Oh, and my real father pawned me off on his brother. But, hey, I'm still related to a Mickey Mouseketeer, so thrills, chills, and peanut butter." So her real father is Uncle Iggy? Is *that* what she's saying?

It's weird that the room has grown so quiet. Why isn't Dr. Wen Head saying anything? Isn't he in charge? My eyes roam the room, trying to find something to look at besides Frances's skull head and that wen of his. There's something cruddy-looking stuck to the doctor's tie—dried oatmeal, maybe?—but who wants to look at *that*? I glance down at my scuffed Buster Brown shoes. The last time Ma and I went shoe shopping, I begged her to let me get Snap Jacks because they didn't have laces, just tongues that you could open or snap closed. Now I'm glad I've got laces. I untie them, pull on the ends, retie them. Double-knot them. Why do Simone and I even have to be here? *We* didn't do anything. It's Frances who's causing all the trouble. And anyway, I'm just a kid. Shouldn't I be protected from this kind of stuff? I think I may be getting a headache. I wish we could go home. Then I surprise myself because it's me who breaks the silence.

"Am I adopted?"

"What?" Ma says. "No, Felix, of course not."

"Of *course* not," Frances mimics. "You're the *boy*. The *chosen* one. Sal and Marie's flesh-and-blood son."

"Then how come you always used to tell me I was adopted?" This is the first time I've said anything to Frances in weeks. "Remember that orphanage you took me to? The one you said I came from? We were looking through the fence at the kids who lived there and—"

"Are you mental or something? I never took you to any stupid orphanage."

"Yes you did."

"No I *didn't*. What are you even talking about?"

Dr. Darda asks if we might change the subject. He'd like to know what Frances is feeling about her birth father now that she's had a few days to process the information. Does he mean Pop? Uncle Iggy? I'm still so confused. And Frances's answer is weird. She starts clucking, flapping her elbows, pecking at the air. Oh, I get it. Chicken. Coward. "You said you invited him to this little party, right?" Dr. Darda nods. "So Daddy's a no-show. At least he's consistent. I'll give him that."

Pop starts sticking up for Uncle Iggy, but Dr. Darda puts up his hand like a traffic cop. "Let's stay with Frances's feelings a little while longer. You seem angry, Frances. Is it fair to say that anger is the primary emotion you're feeling toward your birth father?"

She shrugs. "I don't feel anything, to tell you the truth. I couldn't care less about him." Which I *know* is a lie. "It explains one thing, though. My whole life, I've wondered why he can never look me in the eye." Turning to Simone, she says, "You've noticed that, haven't you? The way he looks over my shoulder when he talks to me? He's so ashamed of my existence that he can't even look at me."

Simone tells her she hasn't ever noticed that. But I have. Uncle Iggy shadowboxes and wrestles with me on our braided rug. He let Simone teach him how to do the bop and he taught her the jitterbug. But I can't remember one single time when he danced or horsed around with Frances. What I *have* always been aware of, however, is that he gives her much better gifts than he gives Simone and me. Last Christmas, Simone got a Dave Clark Five album from Uncle Iggy that she already had, I got a can of Lincoln Logs, and Frances got a girl's bike with purple fenders, saddlebags, a front basket, and a silver bell. For Frances's tenth birthday, Uncle Iggy bought her a three-story dollhouse. It had furniture, a carport, and a doll-sized Thunderbird convertible that I kind of wanted even though the car was girlie pink. For my birthday two weeks later, I got a Davy Crockett coonskin cap that Ma wrecked when she accidentally washed it in the washing machine. I'd complained to my mother once about Simone and me getting chintzy presents compared to Frances's and she'd said something weird about not looking in a horse's mouth if that horse gave you a gift.

"She's right. He never looks at her." When everyone turns to look at me, I drop my head and go to work again on my shoelaces. Why did I just stick up for Frances when she's being such a brat?

Dr. Darda asks Fran how Uncle Iggy's lack of eye contact makes her feel. She lies again and says it doesn't bother her. And then, there's a soft knock on the door. "Come in," Dr. Darda calls.

The door opens and there's Uncle Iggy, looking kind of scared. Frances jerks her head away from him, talking to the wall. "What's *he* doing here?" she says, even though two seconds ago she was criticizing him for *not* showing up. My uncle shoves his hands into his pants pockets and jingles his change. His watery eyes stay on Fran. Now *she's* the one who can't look at *him*.

Simone and I are asked to go back to the waiting room, with its chilly metal folding chairs and rippy magazines. "Poor Frances," Simone says, and I think, Poor *her*? What about poor *the rest of us*? She should be *glad* we let her be in our family. Why doesn't she stop causing all this trouble and just eat? And why did she lie about taking me to that orphanage? Or *did* she lie? Was it just something I made up? No, I couldn't have because then I punched her, and the Miss Rheingold box got run over, and Mr. Melady yelled at us. I didn't imagine all that. That squashed ballot box is whadda you call it? Evidence!

Simone tries to read one of the waiting-room magazines, but its loose pages keep falling to the floor. From a plastic basket filled with old toys and junky Golden books with scribbled-on pages, I pull out a banged-up Etch A Sketch. Twisting the knobs any which way, I create a jumble of nothingness on the scratched-up screen. You can sort of hear them saying stuff in the other room, but Frances's words are the loudest and the only ones you can make out. "Because you're all a bunch of liars, that's why! . . . So she was a slut? . . . Well, maybe I *want* to die!"

Despite my belief that sixth-grade boys no longer cry, when I hear Frances admit she may have been attempting a slow-motion suicide—the worst of all mortal sins—I can't help it. My stifled grunts turn into hot tears and choked sobs. Simone puts down her magazine, gets up, and moves over to the chair next to mine. She puts her hand at the back of my head and pulls me to her, promising over and over, "She's going to be okay, Felix. Shh. Don't let them hear you crying. She's going to be okay."

After I calm down, I start Etch A Sketching again. And again, the lines and squiggles on the screen make no sense. Simone says she used to be a pretty good Etch A Sketcher—that she could write her name in cursive. She asks me what I'm drawing.

"Nothing," I say.

"Nothing? Why are you drawing nothing?"

"Is Frances going to die?" I ask.

She shakes her head. Takes a tissue out of her purse and tells me to blow my nose instead of sucking it back up again.

When my parents, Uncle Iggy, and Frances walk out of Dr. Darda's office, I wonder if my red eyes might give it away that I've been crying, but nobody looks at me anyway. I put my coat on and follow them into the hallway. Without saying goodbye, Frances heads down the corridor toward wherever her room is. The rest of us wait at the elevator. No one speaks.

It was still daylight when we entered the building, but now it's nighttime. In the parking lot, we separate from Uncle Iggy, whose car is at the opposite end of the lot from ours.

We get into Ma's Corvair and Pop starts the car, backs out of our parking space, and drives out onto the street. Retreat Avenue, the sign says. We head toward the lights of downtown Hartford.

"You two backseaters hungry?" Pop asks Simone and me. "They've got some decent pizza pie in this city. There's Spinella's and—"

He stops talking when all the lights around us and ahead of us go out all at once. Oh no, I think. First Frances, now this. It feels personal, as if God the Father has flipped a switch and, for reasons I don't understand, cast our family into darkness. Guided only by the two cones of light at the front of our car, Pop drives toward what looks like nothing.

ELEVEN

I step out of the scene and onto the stage, relieved to exit that confusing and difficult day—to relegate it once again to my past. . . .

When we drove away from the hospital and all the lights went out at once? Turns out it wasn't personal; it was the Great Northeast Blackout of 1965. Human error in Canada had triggered a massive power outage from Ontario through New Jersey that left more than thirty million people in the dark. It had happened as most of Manhattan was getting out of work for the day; commuters were stuck on stalled trains and in elevators that abruptly became pitch-black cells. Subway cars were rendered so profoundly dark that travelers couldn't see their hands in front of their faces. . . . And in a faraway jungle of Southeast Asia, a young marine on watch experienced a similar situational blindness. Jeff would later become my brother-in-law, my sister Simone's husband. "I'm telling you, Felix," he once said to me. "When those monsoons hit, the rain would fall so hard you couldn't even see your hand in front of your face."

It was as if that Northeast Corridor blackout and those South Asian monsoons were reminders that, collectively, we were blind to an unforeseen future that's now become our collective history: the murders of Dr. King and Bobby Kennedy; "I am not a crook" and the Fall of Saigon; hanging chads and "Mission Accomplished"; Columbine, the Twin Towers, Sandy Hook. If the future is inevitable, then maybe it's best that we're blind to it. Maybe our blindness is a gift from God, if God exists. If there is an afterlife where angels and saints are real and ghosts reside. . . .

Speaking of which, Lois's ghost seems to have left the building while I was reliving that strange day in 1965. She's neither in the orchestra seats nor up in the balcony. The projection booth is dark. The first time she showed up, she told me I was "educable." Okay. Now that I'm alone, maybe it's time to test that theory—to figure out why these ghosts have been haunting me. I walk to the front of the stage and sit, my legs dangling over the edge, and try to put it all together. Figure it out, Funicello. Think. . . .

In the weeks, months, and then years after that memorable family therapy session, the grim details of Frances's conception and birth were kept from me. Admittedly, I neither sought out the particulars nor eavesdropped in my usual manner, so I remained in the dark voluntarily. Oh, I knew the basics: that Uncle Iggy had fathered Frances and that the woman he'd impregnated had died shortly after giving birth. Through the wall that separated Dr. Darda's office from his waiting room, I had heard Frances use the word "slut," presumably in reference to her birth mother. I therefore presumed, incorrectly, that she had been a prostitute.

Why had I *not* pursued the specifics—inquired, for instance, why there had been police involvement? Was I attempting to forestall my coming-of-age—to put the brakes on the train that was carrying me, inevitably, toward the darker aspects of human sexuality—the messy complications and scandalous secrets that sometimes accompany and taint the natural urges of adults? Whatever the reasons for my elective ignorance, the effort was proving futile as I entered puberty. In the cafeteria and out on the schoolyard, my peers began saying things like, "She goes down for nickels," and "It's Thursday and he's wearing green. Must be a fag." Sometime near the end of seventh grade, Rosalie Twerski passed by my desk and said, "Ick. Who's got BO?" I sniffed my underarm and realized it was me. Humiliated, I began smearing on Pop's Mennen Speed Stick deodorant and dousing myself with his Old Spice aftershave even though, at the time, I was whiskerless. In ninth grade, a girl in my homeroom disappeared from our midst and the rumor circulated that she was pregnant. This confused me; Pauline was one of the quiet ones, not one of the hoody girls you might expect to get "knocked up." Then the worst happened. Roxy Rajewski, the mentally challenged tomboy from our neighborhood, was on the front page one morning. Her raped and bludgeoned body had been disposed of along the litter-strewn riverbank behind the abandoned mill where Lonny and I had once thrown rocks at the windows for the cheap thrill of hearing them smash. To the best of my knowledge, Roxy's murderer was never found, probably because no one looked very hard.

Ready or not, during the head-spinning year 1971, I finally began to uncover the sad details about Frances's origins. That summer, poised between my high school graduation and my first year of college, I discovered the feel-good fun of beer-chugging with my buddies and the sweet release of marijuana-heightened blow jobs courtesy of my first steady girlfriend, Jerilyn, who was two years my senior and, to me, worldly because she was going to community college. Jerilyn stopped short of letting us go all the way but, stoned herself, she would direct me in how to finger her to shuddering ecstasy.

I worked two jobs that summer, helping Pop and Chino at the lunch counter through the noontime rush and then driving back from New London to Three Rivers, where I was an afternoon cashier and delivery boy at a downtown pharmacy called Medical Drug. Two or three times per shift, my boss would send me out on the road in the Medical Drug Volkswagen. "Punch buggy blue!" kids would shout as I passed by, and I'd toot the horn and wave. I delivered medicine to sick kids and shut-ins, honchos and hypochondriacs, the afflicted, the addicted. At eighteen, I was getting my first close-up look at the myriad ways in which people whose last name was *not* Funicello lived their lives, and my first unavoidable realization that life wasn't necessarily fair. "Medical Drug," I'd say when customers came to their doors, and as they went to get their money or bent to sign their welfare paperwork, I'd study who they were via their furniture and framed photographs, the magazines and snacks on their coffee tables, the knick-knacks on their windowsills, the shows on their talking TVs.

Once I had to leave Pop and Chino to their own devices

at the lunch counter and pinch-hit at the drugstore for the morning delivery guy. A customer in the projects, an elderly man who must have been hard of hearing, had been watching a soap opera when I rang his bell. The TV was turned to such a thunderous volume that the actors seemed not so much to be performing their lines as screaming at each other. Glimpsing Joanne Tate, the long-suffering heroine of *Search for Tomorrow*, I was glad to see that she had managed to survive whatever melodramatic miseries the writers had thrown at her since I'd lost track. That was another thing I was beginning to comprehend: the difference between the flamboyant problems of TV characters and the quieter desperations of the afflicted at whose doorways I showed up with their medications.

Sunday was my day off from both my summer jobs—my time to kick back and relax, go to the beach, or, if her parents were away, hang out with Jerilyn at her house. But Pop had developed hypertension by then. On the advice of his doctor to discover ways to relax more, he bought himself a second- or third-hand fishing boat with a cramped little cabin and an unreliable inboard motor. He named his boat *Sweet Marie* in honor of my mother. Honored or not, she refused to come aboard. "I can't swim," she reminded Pop. "And anyways, I just don't see what's so much fun about hooking some poor fish by its mouth and yanking him out of his . . . what's the word I'm looking for, Felix?"

"Environment?" I offered. We were eating dinner. She had made one of my favorites, manicotti and meatballs.

"Yeah, that. Live and let live. Right, Felix?" Rather than take sides, I shoved more manicotti into my mouth. "And besides, Sal, you catch fish, you gotta clean 'em and I gotta cook 'em. It stinks up the house and you don't even like fish that much to begin with. Lobster and clams, yeah. Who doesn't like *them*? But remember that bluefish you caught? You ate about half of what was on your plate, and then the leftovers sat in the fridge until I had to throw them out. And you know how I hate to waste food."

"Plenty of cats in the neighborhood," Pop pointed out. "You shoulda put it out on the back steps for them." In her raised voice of righteous exasperation, Ma reminded him that he *hated* cats. Sometimes in her dealings with my father, Ma could be Not So Sweet Marie.

"Pop, why don't you ask Iggy to go out with you?" I suggested.

"And listen to him bellyache for hours about his sciatica, or the guys he works with that he can't stand, or that piece-of-shit Datsun I told him not to buy in the first place? No thanks. Last time I took him out, he got seasick and we had to come in early."

Rather than see my dad drive off by himself to the marina with his poles, his tackle box, his five-gallon can of gas, and his jug of Chianti, I sacrificed every other Sunday to go fishing with him. I dreaded these excursions, not because I felt about fishing the way my mother did or suffered seasickness like my uncle, but because I had reached an age where I felt uncomfortable being in a confined space with just him, out on the open water for hours, particularly those times when the *Sweet Marie*'s motor conked out and we had to wait around for the Coast Guard to tow us back to shore. I loved Pop; that wasn't it. But the countdown to my going off to college had begun, and I had better things to do than be stranded offshore with his neediness. Still, he had always been a good father so I felt obliged to be a good son. But I rejoiced guiltily on those

Sundays when rain poured down or strong winds made the seas too choppy. Otherwise, on alternate Sundays, we'd drive to the marina, unmoor the *Sweet Marie* from its slip, and head toward the waters off Watch Hill or Weekapaug.

We fished for flounder, fluke, blackfish. If the mackerel were running, we'd chum and jig for them. We never caught much, but Pop did seem to relax out on those open waters, particularly after he got hammered. He always made and packed us lunch: grinders thick with Genoa salami and capicola and provolone cut from the chunk, not sliced. These were accompanied by pickled peppers, summer tomatoes from his garden, and a big bag of Ruffles potato chips we passed back and forth. For dessert, he'd pack Ma's blond brownies or chocolate chip cookies or, if she'd been mad at Pop that week, cookies courtesy of Keebler or Nabisco.

To wash down all this food, Pop would pour himself Chianti from his jug and hand me one of those seven-ounce beers called ponies from the six-pack he'd bought for me. I wasn't able to drink legally yet, so I appreciated this nod to my impending adulthood. Two years later, in a college anthropology class, I would read about the coming-of-age ceremonies of various cultures: circumcisions and scarifications, the Amish rumspringa and the Jewish bar mitzvah, the proselytizing requirement for Mormon missionaries, the wilderness walkabout of Aboriginal male youth. Reflecting back on that summer of '71, I felt fortunate to have gotten off pretty easily. I'd not been cut or dropped off in some wilderness or required to memorize lengthy passages from the Torah. My rite of passage had only required me to be confined out on the ocean with my father, listening to his boring stories, and, one pony after another, enjoying the reprieve of a mild beer buzz.

Along with boating, wine drinking had become another of Pop's relaxation techniques. Out on the water, three or four plastic glasses' worth into the afternoon, Pop would become nostalgic, waxing sentimentally, often weepily, about the past. But it was during one of those father-and-son excursions that his reminiscences turned dark. That was the afternoon he spilled his guts about how and why Frances had become our sister.

"Did you know that my brother and I were partners at the lunch counter at the beginning?" he asked. "It was after your nonno died. We sold his lunch wagon and moved the operation into the bus depot." Pop's boat didn't have a head; the two of us were standing next to each other, pissing into the ocean on the starboard side.

"Yeah, and then you bought out Uncle Iggy and started running it by yourself, right? Ma said it was because you two had a falling-out."

"Ha! It was more like a brawl than a falling-out. I got a sprained neck and a busted coffee table out of the deal and Iggy ended up with a couple of cracked ribs and a swollen schnozzola."

"You broke his nose?"

"Nah. Smushed up the cartilage a little, that was all." He zipped up and smiled. "The fight started in the kitchen. He threw the first punch, but I got him in a headlock and we ended up in the parlor. Your mother wasn't too happy about her three-legged coffee table, but it was worth getting her a new one not to have to put up with his bullshit anymore. After that was when Ig started working in the warehouse down at Electric Boat. Of course, when him and me had that parting of the ways, you weren't even a twinkle in my eye yet. You want to know something, Felix?" Uh-oh, I thought; his eyes are getting watery. Here comes the sentimentality. "I used to get on my knees every night before I went to bed and ask God to give me a son. And then He not only gave me *any* son. He gave me *you*."

I felt more comfortable deflecting his compliment than accepting it. "Yeah, well, be careful what you wish for."

"No siree Bob. I got no complaints. Lotta young bucks your age are out tomcatting, smoking that wacky weed. But not you. You work hard, keep your nose clean. God gave me one of the good ones."

I needed to change the subject as quickly as possible. "So what was the big fight about?"

Pop went over to his jug, poured himself another glass of wine. "He was stealing from the business. We didn't suspect it at first, your mother and me, and it was driving her crazy. You know what a crackerjack she is with the figures. Likes to account for everything, down to the penny. She finally figured out that Iggy was fingering bills out of the register, a little at a time so's nobody would notice. You know, a fin here, a fin there."

"To gamble with?" I asked.

"Well, yeah. That's where some of it ended up, I imagine." Out came Pop's handkerchief. He wiped his eyes, blew his nose. "But mainly it was because he'd gotten this gal he was seeing in a family way and he needed the cash so he could take care of the situation."

"You talking about an abortion?"

"Jesus, I don't even like to hear that word spoken," he said. "But yeah, that was how he was planning to handle it. Marie and I didn't know why we kept coming up short until she figured out he had his hand in the till. We knew he was seeing some little chippy up there at that hotel where he played cards, but not that she was pregnant. And *married*, for Christ's sake. All of that came out later. That was what the fight was about: not only that he was stealing from the business, but that now that he'd had his fun, he wasn't going to do the right thing. Because that's what a *man* does, Felix: he pays the piper, you know what I'm saying? Steps up and takes responsibility. You make a mistake like that, you can't just pay someone to erase it for you. But that's what that jackass brother of mine was planning to do. He knew this guy up there, okay? Friend of one of his poker chums. And he had a sister who knew how to perform that procedure. Nice people, huh? The brother sets the thing up and the sister does the dirty work. They were charging an arm and a leg, too. Them two are probably both roasting in hell right now, or headed there once they kick the bucket."

I was neither pro-choice nor pro-life back then. I wasn't anything. But I'm pretty sure that, even at that age, I could see both sides of the abortion issue.

"But Iggy's girl backed out of having it done anyway. Decided to have the baby after all. Except your uncle didn't know that."

"The baby?" I said. "Are we talking about Frances?"

He nodded. "Hey, hand me that jug of Chianti, will you? You ready for another pony?"

I shook my head and passed him his. "So who was she?"

"The mother? Just a kid, really. She was from the South. Couldn't have been more than a year or two out of high school. If she even *graduated* high school. She didn't exactly come from high society. That much I know."

"And she was married, you said?"

"Yeah. Just barely, I guess."

"Did you ever meet her?"

He shook his head and replenished his glass. Downed about half of it in a single gulp. "I'm telling you, Felix, it was one hell of a mess. In the papers and everything."

I asked him her name.

"Whose name?"

"Frances's birth mother."

"Oh. It was Vera or Verna something. I forget what her last name was."

At first, she had agreed to the abortion, Pop said. Uncle Iggy had convinced her that she had no business bringing a child into the world and he wanted no part of being a father, or a husband either, in case she was getting any bright ideas about a quickie Mexican divorce so they could get hitched. So how was she supposed to explain this baby to her husband when he got back and started counting backwards? "He was a merchant seaman, see? Those guys go out for months at a time. I hate to say this about my own flesh and blood, Felix, but back then your uncle was a selfish, overgrown mama's boy. In his thirties and still living with his mother? Letting her do his laundry, cook his meals? She'd let him slip by on the rent if he'd had a bad weekend at the track, too. She was part of the problem, see?"

Pop drained the rest of his wine and squeezed the plastic glass so hard it cracked. "Your nonna, may she rest in peace, she spoiled him rotten. Of the two of us, he was the favorite, her little angel. When we were kids and she caught me being bad? She'd take out the strap and whale me with it. But if Little Lord Fauntleroy messed up, he'd get a couple of little slaps on the back of his hand with a soupspoon. 'Chicky-chockies,' she called them. I'd get welts on my behind and he'd get chicky-chockies." Listening to him, I was struck by how much Pop's gripes about parental favoritism sounded like Frances's. "Plus, after the old man died, it was me who always had to go over to the house and fix something if it needed fixing. Iggy didn't know the working end of a screwdriver from the handle. He was no mechanic, either. Couldn't even change the oil on that big showboat he used to drive around in. I'm telling you, he was helpless. The only tool he knew how to use was his pecker.

"One time Mama called me up, asked me would I come over and shovel her stairs and her front walk. It had been snowing like a bastard and we had maybe nine or ten inches on the ground. So I said, 'Where's Ignazio? Why can't he do the shoveling?' And she says, 'Well, he's just starting a cold. I don't want him going outside and catching a chill. He could end up with pneumonia.' So, like an idiot, I get in the car, slip and slide over there, and shovel them out. And when I look up, there's the crown prince standing at the window, watching me. When he gave me a wave, I got so pissed I made a snowball and threw it at him. Lucky it didn't break the window because it woulda been me who had to fix that, too. He's grown up a lot since then, your uncle, but I tell you, Felix, back then he was useless—at home and at the lunch counter, too. Partners? Ha! I did about seventy-five percent of the work while he leaned against the counter, kibitzing with the customers like he was the host at some party we were throwing. Believe me, after I bought him out, it wasn't like I had a lot more work to do than I was already used to."

Listening to all this, I recalled what Uncle Iggy had looked and acted like that day when he came late to that counseling session after Frances found out she was his daughter. He'd seemed like a child who'd been caught doing something naughty and was about to get spanked.

After Pop filled in some of the blanks about Frances's origin, I became hungry for more. But then school started, the first semester of my freshman year in college, so I had to shelve my curiosity. When I came home for Christmas break, I resumed my quest for information. Frances was in dental school by then and went back to Boston right after Christmas. I'm not sure I would have pursued the issue with her, anyway. Too sensitive a subject, maybe? Uncle Iggy came over to the house a couple of times while I was home, but I was pretty sure he wouldn't want to go there with me. So I drove over to Simone and Jeff's and asked my newlywed sister what she knew.

Shortly after she and Jeff had returned from their honeymoon the year before, Simone said, Ma had gone over to their apartment to help hang kitchen curtains. And after the job was finished, while they were having coffee and admiring the way the curtains looked, Ma had changed the subject abruptly, dropping her voice to a conspiratorial whisper. "Now that you're a married woman, you know things you wouldn't have understood before," she told her newlywed daughter. "So if you ever want me to tell you about the time your sister came to live with us, you can ask me. I have some stuff I can show you, too."

"Like what?" I asked Simone.

Simone shrugged. "Jeff walked in on us and the subject was closed. And I haven't pursued it since."

We both laughed at our mother's assumption that she and

Jeff had waited until the wedding night to have sex. "She thinks it's still the 1950s," she said.

"Yeah, I bet Jeff was glad when Pop handed over the key to your chastity belt. So Pop's still at work, right? You want to go see Ma now? Hear what she has to say and see her 'stuff'?"

Simone's smile faded away. "I don't know, Felix. Maybe we should just let sleeping dogs lie."

"In other words, deal with it in typical Funicello fashion by *not* dealing with it."

She held my gaze for the next several seconds. Then she said, "All right. Let's go over there. But just remember: This was your idea, not mine."

Ma hesitated, looking back and forth between us. Then she sighed and told Simone to put on a pot of coffee. She had to get something first. When she reentered the kitchen, she was holding a bulging manila envelope. I asked her what was in it. "Hold your horses," she said. She put out some leftover Christmas cookies and went over to the hutch. A bottle of anisette and two cordial glasses came out. She returned to the table and poured shots for herself and Simone. "I'll take one of those, too, while you're at it," I said. Ma gave me one of her who-do-you-think-*you*-are looks and said she'd be happy to pour me one as soon as I was old enough to drink. When I asked her if she wanted to see my fake ID, she rolled her eyes.

Ma told us that, after Frances's birth and her mother's death, she had gone down to the police station to get some answers. She'd been able to read both the initial police report and the later report filed by the investigating detectives. "It helped that Al Martineau had just been made deputy chief," she said. "He was sweet on me back in high school. Asked me to the senior formal, but I'd already told Cosmo Pusateri I'd go with him. Your mother was quite a looker back then, you know? Never had any trouble filling *my* dance card." Simone and I nodded in agreement. We'd seen the old pictures; she'd been a stunner.

She poured anisette into her coffee, stirred it with her finger, took a sip, and smiled. "So that day down at the station, I batted my eyes a little and told Al that I'd always regretted not going to our formal with him. And I *did* regret it, too. That cheapskate Cosmo came to the door empty-handed. I was the only girl at the formal who didn't have a nosegay or a corsage. But anyways, Al hemmed and hawed, said I wasn't really supposed to see those reports. Then he went and got them for me."

"Do you have copies?" I asked.

She shook her head. "We didn't know from Xerox machines back then. We just had carbon paper. So what I did was, I sat in this little room Al put me in and took notes." She reached into the envelope and pulled them out. They looked like lines and squiggles—some kind of secret code. I glanced over at Simone and shrugged.

"Shorthand," my sister said. "She took the secretarial course in high school." Ma told us to shush while she read and refreshed her memory. Then she got up and said she was going to the living room where it was quiet. She'd be right back.

While we waited, Simone slid her anisette over to me. "Here," she whispered.

"Nah, that's okay."

"No, I mean it, Felix. Drink it for me. We don't want to say anything until we're sure, but I may be pregnant."

I broke out in a smile. Slammed back the anisette. I was

still feeling the burn at the back of my throat when Ma returned. "Okay, I'm ready," she said.

When the responding officers got to Frances's mother's room, Ma told us, another woman was holding the infant. Verna, which was Frances's mother's name, was dead in the bed, her body pulled up on its side in the fetal position. The mattress and bedsheets were soaked with blood. The towels between her thighs looked as if they'd been dyed red.

Ma said that the subsequent detectives' report had included an interview with the woman who was holding Frances when the cops got there: a nurse named Nancy Wiggins. She'd been driving from Millinocket, Maine, to Washington, D.C., because she'd taken a new job. Her plan was to stop someplace after New York City, but she'd become hungry and tired, so instead had pulled off the highway, gotten good and lost, and stopped at the first hotel she spotted. She told the detectives she'd gotten up in the middle of the night to use the bathroom down the hall. She saw the mess in and around the toilet, then followed the drops of blood to Verna's room. When she knocked, the unlocked door had opened by itself and she had looked inside and seen that the woman on the bed was in trouble.

The nurse told the police that Verna was alive still, but that she was slipping in and out of consciousness. The infant looked to be a preemie—about six months, she estimated—and the bluish cast of her feet was alarming. She was listless and unresponsive, but when Nurse Wiggins separated her from her mother to pick her up and examine her more closely, the baby "began screaming bloody murder" and her coloring returned with the oxygen she needed to take in to cry.

Nurse Wiggins called downstairs to the desk for help, but

the phone just rang and rang. When she shouted into the hallway for someone, *anyone*, to call for an ambulance, there was no response. She ministered to both the mother and the baby as best she could, listening to what amounted to Verna's rambling deathbed confession. Verna begged her to write to her mother and tell her she was sorry she'd been such a sinful daughter. And to please take care of her baby. According to the report, the nurse said Verna had made no mention of a husband or the baby's father in anything she said.

After the desk clerk finally answered the house phone and called for help, the rescue workers and the police got to the scene simultaneously. But thirty crucial minutes had elapsed and by then Verna had died from hemorrhaging and blood loss. Frances, who was unnamed at that point, was rushed to the hospital. The authorities managed to track down Verna's family somewhere in the South. But the baby's grandmother refused to take her because she was "a child of Satan"—the fruit of her daughter's failure to resist the temptations of the flesh. There were initial concerns about the child's survival, but she responded well to treatment and was released five days later.

"Somebody at the hotel who knew Iggy called him to tell him what had happened," Ma said. "And then he called your father, which was what he always did when he was in a jam. For Sal and me, there was hardly any discussion. We knew Ignazio couldn't care for her, even with his mother's help. Your Nonna Funicello was too old and none too happy that this baby had come about because of your uncle's hanky-panky. None of us wanted her to go into foster care, or to that orphanage over there on Division Street. We felt we had to step in, take the baby and raise her.

"By the time she was ready to be discharged, your father, your uncle, and I had already gone to the probate judge and signed what we needed to. They didn't make it so complicated back then the way they do now. And we'd gotten everything ready at home. You were in your 'big-girl bed' by the time your sister came along, Simone. Poppy went up to the attic and got your crib back down, and your bassinette. I'd saved all your baby clothes, so I washed them and got them ready. You were still in diapers and rubber pants, but I'd been using your smaller-sized ones for dust rags, so I sent Sal out with a list: infant diapers, pins, nipples, baby bottles, formula, baby powder. When the hospital was ready to discharge her, Poppy and I went to the hospital with all the right papers, so they released her to us and we drove off.

"But we didn't go right home. 'Sal,' I said. 'Drive us over to the rectory. We gotta go see Father Fiondella.' And your father says, 'Right now?' and I said, 'No, a year from next Christmas. Come on.' I'm telling you kids, if there was ever a baby who needed to be made a child of God as quick as possible, it was your poor sister. Born premature, out of wedlock, and fished out of a toilet bowl, for cripe's sake. She wasn't even five pounds yet, and it was still touch-and-go as far as I was concerned. I was damned if I was gonna let that poor little thing die and have to go to Limbo.

"So we get to the rectory and Father Fiondella answers the door in his bathrobe and pajamas. He was sick, see? Had the flu or something. But when I said it was an emergency, he let us in. Brought us into the kitchen and baptized her with tap water from the sink. Under the circumstances, he said, we could function as both the baby's parents and her godparents. Then, when we go into his office so he can fill out her baptismal certificate, he asks us what her name is. Sal looks at me and I look at him, and I said 'Margaret' at the same time he says 'Frances.' We hadn't discussed what we were going to call her; in the court papers, she was just Baby Girl Funicello. I assumed Poppy wanted to name her after that cuckoo movie star he liked, Frances Farmer, but he said no, it was for Francis of Assisi, the saint he always prayed to for special intentions. So I said okay and we went with Frances. Frances Anne, which sounded better than Frances Margaret. You know who Saint Anne was, don't you? Mary's mother. Jesus' grandmother. But anyway, after we'd gotten her baptized, we took her home.

"I'd had my friend Stella Kubat watching you, Simone, and when we got back with the baby, you were down for your afternoon nap. After you woke up, I saw you peeking around the corner. I was in the rocking chair by the window, holding the baby, giving her a bottle. So I said to you, 'Come here. Come and meet your new baby sister.' Of course, you wouldn't remember any of that. But when you came closer to get a look, you bent toward her and gave her a little kiss on the forehead without me asking. And growing up, you were the best big sister a little girl could hope for." Ma looked over at me. "And a little boy could hope for, too. Right?"

I smiled at Simone and said, "Yeah, she was okay, I guess." Simone smiled back and gave me a good-natured poke.

I asked Ma how Uncle Iggy had taken all this.

"The big jamoke was scared skinny when he found out, I'll tell you that much. When the detectives figured out he was the father and questioned him, he thought he'd be in hot water because he'd arranged for that abortion. But there'd *been* no abortion, see? She'd taken the money but hadn't gone through with it. And then that chooch of a brother-in-law of mine breaks it off with her right after he thinks the problem's solved. Gets himself a new girl—a secretary down at Electric Boat. Dolly Charlton, her name was. Kind of a flibbertigibbet, and if that blond shingle of hers didn't come out of a bottle, then I'm a monkey's uncle."

"Aunt," I said.

"What?"

"You wouldn't be a monkey's uncle. You'd be a monkey's aunt."

"Hey listen, smart guy. You want me to tell you this stuff or do you want me to stop so that you can make your wisecracks?"

"Yeah, shut up, Felix," Simone said. "Go on, Ma."

My mother gave me a warning look and continued. "Okay, where was I? Oh, Dolly Charlton. Iggy took her home to meet your grandmother one Sunday dinner and Dolly wasn't exactly the kind of girl you took home to Mama. Your Nonna Funicello had a conniption when she found out Dolly was a divorcée! And she didn't even *know* yet that he'd gotten the other poor girl pregnant. Neither did Dolly. When it all came out and she thought there'd be a child she'd have to raise, she dropped Iggy like a hot potato. You know, Nonna Funicello hadn't exactly welcomed *me* with open arms when Sal first brought me around. To tell you the truth, there was never any love lost between the two of us."

"God, you'd have thought she'd be thrilled to have you for a daughter-in-law. A nice girl from a good family—an *Italian* family, no less," Simone said.

"And I *was* a nice girl, too," Ma asserted.

"Meaning you were a virgin?" I asked.

She shot me "the look" again but answered my question anyway. "You bet your bippy I was! Your father wasn't getting the goods from me until he'd carried me over the threshold. That's the trouble with you young people these days. Nobody waits anymore." She turned toward Simone. "Present company excepted." Looking at my sister, I covered my smile with my hand.

A sadness crept over my mother's face; she seemed to have gone to some other place in her mind. "The poor little thing needed a home and a family," she said. "Parents who would keep her safe and love her like she was our own. And sure, it was a mistake to raise her to think she was ours. I get that now. But we just wanted to protect her from that awful business—the hard way she'd come into the world. We tried as hard as we could with her, no matter how she got later on. How were we supposed to predict that she'd do that to herself? Resent us like she did—me, especially."

"You *couldn't* have predicted it," Simone said. She reached across the table and took Ma's hand.

"I don't know. Maybe I could have. She was always out of sorts when she was little. Hardly ever smiled. You two were a piece of cake next to your sister."

To shift the subject, I patted the envelope. There was still something in there. "So what else you got in here besides those notes you took?" I said.

Ma took the envelope and upended it. A small book with a ragged red cover fell out, and some newspaper clippings—what turned out to be two or three stories she'd clipped and saved about Verna's death and Frances's birth and the investigation that had followed. Simone and I picked them up, read a little of what they said. "What's this little book?" I asked.

"Her diary," Ma said. "Frances's mother's diary. One day, about three or four months after the investigation was all over, the doorbell rings and who's at the door but Al Martineau. He handed me her diary and said that, now that the case was closed, he thought her daughter might like to have it someday. You know, after she was grown up." When Simone asked if Frances had seen the diary, Ma looked down at the table and shook her head. "I didn't have the heart. She writes about how Ignazio wanted her to have an abortion. Arranged for it to be done. But even after she decided to have the baby, she was planning to give it away. I don't know if it was right that I kept all that from her. It's just that . . . it doesn't paint a pretty picture. Of either one of them. At one time, I even thought about burning it. Letting bygones be bygones. That's what your father said I should do. But that didn't feel right either." When Simone asked her if Pop had ever read it, she shook her head. "He didn't want to. So he doesn't know what's in there either. Just me. It's kind of like a secret that me and her share—Frances's two mothers."

I picked up the diary and thumbed through it. Most of the entries were in pencil. She'd printed rather than written in cursive. The dozens of entries looked like the jottings of maybe a fourth or fifth grader. "Can *I* read this?" I asked.

She looked at me, but I think her mind went somewhere else. "If anyone should have the chance to do that, it should be Frances. Don't you think?"

"I'll tell you what," Simone said. "Why don't we put everything back in there and you can let me have the envelope? I'll take it off your hands and maybe someday I'll let Frances know I have it and ask her if she wants to see it."

"You mean someday when I'm six feet under over there at

the cemetery?" There was a sly smile on her face when she said it. "Okay, let's do that. To tell you the truth, it will be nice to get it out of here so that I don't have to have it weighing on me. Yeah, here. Take it."

My assumption, driving back to Simone and Jeff's apartment, was that she and I were going to read Frances's mother's diary that afternoon. I was wrong. Simone informed me that she would honor the agreement she had just made with our mother. The diary was not mine or hers; it was Frances's. If, at some point in the future, Fran chose to read her mother's words and share them with us, then fine. But until then, Verna would remain silent. I tried cajoling Simone, of course. Called her Goody Two-Shoes. Begged a little. I even tried to enlist Jeff's support in getting her to capitulate and let us crack open that diary, but she stood firm. And so, once again, the truth was being held at a distance from me. It was as if I had been exiled to Dr. Darda's waiting room once again, the full story withheld but nearly in reach. . . .

I'm not sure how long I've been sitting at the edge of this stage, looking out on the empty orchestra seats and pondering my past—the apparitions that have appeared to me, the filmed history I can not only watch but also reenter, and what it all means. Well, my watch says it's 3:06, and *that* means I'd better get the hell out of this theater, go home, and grab some dinner before I have to get back here for the Monday night group. I run upstairs and kill the auditorium lights. Come back down, lock up the front entrance, and head for my car. Putting the key in the ignition, it dawns on me that I've forgotten to bring the ghost light out from backstage and turn it on. I guess I could skip it; I'll only be gone for a few hours. But who am I to screw around with theatrical superstitions after what I've been experiencing. It's not like I *suspect* visitors from the spirit world haunt the Garde; I *know* they do.

Reentering the building, I hurry into the auditorium, then wait for my eyes to adjust to the darkness. I make my way down the aisle, stumble up the steps to the stage, and feel my way past the curtain. Backstage it's pitch-dark, but I grope around until my hand touches the wire cage that surrounds the bulb. I'm in luck when I click the switch and the thing lights up. Someone's left it plugged into an outlet. I gather the cord, grab the lamp pole, and carry it out front to center stage.

Hustling back up the aisle, I'm stopped by a familiar voice behind me.

"Felix? Felix, wait."

Looking back, I see them up on the stage, to the left of the ghost lamp: Lois Weber and the apparition of a young woman I don't recognize.

TWELVE

This new ghost is wearing pedal pushers, bobby socks with saddle shoes, and what looks like a maternity top, although she doesn't appear to be pregnant. Her hair's in a ponytail. Whereas Lois's ghost is silvery gray, this new apparition has a sepia tint to her. I'm guessing she might have been a redhead when she was alive.

"Are we at that petting parlor yet?" she asks.

Lois purses her lips. "We're at the movie theater, yes, if that's what you mean. But I would prefer—"

"Is that the brother?" she asks, pointing at me. "Hey, brother! Where y'at?"

Moving closer to the stage, I say, "I'm right here."

She laughs. "I can tell *you* ain't from N'Awlins. When we say, 'Where y'at?' it means 'How you doin'?'"

"Oh, well, I'm doing okay. And you?"

"Awright," she says.

Lois stage-whispers a reprimand that I can hear clearly. "May I remind you that you are here for the singular purpose of telling your story. You do *not* have clearance to converse with a living. Please remember your status and act accordingly."

The bobby soxer pokes out her bottom lip. "Yes ma'am."

"Lois, who is this?" I ask. "Why is she here?"

"Were you not just recalling your frustration about having been denied access to Frances's birth mother's diary? Well, I could not produce that, but—"

"Are you saying this is Frances's . . . ?"

"Verna Hibbard. Yes, dear."

"This is incredible. And I see the resemblance, especially around the—hey, wait a minute. I didn't *say* I was frustrated about the diary. I was just *thinking* it. Do you mean to tell me you can get inside my head? Read my mind?"

"That's neither here nor there, Felix. The point is, I have brought Verna here so that you can hear her story, full and true, from the source herself. That which had been withheld from you will no longer be withheld. Unless you prefer the protection of being kept in the dark. You certainly may elect to remain so if you wish."

"No, no. I just . . . I mean, it's a lot to take in all at once, you know?" I look back at Verna's ghost. Look her up and down, from her ponytail to her saddle shoes. She looks so much younger than I'd imagined. She was just a kid. "So she's just supposed to talk and I'm just supposed to listen. Is that it?"

"That's correct."

"But let's say I want to ask her a question about something

she's just said. Can she answer me?" Lois shakes her head. "Why not?"

She sighs wearily. "Well, Felix, if you must know, in the shaded realm, there are different ranks and classifications. These determine the rights and privileges that are granted. Verna is a lower-level spirit, and lower-levels are not allowed to have verbal exchanges with livings such as yourself."

"So it's like a caste system?"

"Well, no. But our time here is limited. Do you wish us to spend it on the complexities and nuances of the shaded world, or would you like to hear Verna's story?"

"Her story. But just tell me. Is she a lower-level because she's waiting in purgatory or something?"

Verna's ghost laughs out loud. "You're a Catlick, ain't you? When you pass over, you'll see all that purgatory stuff's just a bunch of hogwash."

"That will do," Lois chides her. "If you persist in speaking to him directly, I shall have to take you back. Understand?"

"Yes'm."

"Then why don't you begin your testimony?"

"My what?"

"Your story." Turning to me, she adds, "*Without* interruption."

"Now?" Verna asks.

"Now."

"Where shall I start?"

"Wherever you'd like."

"Okay then. Here goes nothin'."

She says she was born Verna Mae Shoop in 1933, but that she was Verna Hibbard when she met my uncle in January of 1950. "I was a seventeen-year-old married lady, and he was almost twice my age, but he was a real gentleman. The first time I laid eyes on him was in the bar at the hotel my hubby stuck me at while he was out to sea." When Iggy asked her to sit down with him and have a drink, he got up and pulled out her chair. "No man had ever done *that* before, and it tickled me pink. Looks-wise, he was nothin' to sneeze at neither. 'Anyone ever tell you you look like Samson in that movie *Samson and Delilah*?' And he said yeah, but he looked even better in a toga than Victor Mature." That was another thing she liked about him: he was comical. He even had a comical name: Iggy. "T'wudn't no one in all of Luziana had *that* for a name. No one I knowed, anyways."

Verna said the first part of her childhood had been spent in New Orleans where her mother, RuthAnn Gautreaux, was from, and the second part had been spent in Shreveport, where her father, Vernon Shoop, had grown up. Her mother was part Cajun and part Acolapissa Indian, and on her father's side, all she knew was that he had come from sharecroppers.

In Shreveport, Vernon worked as a garage mechanic and a weekend banjo player on a popular country-and-western radio program called *The Louisiana Hayride*. But after a cypress swamp was drained in Metairie on the south shore of Lake Pontchartrain, cheap land and low taxes lured the Shoops back to New Orleans. "My daddy and my PawPaw Gautreaux built us a shotgun house and, the next year, put a camelback on the back of it. None of the other houses around had a *up*stairs, so we thought we was somethin' special!" But just when things were looking up for the Shoop family, Verna says, her father was killed in an accident at the garage where he worked. "He was under a big ole Buick Roadmaster, patchin' up the muffler, when the jack give way. We waked him in the front room of the house he'd built—closed casket since his face had got stoved-in so bad."

At the time of her father's death, Verna was fourteen, the oldest of three girls. Her mother had been a homemaker, but now she needed to earn a paycheck or else go on government relief, which she was too proud to do. She took a part-time job as a church secretary at Abide the Coming Baptist where the Shoops worshiped. "That wudn't enough for us to get by on, but PawPaw built us a chicken coop behind the house so's we could raise chickens and peddle the eggs." Advised that leghorns were good layers, RuthAnn purchased seven hens and one rooster and put her eldest daughter in charge of caring for the brood and selling the eggs in town. After RuthAnn took a second job as a night-shift hotel desk clerk, Verna was obliged to look after both the chickens *and* her younger sisters.

When Verna was fifteen, without the knowledge of her mother, who would have forbidden it, she entered a beauty contest to become Miss Crawfish of Jefferson Parish. She won the swimsuit competition ("I had a shape on me by then and got more'n my share of wolf whistles") but lost the crown when, during the interview portion of the program, she failed to identify "deadmen's fingers" as the spindly, inedible lungs of a crab, and then incorrectly named dill weed as one of the seasonings employed for a crawfish boil. "I was a big dummy for not gettin' that one right, cuz a crawfish and a dill pickle don't taste nothin' like each other," she lamented.

Nevertheless, Verna's beauty contest exposure parlayed her into a clerking job at the Pak-A-Sak, an all-purpose store famous for its takeout cheeseburgers and barbecue sandwiches. "My sister Nettie took over the egg business, but she was *turrible* at the peddlin' part cuz she never smiled, and flirtin' didn't come natural to her. She told me she preferred the company of the chickens to the people who answered their doors when she knocked cuz the poultry was more polite. Mama had told me more'n once that Nettie had been a colicky baby and that was probably why she didn't have my sunny personality."

It was at the Pak-A-Sak that Verna met Yancey Hibbard, a recently discharged U.S. Navy man who liked barbecue and worked at the nearby Esso filling station. "He come struttin' in like he was God's gift to girls instead of a grease monkey in a filthy jumpsuit. But truth be told, I couldn't keep my eyes offa him. First thing he said to me was, 'How many meats y'all put on them double cheeseburgers of yours?' and the second thing he said was, 'How 'bout after work I go down to Fat Harry's, pick us up a coupla rum-and-Coca-Colas in go cups, and you and me can go for a ride?' Well, he was bold, but I was just as. My answer to his first question was, 'You got a 'rithmatic problem, baybee? How many meats do you *think* double means?' And my answer to his second question was, 'Maybe yes and maybe no. Come by at six and I'll let you know what I decided.' Flirtin' may not have come naturally to Nettie, but I was born knowing how to do it."

Yancey was twenty-five and, by Verna's standards, worldly. The two began seeing each other—Verna told her mother she was working extra shifts—and Yancey introduced his new sweetheart to the kinds of things devout Southern Baptists were dead set against: jitterbugging, gin rummy, gin rickeys, and heavy petting. When Verna's baby sister Lucy Jean tattletaled to RuthAnn about what was going on between her sister and the grease monkey, RuthAnn went to her employer and spiritual counselor, the Reverend Galliehue T. Blevins. He affirmed what RuthAnn had always heard: that redheads and left-handed females were more vulnerable to the devil's wiles than other women. Because RuthAnn's firstborn was afflicted with both of these traits, Reverend Blevins promised that the following Sunday he would lead the Abide the Coming congregation in prayer that Verna's soul be rescued from the devil who had taken the human form of one Yancey Hibbard. The day after RuthAnn told Yancey to his face that the devil had entered him, she found three of her best layers flopped over on the ground outside the coop. Their necks had been wrung. RuthAnn was adamant that Yancey had murdered the leghorns. Verna was just as sure that he was innocent.

When Yancey asked Verna to run away with him and elope, she said yes. By then, heavy petting had turned into "man-and-wife love" without benefit of a marriage license. Sex was something Verna discovered she really liked. "When Yancey would put his thing inside o' me, it was like two puzzle pieces was fitting together just right, except that makin' a jigsaw puzzle on our rickety ole card table never felt anywhere *near* as good." She wanted more of Yancey inside of her, and regularly, and she could have it, guilt-free, if she was Mrs. Yancey Hibbard. She might like to have a baby, too—Yancey's baby.

Two days after Verna disappeared, she called her mother from the Plantation Motor Court on Route 17 in Savannah, Georgia, to let her know she was a newlywed. RuthAnn informed her daughter that she should consider herself disowned. "Now that I had made myself the devil's bride, Mama told me, I was welcome to the hell I had brought down upon myself, but I was no longer welcome in what had used to be my home. And she meant it, too. From there on in, every letter I wrote to her and my sisters come back marked 'Refused.

Return to Sender,' and every call I made to Metairie got hung up on. I heard the click in my ear so many times that I finally got the message that forgiveness wudn't about to come *my* way, so I stopped calling. It hurt me somethin' turrible, which I guess was what my mama was after."

To cheer up his bride, Yancey began taking Verna to Le Bon Temps, a French Quarter dance hall and burlesque bar where they could drink, dance, and watch the nightly performances of the two resident strippers, Alouette the Tassel Twirler and Oona the Oyster Girl. One night, Alouette and her manager, Hubie, approached Yancey about Verna becoming a stripper. "I was standing right there and they was talking *about* me, but it was like I was somewheres else. 'She got the figure for it and then some,' Hubie said. 'There's brick shithouses that wish they was built as good as she is.' Well, I didn't take kindly to being insulted like that and was rearing back to slap his fat face, but Yancey grabbed my wrist and said that Hubie'd just given me a compliment. I didn't see how, but I took his word for it. Alouette told Yancey that men would tip any girl on that stage who'd bump and grind and show her titties, but the biggest tips went to those who knew how to lift up their act so it became artistic. Then she turned and spoke right to me. 'Here's the secret, hon. It's more about the teasing than the stripping. I can teach you how to get the fellas eating out of the palm of your hand. And when that happens, you can make thirty or forty dollars a night in tips.' Well, Yancey got dollar signs in his eyes when he heard that. 'I guess she can give it a try,' he told Hubie. 'Ain't that right, honeybun.' I didn't bother to answer him because it wasn't a real question. It was a decision he'd already made. Driving back to the room we was renting, he started talking about how, if I got real good at stripping, we might be able to afford one of them MG Midgets he was always jawin' about—a red one with a convertible top, he figured. See, Yancey had a gnawin' and a cravin' for sportscars, let *me* tell *you*. He'd look at his *Motor Trend* and *Hot Rod* magazines the way other men looked at the girlie magazines we sold under the counter at the Pak-A-Sak.

"So I gave stripping a try, but just once. Back when I was trying to win Miss Crawfish, it made me feel like I was someone special, walkin' all dignified past them judges in my plaid bathing suit and the open-toed high heels I had swiped from Grumbacher's and was fixin' to bring back after the contest. But walkin' around on the stage at Le Bon Temps in nothin' much more than my birthday suit made me feel like cheap goods. They give me a fake name, Fanny Feathers, and a bunch of ostrich plumes that was dyed colors no natural-born ostrich woulda been growin', not that I ever seed any ostriches. I was suppose to kinda play peek-a-boo with the feathers and shake my fanny at the customers cuz my name was Fanny. But I didn't 'preciate the rude things those boozed-up jackasses was yellin' at me, and neither did Yancey, who started lookin' more and more like he was gonna blow during my performance. See, he liked the me-making-money part, but he hadn't thought much about how I had to make it until he watched all those men eyeballing what was rightfully his. The Miss Crawfish judges hadn't seen anywhere near this much of me and they had been classy people—a bank president, a guv'ment lawyer who worked for 'Uncle Earl' Long up in Baton Rouge, and Miss Luziana of 1946, Marguerite McCleland, who got third-runner-up that year for Miss America! But the audience watchin' me was justa buncha drunken knuckleheads.

"Truth to tell, I wudn't no good at strippin' neither. I only got three dollars in tips that night, plus a fake five-dollar bill that had Bugs Bunny's picture on it instead of Lincoln's. Alouette said I would get better at stripping if I kept at it, but I put my foot down and told her and Hubie that I might be headin' to hell when my time came for the things I done, but I was durned if I was gonna arrive there wearing pasties and one of them skimpy G-strings. 'It's probably just as well,' Yancey said. 'You're a banshee in bed, but up on that stage, you looked like you was imitatin' a two-by-four.' It was hurtful, him sayin' that, but I kept my mouth shut. We hadn't been Mr. and Mrs. for very long, but I already knew it didn't do no good to act teary-eyed in front of Mr. Yancey Dale Hibbard. Cryin' made him orneryer than a hornet with a headache."

One night at Le Bon Temps, Verna said, Yancey began talking with a Merchant Marines recruiter who was looking to sign up sailors for a commercial shipping company—engine men, especially, which was what Yancey had been in the U.S. Navy. The catch was that the company was located in New London, Connecticut. Yancey hesitated; he'd been stationed in nearby Newport, Rhode Island, and hated the cold. But when the recruiter told him how much he could make on a ship bound, say, for Hong Kong or Singapore, he signed a contract then and there, probably because that recruiter had bought him two Obituary Cocktails, the strongest drink they served at Le Bon Temps. Verna had taken a sip from Yancey's glass; it tasted like turpentine, and even that amount made her feel tipsy.

The newlyweds drove north on the first of November 1949. Yancey docked his bride at the Hewett City Hotel. He gave her an allowance of five dollars per week and paid in advance for the room where she would live and wait for him for the next four months. Then he shipped off for the Far East. Verna, who had never seen snow before, now faced an endless winter all by herself, cooped up in her second-floor room with nothing more to do than look out at sleet storms, squalls, and nor'easters.

To fill up the hours of the day, she took walks up and down the two main streets and usually ended up in the public library, reading movie magazines, ladies' magazines, and magazines about true crime. "I was partial to stories that had murders in 'em, the bloodier the better, even though they sometimes scared me. Whenever the library closed for the day and I had to go back to the hotel, the lonesomeness would hit me hard and I'd sit in the lobby for a spell, just so's I could listen to the music from the radio they kept going behind the check-in desk. I made groceries at the A&P twice a week—bread, bananas, and peanut butter mostly, but I got so sick of peanut butter and banana sandwiches that I started taking my evening meals at Woolworth's—a bowl of tomato or vegetable soup more often than not, because it was cheap and came with crackers. Sometimes, though, I'd pay the extra and order me some pork sausages and lost bread—or as you Yankees call it, French toast. I was partial to a lot of syrup on my order, and if there was a puddle of it still left after I'd sopped up the rest with the bread, I'd look around to make sure no one else was watchin' me, then pick up my plate and lap up the extra. 'Waste not, want not,' as my mama used to say."

Back in her room after it got dark, Verna wrote love letters to Yancey that she would mail to the shipping company for forwarding. Yancey began to seem like the next thing to a stranger. Why had she done something as crazy as running away with him? "I took to my diary to answer that question, and the answer was S-E-X. I drove away with him that night because I liked the way his body made my body feel, plain and simple. Maybe he *had* bedeviled me into enjoying that kind of thing—turning me from a nice girl into a wicked one who was as full of sin as a carbuncle is full of pus, which was what Mama said had happened to me."

Verna began to wonder if Yancey *had* wrung the necks of those poor chickens. And if he had, did he also have it in him to murder *her*? There were plenty of wife killers in those true crime stories she was always reading. One crazy so-and-so had ax-murdered his wife, chopped her to bits, and put them in their Frigidaire so they wouldn't stink. Yancey would never do something as bad as that, she figured, but he *did* have a mean streak; it had shown itself twice on the long drive up from Louisiana. At that diner in Pennsylvania where they both ordered the meat loaf special, Yancey had shoveled down his own mashed potatoes and gravy and then had moved his fork across the table and started in on hers. When Verna told him mashed potatoes was her favorite food and she would just as soon eat them herself, he had sulked and said okay then, fine, but he sure hoped his wife wasn't going to turn into a fat cow like her mother. When she started to cry, he laughed at her, so loudly that the waitress stopped right in the middle of pouring someone else's coffee and stared at them. After Verna gathered herself, she scraped her potatoes onto Yancey's plate and he gobbled them up without so much as a thank you. And so, she ended up having her feelings hurt *and* not getting to eat her mashed potatoes either.

The second time his mean streak had shown itself was when he told Verna she was "dumber than a retarded mule" for asking him if New Jersey was part of New England. Well, now she *was* in New England, stuck in some boring Connecticut town where she had no friends, no family, and nothing to do but watch snow fall or, after it stopped, people down there on the sidewalk shoveling it. How in the world had she ended up in this cold, unfriendly place where people talked funny and everyone seemed so grouchy? Was her Lord and Savior Jesus Christ punishing her for the ungodly things she'd done? She got down on her knees beside the bed and tried praying but got distracted by the fact that the mattress smelled funny and a doodlebug was scooting across the wall on the other side of the room. Praying seemed useless. She could almost hear Jesus saying to Himself, *That* one wants forgiveness? After she dishonored her mother and the Shoop family name so that she and Yancey could rut like a couple of animals? Verna got up off her knees, picked up her shoe, and slammed it against that doodlebug, splattering its guts against the wall. It was no use asking for divine forgiveness because she didn't deserve the Good Lord's grace. She deserved what she had gotten: Connecticut.

By mid-February, Verna was suffering bouts of panic and crying jags that could last for hours. Some days she couldn't get out of bed until afternoon, except to go down the hall to use the toilet. She had to do something or she'd go crazy. Or had that already happened? Her money was dwindling because, even though she tried to be careful, she had trouble staying within the weekly stipend that Yancey had left for her and had to keep borrowing from the weeks that hadn't happened yet. Maybe *he* should try living on what he expected *her* to live on. She was sick to death of waiting for his letters back, and sick of Woolworth's junky old canned soup.

Fat cow? That's how much *he* knew. She was hungry half the time and skinnier than she'd ever been. Her dungarees felt baggy on her now and her bobby socks, instead of staying up where they belonged, kept drooping down past her ankles. If this kept up, she'd start looking as scrawny as the blank-faced models she saw in the fashion magazines.

THIRTEEN

One afternoon, despite her financial situation, Verna decided to splurge by going to the picture show up the street from her hotel. *A Life of Her Own* was playing and its star was Lana Turner, her favorite actress. Feeling defiant, Verna bought a box of gumdrops and a Hershey bar at the candy counter and got charged twice what she would have paid at the Pak-A-Sak for the same two items. Everything was more expensive up here! Either that or these Yankees were out to gyp her.

Verna liked the movie at first; Lana Turner played a small-town Kansas girl who moved to New York and became a glamorous fashion model. Shortly into the story, however, it got depressing. Lana's friend, another model, jumped from her apartment window and killed herself because she was a has-been. Then the married man Lana had fallen in love with (Ray Milland) left New York and went home to his wife. Lana missed him the same way Verna sometimes missed Yancey when she wasn't thinking ill of him. When Ray Milland finally returned to New York, he brought the wife back with him. "And she was a cripple! I like a good sob story as well as anyone, but *A Life of Her Own* had enough gloomy stuff for three different movies. After a while I just sat there not even watching it." Instead, Verna began to scare herself about how much she had spent on this outing. . . . And about how, when Yancey got back to port—*if* he ever got back—he might tell her *he'd* had an affair with some beautiful Lana Turner type. Would Verna seem as pathetic to him as Ray Milland's crippled wife? *A Life of Her Own* made her feel so sad that she walked out before it was finished, forgetting that, filled up on gumdrops, she had put her Hershey bar on the arm of the empty seat next to her for later and then had left it there. She cried herself to sleep, woke up an hour later, and then stayed awake half the night, convincing herself that Yancey was an unfaithful cad or, at the very least, a chicken murderer.

To quell her desperation, Verna gave herself a stiff talking-to. Then she ratcheted up her courage and went out looking for a job. She found one waiting tables a few blocks down the icy street from the hotel at Charlene's Diner. She worked the supper shift, after which she would trudge back to the hotel. Dreading the thought of climbing the stairs back to her gloomy little room, she began lingering downstairs at the hotel bar. Fueled by loneliness and a relaxing cocktail or two that she could now afford to treat herself to thanks to her tips, Verna started conversing with the clientele—mostly traveling men. Yankee men were much more friendly than Yankee women, she noticed. Even the hotel's colored maids acted like they were better than she was, something that a colored maid down South would *never* try to get away with. Maybe all these Yankee women were just jealous of her looks and her shape and the color of her hair which Buddy, her boss back home at the Pak-A-Sak, used to call *flaming* red. She was no movie star, but she could probably fix herself up pretty enough to be a model if she lived in New York. After all, she'd been in the top three for Miss Crawfish. She might even have won if she'd batted her eyes and wiggled her *be*hind at the judges the way the winner, that homely Phyllis somebody with her yellowy buckteeth, had done. Verna doubted that Phyllis had ever been told she had the face and figure to become an exotic dancer of the artistic sort.

The men at the hotel bar bought Verna drinks and made her laugh. She got embarrassed at first when they talked sugar to her so openly. It wasn't like she was hiding her wedding band or they were hiding theirs. After a few Pink Lady cocktails, though, Verna would sometimes surprise herself by talking sugar back at them. Or sass, which they seemed to like just as much or even more. Flirting was fun and she'd been starved for fun. This one man named Royal something, who she'd seen before at the bar, told her that, with that red hair of hers, he thought for a minute that she was Rhonda Fleming. And she told him that with that name of his, she thought he might be Prince Charming. He laughed and bought her a drink. After a while, Ronnie, the bartender, started making her *free* drinks when she came in. She was good for business, he told her. She began slipping off her wedding band and putting it in her pocket before she entered the bar. "I figgered that Yancey, wherever he was, was passing *his*self off as a single man instead of one who had stood before a justice of the peace and made vows. So if he could do it, why couldn't I?"

One night, Verna got drunk enough and flirtatious enough with a smooth talker named Frank that one thing turned into another and she led him up the back stairs to her room. He was a good-enough kisser; she liked that part. But after their clothes came off, Frank failed to bring her to the wild and pleasurable places Yancey had. "He was only in a big rush to finish, and after he did, he popped up like toast from a toaster, pulled up his undershorts, got the rest of hisself dressed, and left. I might as well have been a toilet."

The next morning, Verna woke up with a hangover that was so bad she had to drag herself down to the drugstore for a bottle of Bayer aspirin "or else I'da had to cut my head off to make the hurtin' stop." After she returned to her room and took the aspirin, she began to feel better—good enough to make her bed, which she did every morning so she wouldn't have to deal with that uppity colored maid. That was when she found money in the sheets: a five, a single, and two two-dollar bills. "For ten dollars, that bum had turned me into a cheap hooker, and it made me feel so ashamed and trashy, I started thinking that maybe I'd just end my life like Lana Turner's has-been model friend in *A Life of Her Own.* But that woman had jumped out of one of them New York skyscrapers, and I wudn't sure you could kill yourself if you were only on the second floor. You might just end up a cripple. Maybe jumping headfirst instead of feetfirst would do the trick. Then I got to thinking of my daddy's head squashed under that Buick and it almost give me the pukes." Perhaps she could commit suicide by swallowing an overdose of laudanum like that jilted girl she'd read about in a *True Story* magazine. But where in the world would she get ahold of laudanum? Would an overdose of Bayer aspirin work? Probably not. She'd always had trouble swallowing pills and might start gagging after the first six or seven and upchuck them. After she died, she was surely going to the fiery place because of the things she'd done. She was in no rush to get there. She might as well just keep living.

She wasn't about to spend that ten dollars that Frank had left her, though. That would *definitely* make her a common tramp. She considered ripping up the bills and flushing them down the toilet at the end of the hall, but that seemed wasteful and hadn't she heard one time that destroying money was illegal? Then she thought of what to do. Designating the cash as her emergency money, she hid it in that Bible the Gideons had placed in the nightstand—specifically, the Book of Leviticus, which seemed somehow fitting, although she couldn't exactly say how. "The only parts I recalled from them chapters when Mama read them out loud at the supper table was how it was sinful to have relations with animals or family members, or with another woman if you was a woman or another man if you was a man. At least I couldn't be faulted for doing any of *them* things."

A few days later, while Verna was thumbing through a stack of magazines at the library, she came upon a full-page *New Yorker* advertisement that made her stop turning pages. It said, HOW WOULD *YOU* LIKE TO WIN $5000 IN CASH, ANOTHER $1000 IN MODELING FEES, $500 IN UNITED STATES SAVINGS BONDS, AND A TRIP TO HOLLYWOOD? A beautiful redhead identified as Miss Rheingold of 1950 was pointing her finger, Uncle Sam style, right at Verna. The small print said any pretty girl in the US of A who was twenty-one years or over, married or single, was eligible. All she had to do was fill out the entry blank at the bottom of the page, enclose it in an envelope along with a full-face photo of herself, with her *accurate* weight and measurements listed on the back of the picture, and mail her materials to the address listed. Entrants selected for the next round of judging would be notified by mail, it said, and had to be available to travel to the Waldorf-Astoria Hotel in New York City on the twelfth of May. From this pool of lovely ladies, six would be chosen as Rheingold girls for the public to vote on. After the votes were tabulated, the winner would be notified and she would reign as the people's choice, Miss Rheingold of 1951.

Well, Verna figured, the people's choice had been a redhead the year before, so they must like redheads. Married girls could compete, so that wasn't a problem. All she had to do was get her picture taken and fib about how old she was. Her measurements would speak for themselves. She hadn't gotten *that* skinny, and she could always roll up her bobby socks and stuff them inside the cups of her brassiere.

Verna looked over at the desk to make sure the librarian was busy. Then she ripped the page out of the magazine and left. She went straight across the street to the Loring Photo Studio, where she sweet-talked a photographer's assistant into taking some photos of her while his boss was home having his lunch. The next day, at lunchtime, she returned for her free head shots. "I had to smooch with him a few times before he'd cough 'em up, but that wudn't anything, 'cept I had to throw out a perfectly good piece of spearmint gum that hadn't even lost its sweetness yet." She wrote her measurements on the best of the photos, slid it into the envelope with the form, and sealed it. So that her entry might get noticed among the ones from other hopefuls, she pressed a lipstick kiss on the sealed envelope flap and beneath that wrote that she was often mistaken for Rhonda Fleming (an exaggeration) but that she herself thought she looked more like Maureen O'Hara (an out-and-out lie). She decided that, as soon as they notified her that she needed to report to that hotel in New York, she would use some of the money hidden in the Gideon Bible for bus fare. An investment was a kind of emergency, she reasoned; why not spend $10 for the chance to win $6,500 in prize money? With a fortune like that, she'd probably be able to buy Yancey one of those MG sports cars he was so crazy about and herself some diamond earrings "and maybe even one of them mink stoles that rich ladies wore." She might also buy her mother an electric stove to replace their old wood-burning one. She would have it sent to her for a big surprise. RuthAnn surely would forgive her then, and tell her to come back home for a visit any old time her busy schedule allowed, "long as she didn't get wind that Rheingold was a kind of beer, cuz Mama was dead set against spirits of any kind."

Verna waited to hear back from the contest people. And waited. And waited some more. "It began to feel like hell was gonna freeze over before I got my invite." The day before semifinalists were to report to the Waldorf, Verna decided her invitation must be stuck in some dead letter office, or that maybe she'd written her return address incorrectly, or that maybe she'd even *forgotten* to put her return address on the envelope. She decided she had better get herself to New York that very next day so that, whatever the mix-up was, she could straighten things out.

"I called Charlene and told her I was gonna be too sick to get to work that night and maybe the next night, too. I figgered I could wear my mint green getting-married-in dress and the open-toed high heels I'd tried out for Miss Crawfish in. I'd come in third in *that* contest, and all I had to do to become a Rheingold girl was get into the top six. Maybe those same shoes would bring me luck. At Woolworth's I was planning to swipe some Hazel Bishop makeup, but that saleslady with the cat's-eye glasses musta been onto me. She kept watching me like she was workin' for the *po*lice instead of for the store, so I had to shell out instead of liftin' it. Another investment, I figured. Once I was a Rheingold girl, I'd probably get all the free makeup I wanted."

Back at the hotel, Vinnie the bellhop told her how to get to New York. When she went up to her room, she plucked her eyebrows, set her hair in curlers, and went to bed early to get her beauty rest. But her riled-up nerves wouldn't let her sleep, so she got out of bed, got dressed, put a kerchief over her curlers, and went downstairs to have a drink. When Ronnie asked her what was new, she told him she was going to New York the next day to be a Rheingold girl. "You are? Well, good for you, honey," he said. "Guess you won't have much use for that waitress uniform anymore, huh? Or this hotel either. You know, the salesman from Rheingold puts one of those ballot boxes here in the bar every year. I'll get you all the votes you need. What are you drinking tonight?" A martini was the fanciest drink Verna could think of, so she said she'd have one of those. She wished she hadn't, though, after he started asking her all these questions she didn't know how to answer. Gin or vodka? Olive or twist? Shaken or stirred? "Surprise me," she kept saying. But what surprised her the most was how terrible martinis tasted. But the second one went down easier, and having two did the trick. Not five minutes after she got back to her room, she dropped into a deep sleep.

The next morning, she took her emergency money out of the Bible and put it in her purse along with some of her saved-up tip money. Then she fixed her face and hair and got dressed up as nicely as she could, given the limitations of her wardrobe. "Wish me luck," she told the girl in the mirror. Then she smiled, wiped the lipstick off her front teeth, and left. Taking the early bus out of Hewett City felt like she was being released from prison.

In New London, she waited over an hour for the Boston–to–New York train, and when it finally arrived, she took a breath, laughed out loud at herself for being so brave, and got on board. She was on her way!

Verna recalls that the train made many stops along the way, and at each one, things got more crowded. "The seat next to mine had went unclaimed for a while, and I was glad for that. But when we stopped in New Haven, a fat lady eyeballed that empty seat, aimed her big *be*hind over it, and landed like a ton of bricks. She took up all of her own seat and half of mine so that I was kinda pushed up against the window. At first I didn't see she had a lapdog with her, but then I did. It was bulgy-eyed and snaggletoothed and not much bigger than rat-sized. The fat lady kept talkin' baby talk to it, sayin' stuff like 'Mommy wuvs Java and Java wuvs Mommy.' From time to time, she'd kiss it on the lips and let the dog lick her neck. Neck-licking was one of Yancey's lovemakin' techniques, so it made me kinda queasy to witness it. If I'da had the nerve, I woulda told Mrs. Fatso to go home, open her Bible, and read the Book of Leviticus, or else get herself a fella that she could neck with instead of a dog. I didn't have it in me to say it, though, so I just sat there and looked out the window, trying not to see the reflection of her and her dog all but having relations with theirselves."

By the time the train pulled into Grand Central Station, Verna was feeling more haggard than beautiful. "I was sweatin' like a sow in heat, covered in dog fur, and most likely smellin' like dog, too. Luckily, I remembered the little bottle of Evening in Paris perfume I'd put into my purse the night before. So I went to the ladies' and doused myself good before I walked outa that station and into the crowded street.

"Tramping around looking for that hotel I was suppose to be at, I got to thinkin' that whoever set up New York City must have been *tryin'* to confuse people. Every street had a number, but some of them numbered streets was called avenues, not streets, and I couldn't figger out the difference. It didn't make no sense, no matter how many people I stopped and asked. I got so confused that I kept walkin' past places I'd already walked past." She would have flagged down a cab to take her where she needed to go, but she had no idea how much that would cost and didn't want to waste her money or get flimflammed. When Vinnie had told her how to get to New York, he'd warned her that the city was full of swindlers.

"When I finally got to the right place, my feet was burning and blistered somethin' turrible from them high heels of mine," she says. "If they was lucky shoes, then it musta been *bad* luck." Outside the hotel, she approached two elegantly uniformed doormen. "This the place where they're pickin' the Rheingold girls?" she asked them. They looked her up and down like she was a curiosity. Then they looked at each other. Then back at Verna. Finally, the younger of the two said yes, this was the place, but they'd been at it for a couple of hours already. "'Well, then they're probably wondering what's become of me,' I said. 'Where should I go?' He gave me directions to the ballroom, but I coulda done without that smirk on his face. Or the other one rolling his eyes. What made those two think *they* was so special?

"I made a beeline through the lobby, although if I wudn't so late, I'da loved to gape at how beautiful everything looked. It was like the inside of a storybook palace! Maybe after I got picked to be a Rheingold girl, I'd get a postal card of the place and send it back to Mama, Nettie, and Lucy Jean. Turns out that doorman's directions stunk. It took me having to ask three more people before I found it."

All the doors into the ballroom were open, and there was a lot going on inside—men in suits sitting at tables, pretty women chatting with them or else waiting in line for their turn. Photographers flashed pictures. Waiters carried trays of drinks and little sandwiches. Then two famous people walked right by, not ten feet away from her, chitchatting with each other. One was that woman from the ad that had brought her there in the first place: Miss Rheingold of 1950. "The other was Mr. Errol Flynn hisself, looking even handsomer than in all those moving pictures I had seen him in. He was a tall drinka water, too, and that gray suit he was wearing was a humdinger—had a little polka-dotted handkerchief pokin' out of his jacket pocket that matched his necktie. 'Hey, y'all!' I called. It come out of my mouth before I could think the better of it. Miss Rheingold raised her eyebrows and kept walking and talking, but Errol looked over his shoulder and gave me a wink and a smile. I was lucky my heart didn't explode when he done that!

"In the middle of the ballroom was three signs held up on poles. They had arrows on them that said which line you went in if you were a blonde, a brunette, or a redhead. My line was the shortest, but when I started making for it, a bald man grabbed my arm and stopped me. 'Hold on there, toots,' he said. 'Who might you be?' When I told him, he checked a list and said, 'Well, I've got a Harrison and a Hughes, but I don't see any Hibbard. And anyway, you can't just jump in halfway through the elimination process. It's almost noon. Half the girls have already been handed their pink cards.'

"I asked him what in the dickens *that* meant, and he said it meant *sayonara*, better luck next year. Then he said he needed to see my letter of invitation. 'Well, that's just the thing,' I explained. 'It got lost in the mail, and that's why I'm late. I didn't know what time y'all wanted me to get here.' And he says, suspicious-like as if he was some kinda detective, 'I see. And might I ask where your portfolio is?' I told him sure, he could ask, and once he told me what that was, I could tell him where mine was at. He held his hand out to all them gals in the different lines. 'Sweetheart, these girls have all had extensive modeling experience,' he said. 'You've probably seen most of them on magazine covers. Now your invitation didn't get lost. They never sent you one. Can't you see that you're way out of your league?'

"I tried reasoning with him. Told him I was all the time being mistaken for movie stars, and that I came all the way here from Connecticut. 'And the redhead line is the puniest one,' I added. He said he was sorry, but Connecticut was only one state away and waiting in line would be a waste of the judges' time and mine because I didn't have a snowball's chance in hell of becoming a Rheingold girl. I felt like cryin' when he said that, but I wudn't gonna give him the satisfaction. So I thanked him kindly, pointed my chin in the air, and started back down the hallway. Just in case his beady little eyes was following me, I made myself walk like my feet wasn't killin' me.

"Crossing that fancy lobby with its glittery mirrors and chandeliers and giant vases of flowers, I stopped, sat down on one of them red velvet couches, and took off my damned high heels. My feet was a sight, all blisters and dried blood underneath my nylons. I got up in my stocking feet and headed for the door, holding my head up high like it was the normalest thing in the world to stroll through that lobby barefoot, holding your shoes.

"Outside, there they were again: those two snooty doormen in those stupid-looking uniforms. I marched right up to them and told them to point me back toward the train station, and to make it snappy cuz I'd had a bellyful of New York City and couldn't wait to get out of it. They went wide-eyed like they was scared of me and told me which way to go. But when I was just four or five steps away from them, I heard them funnin' at my expense. 'Maybe Daisy Mae could go back home and be Miss Dogpatch,' one of 'em said. 'Or Miss Cowshit,' the other one chimed in. Oh, they was havin' theirselves a grand ole time on me—until I marched myself right back to where they was. 'Y'all can go to hell in a handbasket!' I screamed. Then I fired my shoes at them, hard as I could. You shoulda seen them two, duckin' like a coupla scared little girls."

Verna says she managed to stay dry-eyed all the way back

to New London, and on the bus back to Hewett City, too. It wasn't until she reached her dreary little room in the hotel where Yancey had parked her that she gave herself permission to let loose. She cried so hard that she could hardly catch her breath. "The tears that come out of me coulda probably filled up a bucket," she says.

FOURTEEN

The second man to follow Verna from the hotel bar up the back stairs to her room was Uncle Iggy, who, she said, was not like the first guy, Frank, or like Yancey either. He was more gentlemanly than both, and his lovemaking was patient and considerate—absent of the highs she'd felt with Yancey maybe, but at least he didn't make her feel low and used like Frank had. And at least he had no plans to join the Merchant Marines, go off somewhere, and never even write her a letter.

After their second sexual encounter, Iggy mentioned casually that he was an "Eyetalian," which surprised her. Her mother had warned her that "those people" were crude and low-class, just one rung up the ladder from the coloreds, if that. Ha! A lot she knew. Iggy was *courting* her. Giving her flowers and taking her places so that she knew their friendship wasn't just about *that*. He took her dancing one night, and twice to the movies: *Guilty Bystander* the first time and *The Asphalt Jungle* the second. They weren't the kind of pictures she liked, but she didn't mind looking at Tyrone Power and Zachary Scott and, while Iggy sat there holding her hand and cupping her knee, imagining what those two would be like as lovers. Or Errol Flynn, whom she had seen in the flesh, which had been the only good thing that had happened in that otherwise miserable day in New York City—one of the worst days of her life.

One Saturday night, Iggy drove up to see her in the middle of a blizzard! Rather than cancel their date, he'd had chains put on the tires of his car—a roomy Hudson Commodore. "Just the kind of auto*mobile* my daddy'd been partial to." They ate at the best restaurant in town, which wasn't saying *too* much given that the town was Hewett City, but because of the snow, they were the only diners there and it was very romantic. Iggy ordered them both a fancy dish called lobster Newburg. It was delicious and, better still, came with Duchess potatoes "which had fancy swirls but was really just good ole mashed potatoes puttin' on the dog. For dessert, we got slices of this fancy cake that had liquor poured onto it. Iggy fed mine to me. He was trying to be lovey-dovey, I guess, but I kinda felt like a two-year-old in a high chair. Between bites, I told him about how, where I come from, we had king cake at Mardi Gras, and how it had purple, green, and gold frosting and a little plastic baby hidden inside it. And how, whoever got the slice of king cake with the baby was gonna get a year of good luck. Iggy kinda snorted and said that getting a baby sounded like *bad* luck to him. And I said, 'Well it's only plastic. It's not like you have to feed it and change its diaper.' And he laughed and fed me another bite of that boozy cake."

When they left the restaurant that night, they walked through the snow back to the hotel and had after-dinner drinks at the bar. By the time they got up to her room, Verna was feeling "drunk as a skunk and silly enough to tell him that I wudn't Verna Hibbard anymore. I was Fanny Feathers. The more of my clothes I flung off, the sassier I felt, and when I was down to just my birthday suit, I told Iggy that now *he* had to striptease for *me*, and he was liquored up enough to do it, too! So I flopped back on the bed and watched the show. When he got down to just his undershorts, I said what everyone says when they want beads or other trinkets at the Mardi Gras parades: 'Throw me something, mistuh!' Iggy tried to drop his drawers, but they got all tangled up with his pecker, which was already jacked up and ready to go. We both broke into giggle fits. Then he got free of his shorts, jumped onto the bed, and the two of us went at it. I suspect that was the night that the baby got started.

"Iggy ended up sleeping over, which he never done before, and the next morning, after the snow in the street got plowed away and he left, I went over to the mirror and spoke sass to it like I was talkin' to Lana Turner. I said, 'Move over, blondie, because you ain't the only gal that's having an *affair*! And my boyfriend ain't married to some poor crippled lady like yours was. He ain't married to no one. He's free as a bird.' But then it occurred to me that *I* was married, which I had kinda forgot about. Then the sass drained right outa me."

When Verna missed her period at the beginning of April, she started feeling "sick as a shaggy dog in an August heat wave." She had lost her appetite and struggled even having to serve food to customers at Charlene's. But when Iggy gave her a solid chocolate rabbit for Easter, eating it appealed to her and she devoured it, headfirst down to its haunches. Fifteen minutes later, she vomited it all back up. She told Iggy it was the grippe. When she missed her next period, she told him the truth.

She shook her head and cried when Iggy accused her of getting pregnant on purpose. Then she reminded him that he'd not bothered to put on a "safe" that night of the blizzard. He apologized to her but made it clear that he didn't want a baby. To further complicate things, Verna received a cable from Yancey that he would be back in port the next month, and that he loved and missed her and was craving to be with her again. She agreed to have the abortion that Iggy said he would arrange, even though the thought of it made her sad and scared. She took the money Iggy gave her to pay the woman who would come to her room and perform the procedure. He offered to be there with her, but she told him no.

Verna had every intention of going through with it, getting it over with, but when the abortionist knocked and gave her the code word, Verna opened the door and lost her nerve. Facing her was the gruff, mannish lady clerk at the store where she bought her groceries. There were two cashiers at that place and Verna always went out of her way to avoid this woman because she was so mean-looking and unpleasant. When Verna told her she had changed her mind about the operation, the woman became angry and pushed her way into the room. She sat down on Verna's bed and said she wasn't leaving until she was paid what she'd been promised. To be rid of her, Verna got the envelope of bills Iggy had given her, shoved it at her, and told her the cash was payment for her silence.

In the hours that followed, Verna paced and wondered what would happen now that she had paid for an abortion she hadn't gotten. She began to imagine that Iggy would come around and be understanding and sweet again. What did she care if he was "Eyetalian"? She had long since given up trying to please her mother. She would divorce Yancey quickly and quietly. Then she and Iggy would marry and get a nice little place, get all the things that a baby needed—a bassinet, a crib, a carriage. He would grow to love their child. She was pretty sure she loved Iggy, too, although differently than she loved Yancey. The baby would bind them together. "I begun to think that maybe the Good Lord Jesus had decided to forgive me after all. He worked in mysterious ways, didn't He? Maybe He had sent that horrible woman to my room instead of someone more pleasanter just so I would decide not to rid myself of the life growing inside of me—Iggy's and my little boy or little girl. It would all work out, I figgered. And maybe a grandbaby would even soften my mama's heart, especially if the child didn't look too dark-haired and dark-skinned and I could keep it from her that it was half-Eyetalian.

"Iggy brought me get-better flowers that evening when he drove up from work to see how I was doing. I meant to admit the truth from the git-go but, instead, I heard myself lying—telling him that I was tired and sore from the p'cedure but that I'd feel better after I got some rest. I got confused at first when he changed the subject and started talking about some secretary he knew from work, and how she'd been having marriage troubles and would be getting a divorce. What in the world did that have to do with me? Then, suddenly, it came to me like a punch in the head: he had taken up with that secretary and was throwing me over. I threw his flowers back at him and told him to get out of my room and go to hell. The anger was what came first, the tears later. I watched out my window as, down below, he got in that big old Hudson of his and drove away. He had no inkling that I was still carrying his child. Maybe I coulda gotten him back if he knew, but now I didn't even want the big dope. Good riddance to bad rubbish, I thought, which was somethin' Mama always used to say when she was mad at someone."

Luckily, Verna was hardly showing by the time Yancey returned from his travels, talking a blue streak about all the places he'd been to, all the things he had seen. Silence had nearly driven her insane in the first months she'd lived in this room, but now she wished she had a little of it back again. "It was like these talking walls was closing in on me from all four sides." Yancey was not only more boring than she'd remembered, but he was less handsome, too. He had bought her souvenirs at every port of call: mostly dolls in native costumes—saris, sarongs, "the kind of clothes Dorothy Lamour wore in those dumb ole *Road* pictures with Bing Crosby and Bob Hope." He'd bought Verna a life-size silk kimono as well. It was headache-red and egg-yolk orange and had angry-looking dragons embroidered on the front. She wore the kimono as a bathrobe, even though, for some reason, it made her feel cheap and trashy to slip it on. She stood the dolls up on the windowsill like they were contestants in a beauty pageant and took Yancey's naïve ribbing about the little potbelly she'd developed in his absence. That observation caused her to abandon the idea that she might pass off the child as his. She blamed her frequent nausea on a stomachache that just wouldn't quit her. When Yancey suggested he take her to see a doctor, she panicked. She wanted no part of doctors! Luckily, she was able to talk her way out of it. She still enjoyed sex with Yancey, but not as much as before now that she had some basis for comparison. She seemed to want tenderness more than wildness now. Sometimes when he was moving urgently inside her, she was reminded of the ugly encounter she'd had with Frank. When Yancey attempted to pleasure her down there with his tongue, she found herself missing the way Iggy did it and wished her husband wasn't lapping at her like a thirsty dog. Waiting for the slurping to be over, she looked at those dolls on the windowsill. Instead of beauty contestants waiting for the judges' decision, now they looked to her like women in a police lineup. By all rights, she should be standing in that lineup, too. After all, *she* was the guilty one. Was she that good at deception or was Yancey what he had once accused her of being: dumb as a retarded mule? Whatever the reason, he couldn't seem to read any of the signs that he had a faithless wife.

Yancey shipped out again three weeks later. It was a good thing, too, because now she was beginning to show in earnest. She could feel some fluttering in her tummy. Car coats, long sweaters, and loosely tied waitress aprons helped Verna hide her condition for a while longer. She saw Iggy once during this time, after he'd had a spat with his new girlfriend—that secretary he had dumped her for. Verna wasn't about to let him inside her room, so they talked outside in his parked car. He said he thought about her all the time, even when he was with his new floozy. She knew what he was going after with that kind of talk. Without having to disrobe or even take off her car coat, she managed to satisfy him with her hand. He drove away with his pants undone and his goop on his shirttails. "Better there than inside of me, I figger. I'm fed up with men and their stupid needs. The only thing I care about is the child who's gonna come outa me and who I'm gonna love and protect."

At work, Charlene guessed that she was pregnant but not that she was carrying the child of a man other than her husband. Verna had no game plan. She had seen no doctor. She got no advice from the mother who had disowned her and continued to hang up in her ear. She had no girlfriends in this unfriendly town—no young mothers of babies she could consult. Her own baby's kicking made her nervous. Was it normal that it should be so restless in there? Would it come out normal or strange like that pinhead girl she'd seen at the carnival Granny Shoop had taken her to when she was little? "That poor thing's mother must have been full of sin to grow a child like that one in her belly," Granny had said. Every once in a while since that long-ago day, when Verna thought about the pinhead girl, she had prayed for her. "But that was back then, before I lost the right to pray for anyone, least of all myself."

Charlene gave Verna a baby shower on her last day of work. The morning and afternoon waitresses, Margie and Linda, had left gifts but said they couldn't come back for the farewell. So it was only Charlene and her daughter-in-law, Edith, who attended. The gifts Verna opened—receiving blankets, rattles—suddenly made the baby more of a reality than all those months of kicking had. "And that made me good and scared. But I had wrote down the date when I started missing 'my friend' and figgered I had another whole month to make a plan. Maybe I could go see some nice minister and ask for help—or even that old priest with the bushy eyebrows who showed up at Charlene's for supper like clockwork whenever the special was shepherd's pie." Her mother would be horrified at that idea. She'd warned Verna not to trust "Catlicks" in general, priests and nuns specifically. They were as shifty as Gypsies, she told Verna, and would sweet-talk their prey until they'd gotten the conversion they were after. Then they'd show their true colors once you were owned by the pope. The more Verna thought about it, the more she figured she would avoid the clergy altogether. She could put the baby in her wicker laundry basket, tuck blankets around her, and carry her to an orphanage. Ring the bell and run. Yes, that's what she would do. She was relieved that she finally had a plan.

Her water broke at around one the next morning. Either the baby was coming early or Verna had miscalculated. For a while, she lay there on the warm, wet mattress, shivering but otherwise immobile. Then the contractions came. Frightened by the pain, and by what was happening, she was nevertheless grateful that the baby would arrive while the rest of the hotel's second-floor lodgers were asleep. She got up, paced the room, and endured another two hours' worth of the baby's fight to come out. When she convinced herself that it was time to push—that she would either push the child out of her or else die from the pain—she walked down the hallway holding onto the walls as she went. Reaching the bathroom, she entered a stall and locked it, sat herself down on the toilet, and stuck her fist in her mouth to stop herself from screaming out in pain. She began to push with all of her might.

Verna stops her testimony there. Lois thanks her and the two begin to fade. "Wait! Don't go yet! Verna, I need to tell you something."

"Remember the rules, Felix," Lois's ghost says. "She has

been here to give testimony, not to converse with a member of the living world."

Ignoring her, I look directly at Frances's mother's ghost. "Thank you! Thank you for my sister! Thank you!"

In Verna's fading image, I'm pretty sure I catch a grateful, quivery-lipped smile.

FIFTEEN

That day at the Institute of Living? When Simone and I were asked to go to the waiting room and I cried, finally having realized that Frances's anorexia might kill her? Simone had sat down beside me, drawn me to her, and promised that our sister was going to be all right. I guess that's the difference between faith and doubt. When I twisted the knobs of that Etch A Sketch as we waited for the others to emerge, a jumble of nothingness had appeared on the screen. But Simone told me that, one time when she had played with an Etch A Sketch, a linear Blessed Virgin Mary had presented herself to her. "Frances is going to get better and be okay," Simone promised me that day. "You'll see."

She was right. Guided by Dr. Darda, Frances brought herself back to a healthy weight and learned how to release much of the anger and fear that had thwarted her and driven her worst behavior. In the months following her hospital stay, by degrees, she underwent the process by which she forgave my parents their well-intentioned but misguided deception about her origins. As Pop had pointed out to her during that therapy session, she was, after all, still a Funicello. Maybe that was why she forgave him first. Forgiving Ma took longer, forgiving herself longer still.

Frances's grades had never suffered during her illness and she graduated from high school with high honors and a full scholarship to Boston College. After vacillating about whether to pursue a career in medicine or law, she settled on BC's predental program. She became friends with a pre-veterinary student, a freckle-faced redhead named Molly Nickerson. Molly and Fran were dorm mates first, then roommates. Boston was a comfortable fit for them both, so in their senior year each applied to Tufts for graduate work, and each was accepted in her chosen field. "Molly's school is in Grafton and mine's in Chinatown, so it only makes sense that we get a place in between. We've found a pretty nice apartment in Framingham."

"But if your school's in Chinatown, wouldn't it make more sense to live there?" I asked, straight-faced. I was teasing her.

"Well . . ." she said.

"Hey, love is love. I think it's cool." She looked stunned that I'd figured it out.

Simone was accepting of Fran and Molly's relationship, too, despite the dictates of Roman Catholic dogma. If not exactly enthusiastic at first, Ma was okay with Frances's coming out. She recognized that her complicated daughter was happy, and that's all that mattered. Pop's acceptance took a little longer.

He was eventually won over by Molly's chainsaw skills after a bad storm felled a willow tree in our backyard. It helped, too, that Molly was a baseball fan and Frances wasn't. When the Red Sox (Molly's team) played home games against the Yankees (Pop's), she sometimes managed to score tickets. She and Pop bonded over Fenway franks, Hood ice cream bars, and their good-natured arguments about this classic American League rivalry.

For a number of years, Frances and Molly lived and worked in the Worcester area in their respective fields, Molly at an animal hospital in Shrewsbury and Frances for a dental practice in Auburn. When they could afford to do so, they bought a nice piece of property in the Berkshires and built their home, a two-story log cabin situated on a ridgetop. Frances's dental office and Molly's animal clinic, twin wood-shingled ranch-style buildings with a parking lot between them, sit at the base of that ridge. It has taken a while for them to grow their respective practices, but at this point they're both successfully established in the North Adams community. To get to their place, you take a left off Route 8 onto Hunter Foundry Road, cross over the brook, and you'll see the sign on the right: Happy Tooth Dentistry and Happy Pets Veterinary Clinic.

When the Massachusetts Supreme Court okayed gay marriage in 2004, Molly and Fran said their "I do's" at the North Adams City Hall. Pop had died by then and Ma was too out of it to attend, but Simone, Aliza, my ex-wife Kat, and I were all there. It was a day to celebrate, and celebrate we did at the reception afterward at a nearby Grange hall—even the brides' three pooches, Curly, Larry, and Moe. The dancing went on until midnight.

Simone had made Frances aware of the existence of Verna's

diary many years earlier, warning her that it might upset her to read it but assuring her that she could take possession of it whenever she wanted. "You keep it," Fran had told her. "I might want to look at it someday, but not right now." The issue of the diary came up from time to time after that. Frances's response was always the same. "Maybe someday. I'll let you know." Then, three or four years ago, when Fran and Molly were down at Simone's for a visit, Molly asked if *she* could read it—that Frances had asked her to. Simone said sure. She retrieved it from an upstairs closet, came back down, and handed it to Molly. Simone told me later that Frances avoided looking at it. "What a gorgeous day!" Fran had said. "I think I'll go for a walk." Did she want company? Simone asked. "No thanks." Fran and Molly drove back to North Adams that night.

The next day, Frances called Simone to say that she'd decided she didn't ever want to read her mother's diary. "Are you sure?" Simone asked her.

"It's funny," Frances said. "There's a part of me that's waited my whole life for her to come back. But she's *not* coming back. Molly thinks it would be better if I didn't have to hear what she went through, so I decided not to read it. And you know what? It's like I've let go of this heavy weight I've been dragging around forever."

"Then what should I do with it?" Simone asked.

"Her diary? I don't know. Throw it out, I guess."

Simone told me that, after she hung up, she sat down and read each of Verna's entries. "It sounds weird, Felix, but it was almost like she was speaking. Bearing witness from the dead or something. If I threw it out, it would be like silencing her. And I got to thinking that it wasn't me who needed to hear her."

"Yeah, but if Fran doesn't want to hear it, she shouldn't have to."

"I'm not talking about Frances," she said. "I don't know if it was right or wrong. But what I did was, I put it in a padded envelope and sent it down to Boca."

"You mailed it to Uncle Iggy? Why?"

"Because I thought it was time he bore some responsibility for everything that had happened. Way *past* time, actually. I almost called you to ask if I should send it to him, but then I decided not to because I didn't want you to tell me I shouldn't."

"Well, for whatever it's worth, I don't think I would have. Pop used to complain about how everyone treated his brother like an overgrown baby, but he used to enable him, too. Did you write Iggy a note or anything?"

She shook her head. "*I* didn't have anything to say to him. *She* did. I put my return address on the envelope, so he knew who'd sent it, but . . . Oh, I don't know. Was I an awful person to try to make him take some accountability after all this time?"

"No, you weren't. In fact, you're the *least* awful person I know. What was his response? Did he call you? Write to you?"

"Neither one. I have no idea if he even read it. His only response is that now, whenever I call him, all I get is his answering machine. And I know he has caller ID."

SIXTEEN

That day back in 1965 when Uncle Iggy arrived at Frances's family therapy session, a door had opened onto the possibility that he might bond, belatedly, with his daughter. But neither Uncle Iggy nor Frances chose to make that happen. Oh, they were polite to each other when we were all together for holidays at the house on Herbert Hoover Avenue. You could tell, though, that the close proximity made both of them uneasy. After he retired, Iggy relocated to Boca Raton, Florida, making their estrangement geographical as well as emotional. Iggy's pattern continued: card games with cronies, a succession of lady friends, no commitments, no wife. What mere spouse ever could have doted on him the way Nonna Funicello had?

Cigarette smoking and heart disease claimed my father in

2001. Cursed with stroke-related dementia, my mother lingered without him until 2005. My brother-in-law Jeff's passing came soon after. And as if that wasn't enough sadness for my sister Simone to abide, Luke, her only child, was diagnosed the following year with multiple sclerosis, the same disease that claimed our famous cousin, Annette. Bedridden near the end, Luke died from asphyxiation, choking on his breakfast while his mom vacuumed the living room. Simone's path in life has been a difficult one, but she's handled the heartaches and challenges with grace, good humor, and a faith so firm that she believes God's plan, as unfathomable as it might be, is merciful.

Uncle Iggy would call me from time to time from Florida, asking how I was doing and what I was up to. Somewhere in the middle of those conversations, he would want to know what I'd heard from my sister lately, and I always knew which sister he meant. He had met Molly at my parents' house one Christmas and later, in a call to me, had asked just how "friendly" Fran and Molly's friendship was.

"If you're asking me if they're a couple, yes. They are."

"Yeah, that's what I figured. Well, it's none of my business."

Fran and her father were both in town for Pop's funeral in 2001, but I can't recall that they had much of any interaction during those two or three days. She didn't invite him to her wedding. He did not fly up from Boca for my mother's funeral the following year. His calls to me became less frequent and I got careless about calling him. Little by little, he began to fade away.

And then one day I got a call from someone at his condo complex—one of his pinochle buddies. Iggy had been having some trouble with his balance, he said. He'd fallen twice, no serious injuries. He seemed mixed up sometimes, a little bit afraid of things you wouldn't think he'd be afraid of. When he played cards, he couldn't seem to concentrate. "He told me you're his next of kin," he said. "He didn't want me to bother you, but I figured you'd want to know what's going on."

After we hung up, I picked up the phone and called Frances's office. "Can I speak with Dr. Funicello?" I asked. The receptionist said she was in the middle of a root canal. "Then would you tell her to call her brother?" I asked.

"Of course. May I tell her what this is in reference to?"

"Sure. It's about her . . . about our uncle."

Fran and I flew down to Boca together. Although I assured her I could handle it myself, I was relieved I didn't have to. Tests were taken and retaken, followed by further tests. Whenever Iggy smiled at her, Frances wouldn't or couldn't smile back. We hired him a home health care aide and flew home after a couple of days while we waited for all the test results to come in. We were summoned back to Florida a few weeks later.

At the medical center that housed the neurology team to which we'd been referred, Frances and I sat on either side of Iggy and listened to a middle-aged doctor whose name I've since forgotten. "It's often misdiagnosed as Parkinson's or Alzheimer's because it has symptoms common to both," she told us. "But we're confident that Mr. Funicello is suffering from Lewy body dementia." I looked out the window behind her, focusing not so much on what else she was saying as I was on the way the wind was tossing the fronds of the palm trees that lined the medical complex's driveway. When I looked to my left at my uncle, he seemed not to be registering that the doctor was talking about him. Then I looked past him at my stricken sister.

After we dropped Uncle Iggy back at his place, I said, "That doctor reminded me of someone, but I can't figure out who."

"I know who it is," Fran said. "Joanne Tate from *Search for Tomorrow.*"

"That's it! Shit man, all those problems she had to face. Who knew she was a neurologist on top of all that?" Our shared laughter relieved a little of the tension of the hour before.

We worked as a team, Frances, Simone, and I. Two more trips down to Florida and several phone conversations later, we had accomplished everything we needed to: our uncle's bills were paid, his bank accounts were closed, his things were packed up or donated, and his condo was put on the market. I looked for Verna's diary among his possessions but didn't find it. If he'd gotten rid of it, had he at least read it first?

For the flight north, Iggy was sedated, the better to calm his anxiety and fend off one of the hallucinations that could throw him into a tailspin. At LaGuardia, Simone and I waited with Fran and our uncle during their layover. After they handed the agent their boarding passes and disappeared through the gate, Simone said, "I sure hope she'll be able to handle this." I reminded her that she'd have Molly's help, and that it had been her decision to assume his power of attorney.

Frances had secured her father a room at the Williamstown Commons Nursing Home. After a difficult first week, he more or less acclimated, or at least surrendered to his powerlessness. His fear-based tantrums subsided, but his balance became further compromised. With Frances's reluctant okay, the staff began restraining him overnight so that he wouldn't get out of bed, fall, and injure himself. Fran checked in on him three or four evenings a week, usually by herself but sometimes with Molly. One early Sunday morning about a month after he'd been admitted, the nurse on duty called to let Frances know that her father was close to the end. She and Molly hurried to the facility. Molly called later to tell me my uncle was gone. "Fran was holding his hand when he passed," she said. "She was a trouper through this whole thing. I'm really proud of her." I told her I was proud of her, too.

Per his pre-Lewy body instructions, Uncle Iggy's remains were transported back to Three Rivers for burial alongside his parents in the Funicello family plot at Good Shepherd Cemetery. For his wake, he was laid out in a charcoal gray suit, a periwinkle blue shirt, and a blue-and-gray-striped tie. Although he had never been a very religious man, his folded hands clutched a set of gold and amber rosary beads. His thumb, flattened long ago in the wringer of the family's washing machine, was prominent.

There were two wakes at the Labenski Funeral Home that evening: Uncle Iggy's and, from the old neighborhood, Chiki Shishmanian's. Chiki was the 101-year-old father of Shirley, JoBeth, and their brother, whom everyone still called Little Chiki. Before calling hours began, we chatted in the hallway with JoBeth, now a divorced grandmother whose face had the rosy flush of the alcoholic. "Is Shirley here?" Simone asked.

JoBeth shook her head. "Couldn't make it. When I called to tell her that Baba had passed, she had just come out of surgery. She sent an extravagant casket blanket, though: red, blue, and orange roses—the colors of the Armenian flag."

"I didn't know there *were* blue roses," I said.

"Me neither," JoBeth said. "Must have cost a fortune. Oh well, I'm sure she can afford it."

Simone said she hoped Shirley's surgery wasn't anything serious.

"Face-lift number three, but who's counting?" JoBeth said, smirking. "She told me she couldn't be seen in public while she was still bruised and swollen like a battered wife. God forbid she'd just let gravity take its toll like the rest of us." Her laughter sounded so bitter that it triggered nervous laughter in my sisters and me. We looked at JoBeth's cell phone photos of her grandkids, reminisced a little about the old neighborhood, exchanged hugs, and then departed to our respective viewing rooms.

"*Three* face-lifts?" Frances whispered to me.

"Vanity, thy name is Dulcet Tone," I whispered back. Shirley was still chasing beauty, surgically at this point. And who knows what toll it had taken on JoBeth never to have been able to grab the golden ring like her preternaturally beautiful sister had? If Frances had not gotten off that same merry-go-round, she could have starved herself to death trying to become . . . who? Simone? Miss Rheingold? A lesbian hiding in a conventional marriage?

"If Shirley's inherited her father's longevity genes and makes it to *her* centennial, they'll need a block and tackle to lift that face," I noted. Fran guffawed.

"Stop it, you two," Simone scolded. "Be nice."

Calling hours went from five to seven. Across the hall, the local Armenians came out in force for Chiki Shishmanian, but attendance on our side was sparse. Most of the people who showed up had done so to pay their respects to Simone, the Funicello sibling who had remained in Three Rivers. I was pleasantly surprised when Aliza and her mother arrived. Kat had known Iggy, but she was certainly not obliged to pay respects to the uncle of her divorced husband. And by the time Aliza had come along, Iggy had already moved down to

Florida. She'd met him once or twice, I guess, but that was it. Clearly, she and her mom had made the effort for me.

Once calling hours were over, the six of us—Fran and Molly, Aliza and Kat, Simone and me—went back to Simone's house. She'd made a big salad and a couple of antipasto platters and I opened the bottles of wine I'd brought. We had pizza delivered. There was a lot of laughter and remembrance during the meal, and Aliza seemed to get a kick out of listening to the old Funicello family stories: the time Pop had had to cut into the living room ceiling and pull out Winky's kittens; my ill-fated appearance on the *Ranger Andy* show when I'd unwittingly told a dirty joke on live TV; Ma's trip to California for the Pillsbury Bake-Off, courtesy of her culinary creation, Shepherd's Pie Italiano. Simone said she still made that dish sometimes for potlucks at church. "But I use 93 percent lean ground beef and reduced-fat ricotta and mozzarella. And for the crust, I substitute olive oil for Crisco."

"You mean Fluffo," Frances said. "Ma used Fluffo."

"Except when Crisco was on sale," Simone said. "And I don't even want to think about what Pop used in the fryolator down at the lunch counter. Whatever it was, it came in those unmarked one-gallon cans."

"Quaker State motor oil"—I said—"10W-30."

"Except when Valvoline was on sale," Frances added.

Simone turned to Aliza. "Your nonna and nonno had come of age during the Depression," she explained.

"So had your Bubbe and Zayde Schulman," Kat said. "I once caught hell for throwing away a piece of tinfoil. You never tossed that. You flattened and saved it."

I contributed that Ma was a cheapskate about tape: Scotch tape, masking tape, Band-Aids. "If you cut yourself and it didn't need stitches, then you didn't need a Band-Aid either. Put a little Mercurochrome on it, then stop whining and go back outside and play." It was fun sharing these laughs over our forebears' Depression-inspired thrift.

At one point, Simone, the keeper of family pictures, disappeared upstairs and came back down carrying a large carton filled with scrapbooks, loose photos, and other memorabilia. Molly pulled Frances's old 45s out of the box and said she and Fran must have been destined to end up together—that they had bought a lot of the same records. "Oh wow! I haven't heard 'Under My Thumb' in forever. Simone, do you have anything that can play this thing?"

"I think that old thing still works," Simone said, pointing to the stereo housed inside the Pennsylvania Dutch–style cabinet she and Jeff had bought back in the seventies when they were setting up house. She removed the African violets and the doily from the top of it and I reached behind the console for the cord, fished it out, and plugged it into the nearest outlet. When I opened the lid of the cabinet, it creaked. But a flip of the switch started the turntable rotating and a minute later the Stones were coming through the speakers. It was 1966 again—the year of recovery for my anorexic sister. Molly started dancing by herself, then she pulled Frances off the couch and the two were dancing together. Aliza, a fan of old-school rock, got up and joined them. Simone, Kat, and I were smiling from the sidelines. At least I *assumed* Kat was smiling along with Simone and me until the music stopped abruptly and I looked over at her. She had pulled the plug.

"Hey!" Molly protested.

Kat had that adamant, lockjawed look on her face; as much as anything else, that look and my stubborn resistance to whatever it meant was responsible for our having reached the point of no return and divorced. "Don't you people realize how demeaning those lyrics are?"

"You want poetic lyrics, listen to Joni Mitchell," I said. "In a Stones song, the lyrics are incidental."

"Not to me," she countered. "He calls the woman a pet? A squirming dog? She has to keep *her* eyes to herself but *he* can look at someone else? It's disgusting."

"Come on, chill, Mom. It's a fucking *song*," Aliza protested.

"Written by whom? The Taliban?"

"But you can't just unplug it because *you're* offended. You're censoring art the same way as a repressive—"

"If it oppresses women, it shouldn't be *considered* art," Kat snapped back.

Molly took her on. "Look, I'm as much of a feminist as anyone," she said. "Wouldn't be where I am today if it wasn't for the movement. But some of us go overboard with the diatribes and the PC bullshit."

"Some of us? Like me, for instance?"

"Hey, I didn't say that. But if the shoe fits."

"Well, I'm sorry, but I'm not about to let down my guard as long as sexual assault is epidemic, and working women make twenty-two cents less for every dollar their male counterparts take home. And if you're picking and choosing which parts of the movement you support, then that makes you a cafeteria feminist."

"And what's wrong with that?" Frances wanted to know.

"What's wrong with it? It weakens the movement, that's what. United we stand, divided we fall." She turns toward Aliza. "Are you listening?"

"I'm listening, but I don't necessarily agree. Give it a rest, Mom."

Kat shook her head, sighed, and went into the kitchen to cool off. When she came out again, she said, "Well, what do you say, Aliza? You've got a train to catch and I have an eight a.m. meeting in Glastonbury. Don't you think we'd better get going?"

Simone, Frances, and I saw them to the door. Kat said she was sorry if she'd spoiled everyone's fun. Simone waved her hand dismissively. "I never liked the Stones that much anyway. I was a Beatles fan." I kissed Kat on the cheek and said I was glad she still had the fire in her belly. "Damn right I do," she said. "It's not over till it's over."

"Which it never will be," Frances said. "Take it from me, Kat. You need to bend a little so that you don't break. Because what use are you if you're broken?" From what I could see, my daughter was listening more intently to Frances than her mother was.

There were hugs, goodbyes, "drive safely"s. After they drove away and we went back to the living room, Molly said she appreciated Kat's take-no-prisoners zeal, even if silencing Mick Jagger mid-song was damn near unforgivable. "And Aliza? My niece has really come into her own, huh? She's a keeper, Felix." I agreed and thanked her, pleased with her observation.

Molly and I cleared the table and put away the leftovers while my sisters did the dishes. (The old pattern prevailed: Simone washed, Frances dried.) After everything was done, we went back to the old photo albums. Those old black-and-white pictures were like talismans that brought back the past.

Molly got up from the table after a few minutes. "Well, good night, you guys. I think I'll turn in. Have fun." She kissed Frances and went off to bed.

"Nothing more boring than other people's family pictures," I said.

"Pfft. She's going up there to catch the rest of the Red Sox game on her iPad," Frances said. "Hey, Felix, remember that summer we went around with the Miss Rheingold box?"

"Shit yeah. We rang so many doorbells on Shirley Shishmanian's behalf, she should have put us on the payroll."

In my mind's eye, I saw the two of us trudging around with that ballot box. And then, abruptly, I saw the bedraggled boy who had run up to the fence when Frances led me to that orphanage in order to scare me—to project onto her little brother the fear that lived inside of her. She had denied she'd done that once before, and I was curious to see if she would deny it again or, this time, admit to it. But she had been through a lot in her father's final weeks. The next morning we would bury him—the uncle I once had such affection for who had seduced and abandoned Frances's mother, and then participated in the ruse that Fran was his niece, not his daughter. Yet whether he'd deserved it or not, Frances had stepped up to the plate during his final days and had been, if not a loving daughter, then at least a dutiful one. So I kept my mouth shut.

A few days after my uncle's funeral, I received a 9 × 12 envelope that had been addressed to Iggy and forwarded to me. The return address said Ascension Roman Catholic Church, 7250 North Federal Highway, Boca Raton, Florida. The note inside explained that since my uncle had paid for the enclosed items but had never come by the chancery office to pick them up, they were mailing them to him. When I overturned the envelope, six Memorial Mass cards fell out, which indicated that Maryknoll priests would pray at six different Masses for the soul of the departed, Verna Hibbard. Too little, too late? Sure. But Simone and I interpreted his gesture as proof that Uncle Iggy must have read Verna's diary and heard her voice after all.

SEVENTEEN

INVINCIBLE GRRRL

Blogpost # 106: MOM & ME

by Aliza Funicello

The other day, walking along Madison Avenue with my feminist mother, we passed a store that caters to young women, sizes 0 through 6. "Women your age just don't get it," Mom huffed. "Either that, or you're throwing back in our faces everything that women my age fought to give you." Admittedly, the mannequins in the window were wearing outfits that looked pretty slutty.

My mother was born in 1949. Four years earlier, Rosie the Riveter had hung up her coveralls, exited the factory, and retreated back to the kitchen or the secretarial pool—or to the back alley if she needed an abortion. In one of the biggest films of 1949, *A Letter to Three Wives*, a trio of virtuous married women each receives the same letter from a homewrecker named Addie, informing them that she has run away with one of their husbands. The movie keeps audiences guessing about which wife's failure to please her man has resulted in her devastation. Arizona's Jacque Mercer was crowned Miss America of 1949. Asked how she had won, she replied, "I just figured if you could learn how to be a brain, you could learn how to be a woman. Nobody figured I could do anything anyway." Seriously?

So I get it, Mom. You and your second-wave sisters had to work like hell to bust through those stereotypes, procure your reproductive rights, and begin to shatter corporate America's miles-high glass ceiling without getting injured by all those falling shards. I'm neither ungrateful nor oblivious that women my age reap the benefits of your admirable, uphill struggle against a male-stacked status quo.

But Mom, we're not you. We inhabit a world dramatically changed by technology, globalization, and gender politics—a world your generation could not have imagined. Whereas you marched in the streets carrying placards that demanded "Equality NOW!" we take to the Internet where we Facebook, tweet, blog, and access the collective power of #hashtag feminism. One digital campaign convinced Amazon to stop selling T-shirts that promote violence against women. Another campaign cost rapper Rick Ross his lucrative Reebok spokesmanship after he released a single that boasted about date rape compliments of a molly-infused cocktail. Digitized feminist outrage pressured the Susan G. Komen Foundation to reverse its decision to defund Planned Parenthood a mere three days after it announced its decision to do so. When Chip Wilson, the fat-shaming CEO of Lululemon, blamed the flaws of his clothing line on plus-size women whose body shapes were "inconsistent" with his product, the resulting outrage of the feminist blogosphere cost Wilson his chairmanship. And online feminism has gone worldwide in its fight against gender inequality, Mom. Crowd-sourcing apps now track and expose sexual assaults, sex trafficking, and female genital mutilation in places like Syria, Senegal, and elsewhere around the globe. The Internet has removed the barriers of geography and distance, replacing isolation with solidarity. That's grrrl power, right?

Mom, you did your feminist best raising me, steering me away from stories about fairy-tale heroines whose happiness-ever-after was dependent on handsome, well-heeled princes. Instead, you exposed me to feisty female characters like the Paper Bag Princess, Pippi Longstocking, Madeline, and Rosie Revere, Engineer—all of whom I adored and wanted to be. When I was in middle school, you were ambivalent about my affinity for those Nancy Drew mysteries, maybe because Nancy was, at best, only a sort-of feminist and, like me, a daddy's girl. To your credit, however, you didn't tell me I couldn't read them. And you wholeheartedly endorsed my reading of Judy Blume's frank YA novels that took on subjects like menstruation, divorce, and masturbation—realities that Nancy never went near.

Have I ever properly thanked you for your guidance during my high school years? "Politics is personal," you used to say. "Don't wait for someone to hand you power. Just take it." Your advice came in handy when my creepy algebra teacher began teasing me in that flirty way during class. When I finally told him to fuck off in front of everybody, it earned me a detention, but it also got him to back off and leave me alone. I felt as powerful as Wonder Woman. Do you recall when I started becoming preoccupied about my weight and you pulled Naomi Wolf's book *The Beauty Myth* off your shelf? "A culture fixated on female thinness is not an obsession about female beauty, but an obsession about female obedience," she wrote. I copied that quote onto an index card, thumbtacked it onto my bulletin board, and read it every time I had the urge to get back on the bathroom scale. In college? When I decided to major in feminist studies? That was because of you, Mom—and maybe a little because of Naomi Wolf and some of the other feminist thinkers you exposed me to. But Daddy's influence is probably what led me to become what I am: a writer.

You no doubt would have preferred it if I had landed a job with more feminist cred than my gig as a fashion and shopping reporter at *New York* magazine. But do you realize that *New York* was the parent publication from which Gloria Steinem and Dorothy Pitman Hughes launched *Ms.* as an insert way back in 1971? Anyway, a while back, I was assigned my first feature: a nostalgia piece about an East Coast beauty contest that was wildly popular from the 1940s through the early sixties. Each year, the makers of Rheingold beer invited the public to choose Miss Rheingold by voting for one of six pretty women whose pictures appeared on cardboard ballot boxes in stores and taverns. I balked at being dealt such a lame assignment. My generation tends to dismiss beauty contests as silly and inconsequential but not particularly dangerous. Now I'm not so sure.

Aunt Frances, your ex-sister-in-law, may be a successful dentist whose wife is an equally successful veterinarian. But did you know that, as an impressionable girl nearing puberty during the late 1950s, she was both heavy and heavily invested in the Miss Rheingold contest—so much so that she would borrow the ballot box from a local liquor store and ring doorbells to get out the vote? Given who she became, Aunt Fran seemed an unlikely adherent to the ethos that touted beauty queens as the feminine ideal. But when I interviewed her for my piece, she reminded me how few options were open to her and other girls during the 1950s, before the movement. "Mother, teacher, nurse, secretary, librarian, fashion model: that was about it. I didn't want to be any of those things, or a Rheingold girl either," she said. "But at least Miss Rheingold got a title, public recognition, and a hefty paycheck." In retrospect, Aunt Fran told me, she realizes that imagining herself as an icon of femininity seemed like a great way to cover up who she really was: a chubby, brainy, insecure little girl who was already attracted to other girls. With a laugh, she adds, "Still, turning myself into a beauty queen would have been like trying to hammer a square peg into a round hole."

Yet for a while, Aunt Fran did just that. In her teen years, she dieted so aggressively and exercised so obsessively that she became dangerously anorexic and had to be hospitalized and then institutionalized at a facility for the mentally ill. This unrealistic standard that so many women measure themselves against could have killed her. Sadly, idealized femininity and body weight are as interconnected as ever.

Mom, when you and your sisters were young feminists, you had your copies of *Our Bodies, Ourselves* and your consciousness-raising groups that convened in living rooms and coffee shops, where it dawned on you that the anti-war slogan "Women say yes to men who say no to the draft" was a kind of pimping out of your gender for the sake of the cause. You had access to the enlightened political writing of Betty Friedan, Nikki Giovanni, Susan Brownmiller, and the *Village Voice's* Jill Johnston. What you did not have is the power to convene a flash mob with a few taps on your iPhone or to reach an audience of thousands, or millions, by merely hitting Send. At my day job as a writer for *New York*, I write pieces that are assigned, edited for balance, and fact-checked for accuracy. But the feminist blog posts that I send floating into cyberspace are more casual, more personal, and often more fervent and furious.

Our bodies, ourselves, Mom. Whereas you went braless, and, for a while, stopped shaving your legs and underarms as a political statement, some of us shave our pussies, insert "chicken cutlets" in our bras when we go clubbing, and ink our bodies with symbols and statements that may or may not be political. Which brings me back full circle to those "slutty" size 0 dresses in that shopwindow on Madison Avenue.

I'm guessing you might not approve of the global phenom known as the SlutWalk, Mom—or the fact that, not long ago, your daughter dressed herself in a bikini, fishnet stockings, and fire-engine-red stilettos and marched not down a runway in some beauty pageant but down Broadway in solidarity with other feminists of my stripe. (Full disclosure: I put on a hoodie for part of it; I was fucking freezing.) In case you're not up on the history of the SlutWalk, it originated when a Toronto cop advised women that if they didn't want to become rape victims, they should stop dressing like sluts. In response, outraged activists rallied the troops via social media to protest in the streets by dressing provocatively in order to call for an end to rape culture, slut-shaming, and victim-blaming. The point was: women enjoy sex the same as men, and we have the right to signal that in what we wear *without* having to be afraid that we might be sexually violated. Keep in mind, Mom, that you once advised me not to wait around for someone—a rapist, say—to hand me some power. You told me to just take it, or in this case, to take it *back*.

Think about it, Mom. Isn't that what Gloria Steinem, the patron saint of your feminist movement, did when she stuffed herself into a Playboy bunny costume so that she could expose the pigs and fanny-pinchers at these puerile men's playgrounds? Those Playboy Club key holders might not have been rapists, but weren't they propagating a kind of socially acceptable foreplay by taking from women what they weren't necessarily willing to give? Case in point: that frequent guest at the Playboy mansion, Bill Cosby.

Mom, you and your generation took to the streets to demand fair treatment for women in sports, equal pay for equal work, subsidized child care, safe and legal abortion, and an end to domestic violence and discrimination against minority women. My generation supports all the above and, in addition, stands against discrimination and violence toward the LGBTQ community. Born female, I happen to live comfortably as a monogamous heterosexual woman. In the new terminology, that makes me both cisgender and cissexual. But take my boyfriend Jason's younger sibling, Morgan, who he still thinks of as his little sister, even though she identifies herself as "genderqueer"—meaning gender-nonspecific—and prefers pronouns like "hir" and "ze" to "her" and "she." Jason's parents assume this is a rebellious phase their daughter is passing through, aided and abetted by the pricey New England liberal arts college Morgan attends. Maybe so. But maybe in our gender binary society, in which LGBTQ kids are more than twice as likely to attempt suicide as their straight peers, it's something bigger—something positive and life-affirming, even life-saving.

So yes, Mom, we may differ in terms of our feminist coming-of-age and our focus. Nevertheless, we find common ground in fair treatment for all. We rally around nonviolent problem solving. And we join forces against the immoral abuse of power. So maybe we feminists of today *do* get it, even if we go into that boutique on Madison Avenue, credit card in hand, and walk out with one of those dresses from the front window.

And speaking of power, Mom, wouldn't you agree that, when we laugh, we feel more powerful? That laughter is liberating? So let me leave you with this observation from the Taiwanese-American stand-up comic Sheng Wang, who asks, "Why do people say 'grow some balls'? Balls are weak and sensitive. If you wanna be tough, grow a vagina. Those things can take a pounding."

EIGHTEEN

The new semester will be starting soon, so I've been working on the syllabus for my Introduction to Film Studies course at Hunter. I'll be screening several of the usual suspects for my undergraduates: *The Grapes of Wrath, Citizen Kane, The Bicycle Thief, The Last Picture Show*. But I'll also be mixing it up a little, adding a few new films to the roster: that Disney-Pixar movie *Up*, Lois Weber's silent film *Hypocrites*, Terrence Malick's *The Tree of Life*. Most of my young scholars will probably dislike the Malick film, which will confound them and force them to think about the profundity of life and death, the mystery and meaning of family, and the passage of time. But some might watch it a second time, think a little more deeply about it, or catch it again when they're older and wiser and maybe not as sure that they've got life all figured out the way they assumed they did when they were eighteen or nineteen or twenty.

I've had no more direct contact with ghosts at the Garde since Verna Hibbard's translucent image smiled and faded away. I still run the Monday night movie club there and sometimes, although I can no longer *see* Lois's spirit, I frequently *feel* that she is among us. Kenneth dropped out of the club after I convinced him, once and for all, that I would not be screening any of the films of Russ Meyer for us to study, not even *Beneath the Valley of the Ultra-Vixens*, which Kenneth considered Meyer's masterpiece. So we were down by one movie club member until Aliza's boyfriend, Jason, joined us. He drives up from the city every Monday, sleeps overnight on my couch, and sets his alarm for 5:30 a.m. so that he can get back in time for work—proof positive that, as Aliza once told me, Jason is "almost as big a film nerd as you are, Daddy."

Jason will become a daddy, too, later this year. Aliza is due in May. That news she wanted to tell me? That was it. Next week, Kat and I will be meeting our daughter and her husband-to-be at Manhattan's City Hall. Jason's asked me to be his best man and Aliza's maid of honor will be one of the three Js. Jordana, maybe? Jilly? I still can't keep them straight.

A lot has been happening career-wise for Aliza, too. An editor has approached her about publishing one of her blog posts for a collection of essays by new feminist writers. This past winter Aliza was promoted to the position of deputy editor at *New York* magazine. For the most recent installment of their "Yesteryear" edition, she's been given the cover story, a survey of Manhattan's "it" girls, past and present, from Edie Sedgwick and Madonna through Carolyn Bessette-Kennedy and Chloë Sevigny to the current downtown sensation, transgender DJ, artist, and runway model Juliana Huxtable. "It" today, gone tomorrow, alas. Time, as they say, does not stand still.

Lois Weber's ghost said that she and her fellow shades, Verna Hibbard included, appeared to me because I had been deemed "educable." To prove worthy of that designation, I've been reading widely and eclectically: Saint Paul, Søren Kierkegaard, Simone de Beauvoir, Elizabeth Cady Stanton. In preparation for the book on Lois Weber I'm planning, I've also undertaken a study of silent films made by the women who were largely written out of the accounts of the early days of motion pictures—not only Weber but also Alice Guy-Blaché, Hanna Henning, Dorothy Arzner, Dorothy Davenport Reid. I'm hoping to bring these creative filmmakers—the predecessors of contemporary directors like Jane Campion, Lisa Cholodenko, Ava DuVernay, and Rebecca Miller—out of the darkness and back into the light. We'll see. And I've decided against writing that book about Hollywood's secrets and scandals. Who needs another one of those?

My reading and viewing have led me to think more deeply about life and death. About women and men. About faith. Kierkegaard noted one of the central ironies of human existence when he wrote: "Life can only be understood backwards; but it must be lived forwards." I guess that's why historians and Monday morning quarterbacks seem so damned insightful. . . .

Like our parents before her, my sister Simone practices the Roman Catholic faith. Each Sunday and two or three times during the workweek, she attends the 7 a.m. Mass at St. Aloysius Gonzaga where she entreats the Father, the Son, and the Holy Spirit to care for the souls of the departed, especially her parents, her husband, Jeff, and their son, Luke.

Frances and Molly are churchgoers, too, although their attendance, they say, is erratic. They belong to a Congregational church which is "open and affirming." They believe in a God who loves but does not judge.

My ex-wife, Kat, is a Reform Jew who goes to Temple once a year during Yom Kippur. She believes that personal autonomy takes precedence over patriarchal Jewish tradition, but she nevertheless adheres to some Judaic customs as a way to honor those family members who came before her. She is troubled, however, by the chauvinistic assumptions embedded in Orthodox Judaism.

Our daughter Aliza is a nonbeliever who, on Sunday mornings, goes to brunch with her friends or, if she's been out late the night before, sleeps in. She believes that organized religion does more harm than good and that we need to be charitable to one another because it's the right thing to do, "not because it allows us to rack up mileage points for our trip to some imaginary heaven."

Me? I'm not exactly a Catholic anymore, but I'm not exactly a non-Catholic either. I guess you could say I'm stuck in the middle, although Francis, the Jesuit pope from Argentina, offers a glimmer of hope that the church can change. As my sister Frances put it, better to bend than break.

So what *do* I believe in? Equality. Forgiveness. Compassion. Social justice. I believe in the value of family, whether you define it as your blood relatives or the people you draw to you—which is to say that I believe in love.

I believe, too, that art—literature, painting, music, film—has the power to illuminate the human condition.

And I believe in miracles. How else to explain that my sister Frances—born into a toilet, baptized in a kitchen sink, ensnared in the tangled relationship between cruelty and fear brought on by withheld information, and rescued from an eating disorder that nearly killed her—not only survived but later thrived, having inherited the verve of a birth mother she never knew and given the support of the loving family that cradled her and kept her safe?

William Faulkner wrote that "the past is never dead." F. Scott Fitzgerald concluded *The Great Gatsby* with these words: "So we beat on, boats against the current, borne back ceaselessly into the past." But Louisa May Alcott wrote, instead, about the future. "Far away there in the sunshine are my highest aspirations. I may not reach them, but I can look up and see their beauty, believe in them, and try to follow where they lead." I sent that last quote to my daughter a while ago, figuring she'd appreciate it, which she did.

How could I not believe in ghosts, and what they have to teach us about how to learn from the past, fully inhabit the present, and embrace the propulsive thrust of the future, as when Jason holds my daughter's hand and squeezes it, the baby's head crowns, and the obstetrician says, "Okay, Mom. Are you ready? Push!"? I'm told by those in the know that I'm going to love being a grandfather. And I could be wrong, of course, but something tells me Aliza is having a girl.

ACKNOWLEDGMENTS

UNITED TALENT AGENCY'S Kassie Evashevski is much more than my literary agent. She's also my writing coach, my business adviser, and, when I hit the occasional bad writing stretch, my unpaid psychologist. Most of all, she is my good and trusted friend, for which I am enormously grateful.

I'm indebted to Ken Siman, Metabook's publisher and editor-in-chief, for his encouragement and invaluable editorial feedback during the evolution of this novel through several drafts. Benjamin Alfonsi, Metabook's brilliant creative director, built a multifaceted multimedia adventure around my humble story. Thanks as well to Christian Alfonsi, Metabook's president and CEO, and the entire Metabook team.

HarperCollins has been my loyal and longtime publisher and I'm grateful to the Harper imprint team, led by publisher Jonathan Burnham, executive editor Terry Karten, and Harper's affable and expert veeps Kathy Schneider, Leah Wasielewski, and Tina Andreadis. It's always a delight to work with Leslie Cohen, Harper's publicist extraordinaire, and to swap wisecracks with Virginia Stanley, who is HC's library marketing director despite all those overdue books fines she's accrued.

Whenever the members of my writing group provide critical feedback for my work-in-progress, I shut my mouth and take notes as fast as I can; their instincts and observations are always reliable and razor-sharp. These talented writers are Denise Abercrombie, Jonathan Andersen, Bruce Cohen, Leslie Johnson, and Sari Rosenblatt. While writing *I'll Take You There*, I also received useful reactions from Susan Cole, Janet Dauphin, John Ekizian, Doug Hood, Careen Jennings, and the students in my writing class at York Prison.

Doctoral students Matt Jones and George Moore keep things running smoothly in my office. Big thanks to both of these full-time scholars and part-time assistants.

If stories are rivers, this one had two tributaries. One was my involvement with *Beauty and the Beer*, a documentary about the storied Miss Rheingold contest; the other was the premiere showing at the Garde Theatre of Synthetic Cinema's *Wishin' and Hopin'*, an adaptation of my novel of the same name. Thank you to the Garde Arts Center's directors Jeanne and Steve Sigel, who told me about the theatrical tradition of the ghost lamp and about sightings of the spirits that haunt the venerable old movie palace they manage so lovingly. Director and onetime Miss Rheingold finalist Anne Newman Bacal and her *Beauty and the Beer* associates, Leslie Clark, Tom Spain, and Esther Cohen, invited me to participate in their film project which, in turn, triggered this novel's exploration of women's roles and expectations from the 1950s to the present.

For laughter, moral support, and camaraderie, I tip my hat to Joe Leonardi, Mark Croxford, Penny Balocki, Jerry Spears, Ken and Linda Lamothe, Hilda Belcher, and—especially—my best buddy, Ethel Mantzaris.

It still amazes me that, on that first day of July in 1978, Christine agreed to be my partner through life. Of my many blessings, she is the central one.

ABOUT WALLY LAMB

WALLY LAMB is the author of five *New York Times* bestselling novels: *She's Come Undone*, *I Know This Much Is True*, *The Hour I First Believed*, *Wishin' and Hopin'* and *We Are Water*. He has twice been selected for Oprah's Book Club. Lamb also edited *I'll Fly Away* and *Couldn't Keep It to Myself*, two volumes of essays from students in his writing workshop at York Correctional Institution, a women's prison in Connecticut, where he has been a volunteer facilitator for the past seventeen years. He lives in New York and Connecticut.